Funicular

T F Lince

For

Claire, my lovely wife for putting up with me banging on about my latest book all of the time, I even get on my own nerves.

Foreword

Here we go again. My second book is due to be released on more or less the same day as book one, but a year on.

Well, what a ride! *Room 119* has received many great reviews and comments, and it is currently being made into a screenplay thanks to interest from a couple of film directors, so thank you, world. Unfortunately, though, I still have nobody famous to write my foreword. No doubt by this time next year, Hollywood stars will be falling over themselves to provide me with a foreword, but as I quite enjoy writing them myself, I may tell them all to sling their hooks.

OK, back to *Funicular*. The story is set in Saltburn-by-the-Sea, which is situated on the north-eastern coast of England, a mile or so from where I was born and raised in Marske-by-the-Sea. I am very proud of my roots, so I'm hoping the locations I've described in *Funicular* will evoke fond memories in anyone else from the area, and persuade anyone who is not to put a visit on to their 'must do' lists.

Funicular is a detective drama – what was I thinking? We follow DI Bob Dixon as he embarks on the cold case of a young local girl, missing for many years, and it's at this point that he and normality part company. Always a maverick, Bob is quite happy to throw the rule book out of the window – the last thing on our hero's mind is following procedure.

I hope you will hear the sounds and smell the scents of my youth as you join Bob on his bumpy voyage. The more clues he gathers, the less sense they make. Why not try to work out what the hell is going on and solve the mystery before he does?

Er, good luck with that…

Thanks for reading, please leave a review

Trev Lince.

Part One – Crash and Burn

Chapter 1 – Retirement By The Sea

Saltburn-by-the-Sea, as its name suggests, is by the sea, and very proud of it. The sleepy North Yorkshire town boasts a beach eight miles long that joins it to the buzzing seaside resort of Redcar via the picturesque village of Marske, which also wears its by-the-sea tag with pride.

Over a hundred years ago, Saltburn thrived as Victorian holidaymakers flocked in great numbers to enjoy its fabled healing air and bustling pier, the funicular cliff lift saving them the walk back up the steep bank to the grand Zetland Hotel, which towered over the proceedings below. What a sight it must have been back in the day, the steam locomotive announcing their arrival directly inside the hotel's reception, allowing first class passengers to step off the train and receive their room keys more or less in one continuous motion. The passengers in third class had to alight further down the track at what today is Saltburn's railway station, but they were welcomed as warmly as the rich by Saltburn and all she had to offer.

It is now 2011 and the flocks of Victorians are little more than a distant memory.

The train from London was passing through Doncaster en route to Edinburgh. Bob Dixon was trying his best to doze, which was proving difficult with a gaggle of Middlesbrough fans in his carriage. After seeing a less than thrilling draw at Crystal Palace, they were not in a dozing mood, instead reeling through their repertoire of songs for the umpteenth time.

"Do you want a beer, mate?"

Bob had the pleasure of sharing a table with one of the Boro fans. Not waiting for an answer to his question, the supporter took two cans of Tetley's out of a plastic bag and handed one to Bob.

"Do you know what, I will, son, if you don't mind."

If you can't beat em, join em, Bob thought. *And besides, it's easier than saying no.*

His new friend pulled the ring pull with a nod of approval.

"Middlesbrough fan, eh? What was the score?" Bob asked, taking a sip.

"All that way for a bloody nil-nil. Life of a Boro fan, I'm afraid. We're shite and we know we are."

Some of his drunken friends picked up on his last few words.

"We're shite and we know we are, we're shite and we know we are, we're shite and…"

As the tired effort at a song whimpered out to nothing, Bob's travelling companion continued.

"So what's a soft southerner like you heading up here for?"

Bob thought on his feet – as a long-standing detective inspector with the Metropolitan Police, he was good at that. He could say that he was moving to the northeast to wind down into his retirement in sleepy Saltburn-by-the-Sea, but telling drunken football fans that he was a cop did not seem the smartest of moves.

He settled on, "I've got a sales job up here." It was the least engaging answer he could come up with.

"Scraggs." The young football fan held out his hand with all the confidence of an older man.

"Bob Dixon. Pleased to meet you, Scraggs." Bob shuffled uncomfortably out of his seat to shake the younger man's hand. He was good at shuffling. The only thing that could be described as sharp about him nowadays was his mind; all the other elements had joined forces to form more of a rounded shape.

Early-forties had not been kind to him. All the doughnuts and cakes he'd consumed on stakeouts or while looking into cases in the office deep into the night had taken their toll. He still had looks and charm, but they were heading south even as he headed north. At least, one of them was. He would always have charm, but his looks were just about hanging on by the fingertips. Hoping he would join the next gym he walked past, he hadn't. Joined one, that is. He'd walked past many.

Scraggs, on the other hand, was just starting out in life. Early twenties at most, he was tall with angular features, shaven brown hair, and all the exuberance of youth bursting out of the seams.

Oh to be young again, Bob thought as he caught his reflection in the window. Black hair, gelled back rockabilly style, surrounded a much rounder face than he used to see. He sighed. He used to have a look of Elvis back in his younger days. In fact, he still did have a look of Elvis, but more the Las Vegas Elvis than the *GI Blues* Elvis.

Bob sighed again before turning back to Scraggs, allowing his mind to wander away from memories of his youth. They were annoying him.

"So, Scraggs, where are you from?"

The rest of the Boro fans had given up on singing. The day on the booze had taken its toll, so Scraggs and a couple of others who were playing cards at the next table were the only ones still awake. The rest had their heads in their hands on the table and were snoring happily.

"Saltburn-by-the-Sea. It's about twenty miles north of Whitby. It's in Cleveland now, but my dad says it's still Yorkshire and they can bugger off with their boundaries. They needed to break Yorkshire up as we were getting so powerful, they were frightened we would take over the world." Scraggs ended his speech with an emphatic nod. It seemed he agreed wholeheartedly with his dad's sentiments.

Bob's eyes rolled for the briefest of seconds before he reset them to a balanced position, hoping he hadn't given anything away.

What are the chances? he thought. *I speak to one guy on the bloody train and he's from sodding Saltburn.*

"Saltburn, you say? I've not heard of it, son," he lied. All good cops can tell a lie when they need to, and Bob was one of the best.

The train had left York behind and was heading for Darlington. Bob thought better of getting the rattler to Saltburn with Scraggs and his army of football followers. The *I've never heard of Saltburn* line might unravel if he and Scraggs shared a train all the way there. Instead, Bob said his goodbyes to the boy and headed out of Darlington station towards a fleet of red cabs. Their drivers, all wearing matching blue jumpers, were strutting around like peacocks, looking for passengers to seduce into their cabs. Bob walked over to the one he assumed was next in line.

"Saltburn-by-the-Sea, please," he ordered as he climbed into the back seat while the driver attended to his bags.

"Saltburn it is, sir."

Bob was surprised, after witnessing Scraggs's pride in his hometown, that Saltburn was allowed to fly solo without its by-the-sea tag, but he let it go. He was exhausted.

A new start Monday, he thought. *A new Robert Dixon without the hustle and bustle of old London town. I can't wait.*

Chapter 2 – First Day at School

Bob awoke in his hotel room at 5 o'clock on Monday morning; he had to make a good impression today. Saltburn was a far cry from the London streets, where there was crime around every corner. He guessed that life would be a lot gentler up here. There might still be crime around every corner, but the corners would be a lot further apart.

Staying in London had not been an option; he'd put too many rotten eggs inside, and with that came consequences. When his flat was broken into and "You're dead" was painted in red letters on his bedroom wall, he knew it was time to get out. He'd done his bit, he'd earned a break, and he was going to enjoy the last few years of his career in the police in sleepy Saltburn.

His boss in London had arranged for his transfer. She'd known it was time for him to go while there was still something left of him to do the going. DI Bob Dixon did not always play by the rules; he had sent people down, yes, but the evidence had a way of conveniently lining up in his favour. One fewer toe-rag on the street to murder or rape was one thing fewer for the public to worry about. He should have been a DCI by now based on his results, but the guy who cheats in exams never gets the grades.

After a shower and shave, Bob scrutinised his 'Do I look fat in this suit?' pose in the mirror, the shake of his head confirming that he did. He then headed down for breakfast.

On his way past reception, he turned back and asked the young receptionist, "Do you have a gym here?"

She looked him up and down before replying.

"No, sir, sorry."

Bob pulled his stomach in and held his breath before thanking her and heading off to the restaurant. *One more fry-up won't hurt,* he thought, *the diet starts tomorrow.*

It was a crisp, cold October morning. After a hearty breakfast, he set off at a brisk pace to Saltburn-by-the-Sea police station, until the sausages and bacon took their toll on the briskness. At 7.25am he arrived at the door. Bob was a confident man, but your first day at school is your first day at school. He made sure his suit trousers were pulled up and his tie was centred before levering the door handle and pushing forward.

His face nearly hit the locked door.

Welcome to the sticks, he thought, his mind giving him a playful nudge. *What the hell am I doing here? It's the bloody back of beyond.*

He looked over the road and spied a sign of life. More importantly, he spied a sign of coffee. Bob stepped into the coffee shop and placed his order.

"What time does the cop shop open, please?" he enquired of the old lady who was expertly attending to his skinny latte. Bob believed ordering a skinny latte was like ordering a diet coke – it made him feel like he was actually losing weight, despite the huge fry-up still sitting heavily in his belly.

"Normally about nine," she said as she handed Bob his drink.

"What do you mean, normally?" He raised an eyebrow and put extra emphasis on the word *normally*.

"It depends who's on keys."

"Why does it depend on that? What type of…"

The lady stopped him in mid-rant.

"It's David today so it will be about twenty past."

"Why did you say it would be nine o'clock if you knew it would be twenty past?"

"I said *normally*, as I recall. It is *normally* nine, but not when David's on. He lives in Guisborough, you know."

Why does it matter where he lives? Bob thought.

"Do you want a croissant with your coffee, sir?" the old lady offered with a reluctant smile, her head leaning to the left.

"No thanks, I'm on a diet."

She leant over the counter a little to get a better look at him as she rang the price of the coffee into an old-fashioned till. "Really? Is it going well?"

"Am I paying for the insults? To be fair, my diet only started twenty minutes ago when I walked up the hill, but it's a new start, a new me. I can always start tomorrow, though, so I will have a croissant, if you don't mind. I seem to have an hour or two to kill before David shows up."

Realising he may have got off on the wrong foot, he smiled at the old lady, trying to win her over.

"You're the new guy, aren't you? Dodgy Dicko from that London, isn't it?" She smiled back. "I can tell from your accent."

"Dodgy Dicko? The name is Bob, actually. Pleased to meet

you. I guess a lot of the coppers from over the road eat in here, so what's the buzz? What have they been saying about me?"

His croissant was delivered on a plate with a knob of butter and an excessively small jar of jam. It looked like he would struggle to get a knife into it.

"Oh, I couldn't possibly say. Loose lips sink ships, you know."

Ding-ding! The bell above the door announced the arrival of another customer.

Welcome to the madhouse, Bob thought as he took a seat by the window.

He waited and waited, then had no option but to wait some more. Two coffees and another croissant later, he finally saw a uniformed figure ambling up to the door of the police station. Bob headed over the road, safe in the knowledge he wouldn't risk breaking his nose on the door this time. As he entered, he saw a tall beanpole of a man with red hair and thick-rimmed glasses looking pristine in his police uniform.

"Morning. Can I help you, sir?" the police officer asked, looking down at Bob from behind the raised desk.

"David, isn't it?" Bob enquired.

"Yes, it is, Constable David Skelton. DI Dixon, I presume? We're expecting you, sir."

Bob thought better of saying, "You could have fooled me." It was day one, after all. Instead, he settled on, "Pleased to meet you, David."

As David shook the hand of Saltburn's new DI, he said, "We've heard a lot about you. Quite the star down in London. We've not had a DI in this office for years; CID works out of Redcar now. You must have friends in high places to rekindle that position here. Someone must have pulled a few strings for you."

"I guess so. Aren't I the lucky one?" Bob offered a forced smile, which was well received nevertheless.

"Sorry, sir, we had to do a bit of a clear out, but we managed to find you an office… of sorts."

PC David Skelton showed Bob around the small station, finishing at his new office. Bob's jaw dropped.

"David, it's a cell. It's not an office."

"Well it's all we have, sir. You've seen the size of this place. All ten of us share the main office and there are only two desks. Is it a problem? It took us ages to get the desk in and the power hooked up for the computer and everything."

"No, it's not a problem, David. I will make it work. Not sure about the computer, though. I'm old school – notepad and pen all day for me, son."

"Skelly. Everyone calls me Skelly, sir. I guess it's sort of a northern thing – we all tend to have nicknames from school that stick with us till we die up here. Have you ever been to Saltburn before, sir?"

"No, Constable Skelton, I have not." Bob's formal attitude did not go unnoticed by Skelly, who straightened his attire and remembered that a police officer should respect rank.

As sounds of activity came from the front of the police station, they both headed out of the cell-cum-office. By now, it was 10am and it seemed like the rest of the force had decided to make an appearance, complete with takeaway coffees from the café. Uniformed officers were milling around the large shared office, joking and larking about like schoolkids who have had too many blue smarties.

David spoke loudly to be heard above the hubbub.

"Guys, settle down, settle down." He raised his hands up and down to grab everyone's attention, and once the din had abated, he continued, "This is Bob Dixon, our new detective inspector."

One by one, the Saltburn officers shook Bob's hand, introducing themselves. Bob ensured he eyeballed each of them and made a mental note of their names. They only had one name to remember today, but he would make it his business to memorise all of theirs. He knew it would pay him back later in the day.

The nick was run by Sergeant Hopkins, but in the office he was Hoppy to one and all. Bob was starting to realise he was going to have to try harder to blend in. That would take time, though, so to keep the upper hand, he insisted on being addressed as 'Sir' all day.

Day one was all about getting to know everybody for Bob, weighing up whom to trust, whom not to trust, who would be his go-to guy, and who would give him the inside information. But maybe his senses were failing him, because nobody seemed to have a story to tell. It would appear they all had each other's backs. All Bob got was the lowdown on policing in Saltburn-by-the-Sea. Walking round the streets, chatting to residents, seemed to be the main job around here. Real policing, in other words – nipping crime in the bud before it had a chance to happen.

All in all, Bob found his first day as Saltburn-by-the-Sea's own detective inspector quite refreshing. Maybe he could enjoy winding down to his retirement in the back of beyond, after all.

Chapter 3 – On the Beat

Over the next three months, things went from bad to worse for both Bob and his diet. A coffee and croissant in the morning became the norm. Through force of habit, he would still roll up at 7.30am each day, hoping that the police station might actually be open, but it never was. Instead, he would wait in the café, getting to know the chatty old lady, Audrey, better and better.

She had said when they first met that loose lips sink ships, and hers could have sunk an armada. She started every sentence with "I shouldn't tell you, but…" before bombarding Bob with snippets of information about what his new colleagues thought of him or the names they called him behind his back: "Dixon of Cock Green"; "Cockney Dick"; "DI Dicko". Three months in charge had clearly amounted to nothing. Was respect really too much to ask?

He had arrived late one day while he was sorting out his new flat. The lads in the large office were laughing and joking like they had been on day one, until Bob arrived. Then the place went silent. It did not go unnoticed. Bob spent his days in his office cell, feeling like a prisoner in solitary confinement. If he could have started over again with a clean sheet of paper, he would.

The problem was, he was a detective in a place where the only detecting was done on the beach with a machine looking for metal and old coins. He had nothing to do, no cases to answer. He was on a retirement ride organised by friends in high places, and the Saltburn police despised him for it. Bob was even contemplating moving back to London. So what if people were after him? At least he would feel useful again.

He'd been to meet the CID guys in Redcar, which was a well-run outfit, and had thought about transferring over there, but Bob was not a quitter. He was many things, but not that. He got the impression there was still very little to do in Redcar; the officers there were just more organised at doing nothing than the lads in Saltburn.

A lot of water had already passed under the bridge since his arrival in the north, but things were going to change. It was a Saturday, Bob's day off, when he opened his wardrobe and pulled out his uniform, which had not seen the light of day since he had been on parade in London. He hoped it would still fit, and to his surprise, it did. Nearly. It fitted well enough for his needs, anyway.

Bob headed up the hill to the station, booted and suited. No coffee, no croissant – today, he was going to be late on purpose. Why not? Everyone else at the station seemed to turn up late, so if that's what it would take to blend in, so be it.

When in Rome, he thought.

Constable Skelton was on key duty this morning.

"Morning, Skelly."

Skelly looked down through his thick-rimmed glasses at DI Dixon.

"Sir." He looked at his watch, apparently to check the day of the week. "It's Saturday, sir."

"Dicko when I'm in the office, son, and I know it's Saturday," Bob said in his cheeriest voice. "I fancy doing some voluntary community policing."

"Why the uniform, sir? Sorry, D-i-c-k-o." Skelly said Dicko slowly, as if to emphasise the strangeness of it.

"Well, I am a detective, and I don't appear to have anything to detect. So I thought I would get out and about and see if I can remember what real policing is like. It nearly fits." DI Dixon looked down at his attire and gave his tummy a tap.

"It nearly doesn't." Skelly chuckled, and Bob joined in with the joke.

"Look, Skelly, it's taken me a while to acclimatise to your ways here after London life." He left a purposeful gap before adding, "New start?"

Bob offered his outstretched palm to Skelly.

"You have been a bit of a Dick, if you don't mind me saying, Bob." Skelly had three names in his head now and was fumbling for the right one. Dicko did not feel right without an insult wrapped around it, but he now had permission to drop the sir.

Bob picked up on this. "Look, I'm not stupid. Cockney Dick, DI Dicko, and my favourite, Dixon of Cock Green." Skelly lowered his head to hide his smile. "That was yours, wasn't it, Skelly?"

"It might have been. You're a good detective, sir, I'll give you that."

"Can you put me on the beat today with one of the young lads? It'll do me good to walk around all day. My diet isn't really working out, and I can't stand another day in that cell looking for a case that don't exist." Again, he left a gap before adding, "Does nothing ever happen around here, Skelly?"

"I don't think we've had a murder for years, if that's what you mean?" Skelly put his finger and thumb on his chin in the classic thinking pose before continuing, "Apart from the odd burglary, which you've seen… mmm, we get a few jump off Huntcliff. Oh, and the odd missing person, but that's about it, I reckon." Then he pointed to the noticeboard. "She hit the main news on the BBC, poor girl. Still not found her. Lizzy Scraggs."

Bob looked at the poster. Next to the words *MISSING. Help us find Lizzy* was a picture of a young girl adjacent to a computer-generated photofit.

"What's the photo next to her? Is that someone who might have taken her?"

"No, that's a picture of what she might look like now. It's six years since she went missing."

Bob went over to the picture to get a better look.

"Lizzy Scraggs? Has she got a brother?" He turned to face Skelly, awaiting the answer.

"Yep, big Boro fan. Always scrapping in town. Not a bad lad till you get a drink inside him. We give him a break due to his sister… well, you know. I think he was only fifteen when she disappeared. Why, do you know him?"

"Do you know what, Skelly? I think I might."

Skelly looked surprised, but did not pursue it, instead writing in the roster.

"Right, you can take out Constable Higgins. He's over here from Redcar on cover. I doubt any of our lot will want to go out with you." He looked up over his glasses. "No disrespect, sir… Bob, but..."

Bob stopped him. "None taken, Skelly."

"He wants to be over here full time as he's from Saltburn. He's a young lad, sir, look after him."

"OK, Skelly, I will. What name does he go by? Higgy?"

"We can be a bit more inventive sometimes, you know. Hurricane, he goes by Hurricane."

"What, after the snooker player? Does he like that?"

"Not really, but he hasn't got much choice. That's what we call him when he comes over here." Bob laughed; he was really trying. "I'll smooth things over with the lads, sir."

"It's Dicko, remember?"

"That wasn't an accident. You'll get sir most of the time, from me anyway, because you've earnt it. We're a weird lot up here; we don't take very well to being told what to do. Knowing we don't have to call you sir will make all the difference."

Skelly handed Bob a radio and protective vest.

"Thanks, Skelly, that means a lot. When does Hurricane arrive?"

"He's already here. The Redcar office is a little stricter than we are here, so I sent him over the road for a coffee before he heads out. Go join him if you like. He was heading out with Brian Poulter, who will owe you. He's just back from long-term sick leave, and he's got a mountain of stuff to catch up on."

"Let me guess – Poulty?"

Skelly laughed out loud. "No, Brian. He's not from round here, he's from York. We're not all crazy, you know." Skelly closed the roster as Bob went to leave, grinning and shaking his head. "I'll have the Scraggs case sent over from Redcar, if you like, sir."

Bob stopped and turned.

"Do you know what? Yes, please do. I'd like that, son."

"Consider it done, sir."

Bob walked into the café and over to a fresh-faced kid in uniform who was finishing his coffee. He was a wisp of a boy with light hair – a strong wind would probably cause him some damage.

"Pleased to meet you, Constable Higgins, I'm DI Dixon and I fancy a day out on the beat. And you're my lucky guide." If Redcar was stricter than Saltburn, Bob decided he'd better not play nickname games with Higgins straight away.

"OK, sir, do you normally go out on the beat?" Higgins smiled as he finished off the dregs of his coffee.

"No, son, first time for about twenty years, so I am glad to have you with me to show me the ropes. Show me what Saltburn has to offer – a guided tour, if you like."

"I live in Saltburn so that shouldn't be too difficult, sir. I get ribbed by the Redcar lot – they're a bit up their own arses – so I always take shifts over here if they're offered."

Subconsciously, Bob was weighing up his partner for the day as the young man spoke. He liked what he saw. Higgins had spirit and an edge to him.

"Well let's see how you get on today. Maybe I could put a word in for you with Sergeant Hopkins."

The boy's eyes lit up as he stood up, eager to impress.

"OK, son, let's go. You can show me all you know about Saltburn. Lead the way."

Bob instinctively knew he was going to enjoy being back on the beat rather than languishing in his police cell office in Hatesville. He and Higgins headed off around the town, making small talk, before going across the hilltop towards the pier. If any criminal activity was going to happen, it would happen there. Bob's new partner said that Saturdays could get a bit rowdy, with the local surfers and a group of bikers from Whitby having a dick measuring competition.

"So what made you become a rozzer, then?" Bob was falling back into PC Plod mode with ease, adopting the hands-behind-the-back pose that older coppers seemed to favour.

"Rozzer?"

"Rozzer, copper, peeler, policeman." Bob looked at Higgins quizzically.

"Oh, I've never heard rozzer before. My dad was in the police. In fact, he was the last DI at Saltburn. They didn't replace him – nothing to investigate, really. It's very quiet up here, sir." Higgins stopped walking and turned to smile at his partner for the day. "Is that why you're out with me, sir? Are you bored?"

"Well, you could say that, son." The constable's smile was returned with interest as they continued across the bank top.

After three months, this was the first time Bob had really taken proper notice of Saltburn-by-the-Sea's beauty. Lit up by the January sun, the orange hues of Huntcliff served as a backdrop to the sandy beach, the pier and, of course, the famous cliff lift. Saltburn in all its majesty was like a living, breathing postcard.

"What's that thing, then, Higgins?" Bob pointed to the lift, where the cars were currently crossing at the midpoint, making their journeys up and down the steep grassy bank.

"It's our funicular." Higgins said with much pride.

"OK, you've got me intrigued. What is a funicular?"

"Do you want to have a go, sir? My dad will tell you all about it, if you like. He would love to meet you." Higgins looked at his partner before adding, "I think," with a cheeky grin.

"Why is your dad here?"

"He's the brake-man; he's part of a group that keeps the funicular running. It's the oldest water-driven funicular in Europe… I'll tell you what, sir, I'll leave that to my dad. He loves telling people about it. I'm sure he'll let you have a ride, if you're willing to listen to him for twenty minutes."

Higgins laughed, knowing what was coming.

"I would love that, sunshine, and yes, I would love a ride, too. Thanks, Higgins."

Bob gave Higgins a playful tap on the arm. Finally, Saltburn and its people were growing on him.

Chapter 4 – The Funicular

As they approached the cliff lift, a group of customers were exiting the top and bottom rail-cars simultaneously. The brake-man at the top spotted his son and gave a hand signal to the gate man at the bottom to take five.

"Hi, George, I heard you were over here today."

Bob mouthed the name George to Higgins and got a look that suggested it would not be worth pursuing.

"Yes, Dad. This is DI Dixon, the new DI in Saltburn nick."

"Pleased to meet you, DI Dix..."

"Bob, please. You have a good lad there, you should be proud of him."

"He's alright, aren't you, George? He has his moments, but he's a good kid, most of the time."

Higgins gave his dad a 'here we go again' look.

"Keith Higgins. Pleased to meet you." As they were shaking hands, Keith continued, "So, Bob, you've made quite an impression in the station, I hear?"

"Well, you could say that. Maybe not the right impression, but an impression nevertheless. I guess you could say I'm not in Kansas anymore, Keith." As the two older men shared the joke, Higgins looked on clueless. *The Wizard of Oz* clearly wasn't still on every kid's Christmas viewing list nowadays.

"Look, it's not London, Bob, but people are people. I'm sure you'll win them round, and being in uniform for a day, I would say, is a good start. Especially it being a Saturday."

"It might score me a few points in the office, and I've loved being out with your lad today. I'd forgotten what real policing was all about. I've been in a suit to long."

"They're a good bunch, all in all. They just need a bit of loving now and then. I did laugh when I heard they put you in the cell." Chuckling, Keith noticed a group of people that had gathered to the left of them. "Anyway, if you hang around for five minutes, I'm about to take this group of visitors round, telling them all about our famous funicular." Keith outstretched his arms, as if introducing the funicular as an old friend.

"I'd love that, Keith, thanks."

After five minutes, the group had swelled to eight people, gathered next to the sign offering funicular tours. Keith called them over to join him.

"No offence, sir, but I've heard it all a million times, including all my dad's crap jokes. I'll walk down. See you at the bottom."

"OK, *George*," Bob said with a wink.

"Don't you start, sir. My dad's bad enough." Higgins set off on the alternative route: a winding path that snaked its way down the hill to the pier and the beach. Bob joined the crowd heading over to Higgins's dad.

"Ladies and gentlemen, welcome to the weird, wonderful and sometimes mysterious world of Saltburn-by-the-Sea's famous funicular. Listen, I know everyone calls it the cliff lift, but not on my watch. If any of you do, you can walk down now." He smiled before continuing, "So what is it called?"

A couple said weakly, "A funicular."

"Right, that's it, you can all walk. I'm not doing this for the goodness of my health, you know. Let's try again. What is it called?"

"A FUNICULAR!"

"That's better. What is it not?"

"A CLIFF LIFT."

"That's where you're wrong, boys and girls. It *is* a cliff lift, but this one is also a funicular, so let me tell you about funiculars. It works on the principle of the descending and ascending cars being counterbalanced, and ours is one of the oldest in England. We are very proud of that."

Keith had his audience captive now and went on to tell them the history of the funicular, which was opened on Saturday 28 June 1884, and all about the original cars, complete with stained-glass windows, capable of seating ten to twelve passengers.

"Aluminium cars with clear windows replaced the original wooden ones in 1979. The stained-glass windows were reinstated in 1991. The cars were rebuilt as replicas of the originals with wooden bodies, and the whole thing was 'Victorianised' earlier this year. Which cost lots and lots of money."

Keith gave a chirpy smile to each person in the group before continuing.

"Which is why, when you get to the bottom, you will make a donation… won't you?" He paused again, letting the 'won't you?'

hang in the air for a few seconds. "We prefer notes as it takes so much time to count all the coins."

Everyone laughed and nodded as one. Keith could be very persuasive when he wanted to. By the time he went on to say how each of the cars was fitted with a 240-imperial-gallon water tank and ran on parallel standard gauge funicular railway tracks, he had his crowd mesmerised.

"So how does it work, Keith?" Bob asked. He loved knowing not just why things were there, but how they worked.

"Good question, Bob. Obviously, I'm the most important guy here." The crowd had warmed up, so Keith allowed a few sniggers to settle before continuing, "I sit at the top in the cabin and control the brake, just in case, but the funicular runs on its own really. Victorian engineering, Bob, that's all it takes." The visitors all looked impressed, and so they should. It's not hard to be impressed by something that's impressive. "The car at the top has its water tank filled until its mass exceeds that of the car at the bottom. It then travels down the incline, counterbalanced by the mass of the other car, which makes the alternative journey to the top. Simple. When the car reaches the bottom, its water is released, thus reducing the mass of the lower car, and off we go again."

The crowd applauded, which seemed like the right thing to do.

"What about the mysterious bit you mentioned?" one of the visitors asked.

Keith looked left then right, as if to ensure nobody was eavesdropping on their conversation, then his voice turned deeper.

"It is said…" He beckoned everyone in to form a tight group before starting again. "It's said that the centre of the lift, where the cars cross, runs over an ancient ley line that comes out of the sea in Marske, runs through the churchyard there and heads to Saltburn before disappearing somewhere over Huntcliff."

"What's a ley line?" a young woman asked.

"What's your name, my love?"

"Dawn," said the young woman, nervously gripping her boyfriend's hand.

"Oh, I'm so glad you asked, Dawn." Dawn was already wishing she hadn't. "It's a geological line that is thought to have ancient, mysterious qualities." Keith urged the visitors in even closer, as if he was telling a secret that he should keep to himself.

Their heads were now all locked together, forming a huddle.

"OK, the brake-man who worked here before me told me about mysterious goings on, many, many years ago. Late one stormy night, on the last ride of the day, a man and a boy entered this lift at the top, just like you are going to do today. The brake-man gave them their tickets and called to the cage operator, Bill, at the bottom to say that there was one more load for the day."

Keith started to talk slowly and deliberately, like he was running out of batteries.

"When the lift made it to the half way point, opposite the car coming the other way, exactly where the ley line is fabled to be…" he left a pause, the crowd hanging onto his every word, "…there was a blue flash which forced rainbow colours to bleed out of the car through the stained glass windows. When the car reached the bottom… guess what, Dawn?"

"The car was empty?" Dawn whispered.

"That's right, empty. All that was left in the car was a glowing blue ticket on the floor."

Again, Keith left his words to hang in the air. This speech was his pride and joy.

"You will meet Bill at the bottom. He says to this day that the brake-man at the top must have been having a joke with him, but up until the brake-man's death five years ago, he was adamant he put two people in the car that night. Ask Bill when you get down. He might even show you the actual ticket."

There was a crackle of nervous tension in the group as Keith gave Bill at the bottom of the steep slope a wave to tell him to fill his car with waiting passengers.

"So, who wants a go?" Keith's voice was cheery now, as if the last couple of minutes hadn't happened, and he smiled at the group to break the tension. The enthusiasm for the ride had diminished somewhat, so Keith lightened the tone. "I've never seen anything, and I've been doing this… oh, ten years or so. So I think you'll be OK." There were a couple of laughs as people got some of their bravery back. "Just make sure you hold your breath as the cars pass."

Keith started to laugh.

"Well, I'm in," said Bob, not falling for any of the tourist mumbo-jumbo.

"Ladies and gentlemen, you have an officer of the law to

protect you. What could possibly go wrong? Tickets, please."

The visitors formed a line and handed over their tickets, which Keith stamped with the date and punched through the word "out" at the top, leaving the word "rtn" untouched. They then loaded onto the car and took their seats.

"You're on for free, Bob, but make sure they all get down safe," Keith said in a sinister voice, adding a "ha-ha-hah-hah" for pantomime effect before slamming the door with a crash to jangle everyone's nerves even more, if that were possible. Bob could hear the water sloshing around the tank beneath the floor as Keith released the brake, allowing gravity and Victorian engineering to join forces and start the short journey down the steep grassy hill. A young couple gripped each other's hands as the opposite car approached to the right, and to Bob's amazement, everybody *did* hold their breath as the cars crossed – including him. He had to give it to Higgins's dad, he was good. Bob could tell Keith loved what he did.

The journey took all of sixty seconds before the visitors and Bob were safely delivered to the foot of the steep bank. Bill, the cage operator, allowed them out at the end of the pier, and they poured from the car looking as pale as if they had been on a ghost train at the funfair.

"Did you enjoy that, sir?" Higgins was laughing as Bob exited the funicular car. He knew every word of the story his dad had just delivered to Bob and his fellow travellers.

"He's quite convincing, Hurricane, I'll give him that. What a load of baloney, though – blue flashes and ley lines?"

"Not according to my dad, it's not. The guy before him saw it with his own eyes. Ask Bill."

Bob looked over at Bill, who was busy sorting out the queue of passengers waiting for the next ride up.

"Next time maybe, son. I think your dad got to most of them, but not me." Bob nodded at his travelling companions, who were making their unsteady way onto the pier. "I believe in evidence, son. There is always a reason for everything, and everything happens for a reason. It's the rules."

"He's better when he does it in the dark. I think my dad gets a kick out of scaring folk. Weren't you even a bit scared, sir?"

"Don't be stupid, Hurricane. I did hold my breath when the other car passed, though – I thought it would be safer."

Bob gave Higgins a playful punch on the arm before ambling to the end of the pier to have a chat with the fisherman. He had forgotten how proper policing in the community felt, and he felt like he belonged for the first time since his arrival in Saltburn-by-the-Sea.

Chapter 5 – Cowboys and Indians

They walked the pier before walking along the beach towards Marske for a while. The distinct smell of seaweed and the salty air of the sea was being carried toward them on a bitterly cold wind Bob lifted his collar as a small defence against the elements. He asked Higgins where they could get a bite to eat, and Higgins, true to local form, suggested a pub four or five hundred yards along from the pier called The Ship.

Bob was busy taking in the beauty of all Saltburn had to offer. The surfers were heading to shore in their black and grey wetsuits like a pod of dolphins playing in the rolling breakers. They were done for the day and were hitching a ride on their final waves.

"Do you want an ice cream, sir?"

Bob gave Higgins an "Are you mad?" stare and raised an eyebrow.

"Ice cream? It's January! Bloody ice cream."

"Ice cream is all year round here, sir. Have you tried a lemon-top?"

Bob upped his eyebrow to its maximum. "OK, you have my attention. What's a lemon-top?"

"What? You don't get lemon-tops down in London?"

"No."

Higgins smiled. "Next thing you'll be telling me you don't get parmos."

"No, we don't, Hurricane. What the hell is a parmo?"

"One thing at a time, sir. Let's do a lemon-top first, break you in gently. You'll love it, but I don't think you're ready for a parmo yet."

"OK, you're the boss today, son. Two lemon-tops it is."

And so Bob tried his first lemon-top ice cream, fighting through the lemon sorbet before meeting the soft Mr Whippy style ice cream beneath. Yes, it was January, and yes, it shouldn't work, but Bob loved it, and had devoured it before they were even half way to the pub.

The Ship was an old pub with a museum displaying the history of smuggling attached to it. There were pirate figures guarding the entrance of the pub, and all the tables outside were barrels. The surfers had all congregated at the barrels outside, conspicuous with their flowing locks of bleached-blond hair, cut-off jeans and flip flops.

It is January, isn't it? thought Bob, concluding that a man who had just eaten a lemon-top ice cream was in no position to judge.

"Hurricane, I'm just nipping to the toilet. Try not to get into too much trouble while I'm gone."

Bob winked at Higgins as he headed into the pub.

As soon as he'd disappeared, a new noise grabbed Higgins's attention: a deep purring, rumbling noise as not one, but twenty motorbikes, most of them Harley-Davidsons with their long handlebars and drop back seats, wound their way down the corkscrew road of Saltburn's bank. The riders were wearing an assortment of leather jackets, some sporting tassels, others with pictures on the back.

One of the surfers pricked up his ears and turned, followed by the rest. All stood taller like meerkats, trying to get a better view of incoming predators.

"Here they are, lads."

The bikers had clearly decided they wanted a drink in The Ship, too. Of course they did. The meeting of bikers and surfers would never end well; it probably wasn't going to start well, either.

Higgins looked over his shoulder for Bob as the surfers pulled close together, like cowboys being circled by Indians. The bikers parked up on the other side of the road and walked across to the pub en masse. Higgins positioned himself between the two groups. He couldn't radio in now – that would give both groups licence to kick off, knowing they would have at least a five-minute window to rumble.

"I'm surprised you're back for more after last time, girls," one of the surfers said as he and his mates all shifted forward a step.

"Right, we want no trouble, lads. Come on." Higgins puffed out what little chest he had. He was a brave lad.

"And what the fuck are you going to do about it, you scrawny little shit?" asked one of the bikers, not taking his eye off his chosen opponent. "We have unfinished business, don't we, boys?"

Higgins was now wishing he had called in on the radio. *Too late now*, he thought as he looked left and right, waiting for the first move. One wrong move and it would all kick off. He could almost taste the tension.

"I'll handle this, son. Move away and leave it to me." Bob

suddenly appeared at Higgins's side, winking at the young man. Higgins knew that command well – it was his hint to radio for backup.

"They've replaced skinny with fatty. What's this, the Laurel and fucking Hardy show?" The biggest of the bikers, sporting the full blond 'Hulk Hogan' moustache, got a laugh from his tribe. The two groups were no more than two steps away from each other now.

"Charlie Delta four, we request back up, The Ship in Saltburn." Nobody noticed Higgins, who was out of sight, out of mind. There was far too much testosterone flying about and eyeballing going on.

Bob looked at both groups in turn. A barrel table sat either side of them.

"Right, this is what's going to happen." He drew a line with his boot in the sand to join the two barrels. "I don't know what your problem is, and to be honest, I don't care, but the first to cross this line has me to deal with. GOT IT?"

A man shuffled forward from the surfers' group.

That's all I bloody need, Bob thought. It was Scraggs.

Bob eyeballed Scraggs, truncheon poised. Hulk Hogan stepped forward from the bikers' group to face him – he was twice Scraggs's size.

"Scraggs, don't do it, son. I'll take you down. And you, sir… you'll be making the biggest mistake of your life, believe me. Don't fuck with me."

Bob was trying to defuse a bomb that already had its fuse lit. The atmosphere was fizzing.

"You're Bob from the train. Fucking sales? You're all the same, you lying fucking coppers."

"Not now, Scraggs, I can explain…"

"What the fuck are you going to do to stop me, fat-boy?" Hulk Hogan piped up. The bikers all laughed with their leader.

"OK, this is how it's going down. You lot," Bob pointed to the surfers, "back to your tables for a civilised drink, and you lot," pointing to the bikers, "back on your bikes and fuck off to Whitby for the day."

Just then, Hulk Hogan walked across the line to confront Scraggs face to face. Bob flew into action. He wheeled his weapon round, delivering a blow first to the back of one of Hulk Hogan's calves and then on the other. He'd downed him in seconds; the biker was screaming in agony on the ground. Bob stood over him and put Hulk's arm into the pressure point position, inflicting more pain with minimal effort. He then looked up.

"Anyone else?" Bob could hear the sirens echoing from the top of the bank, announcing the arrival of the cavalry. The surfers backed off, and Bob turned to the bikers as they too walked away.

"You have ten seconds to get this piece of shit on his bike and out of my fucking town or he's nicked. Do you understand?" Two bikers broke ranks and walked over to their felled leader. "And you won't be coming back here, will you?" Bob said into the ear of the man squirming on the floor, applying more pressure to his arm.

"No. Noooo!"

"Right. Don't let me see you again."

The bikers helped Hulk up, seating him on the back of one of their bikes as he was unable to ride his own. They then sped off on the road to Whitby, giving Bob 'the bird' as they did.

"Fat bastard," one of them shouted.

"Are you OK, sir?" Higgins ran to Bob's side.

"Fine, son. Is every week like this?"

"No. The bikers have been holding a grudge for a while, though, so it's been coming. You move quickly for… it doesn't matter, sir."

"For a fat bloke? You may as well say it, Hurricane, everyone's been thinking it." The sirens were getting closer. "Call them off. Say it was a false alarm and it's all quietened down now. There will be no more trouble. I need a word with Scraggs."

"OK, sir."

Bob straightened his uniform and walked over to the surfers.

"Right, lads, I don't want to hear a murmur from you lot or I'm on your case. And you don't want me on your case. Scraggs! A word, please"

Scraggs followed Bob to the sea wall, away from the crowd.

"Look, son, I know you've had it tough and lost your sister, but you can't go through life fighting everything and everybody."

Scraggs's bravery left him the moment he heard his sister mentioned. He was holding back the tears with his back to his surfer mates, looking out to sea. Bob put a hand on his shoulder.

"It's OK, son. If she can be found, I'll find her, I promise. Oh, and sorry I lied about the sales job. I am the new detective inspector in the nick, and I was only told today about your sister. I'm going to try to find out what happened, but I might need your help. Is that OK?"

"Yes, anything. I miss Lizzy so much."

"I know, son. Here is the deal: you keep out of bother and I'll have a look into the case, is that fair enough?"

"I would do anything to get her back." Scraggs's shoulders were heaving up and down as the tears poured down his face. He was finally letting out all the emotions he had been bottling up since Lizzy had disappeared.

"I know, son. Look at me." Bob squared his shoulders and eyeballed Scraggs. "I'm on it. Anything you can remember, write it down. I'll read up on the case and come and see you in a week or so."

"OK, thanks."

"Anything at all you remember. You might not think it's important, but let me be the judge of that. Deal?"

"Deal." Winning some of his composure back, Scraggs wiped the tears from his eyes with his jumper before walking confidently back to the lads. But they all knew where Scraggs's anger had come from, too.

Despite Higgins radioing in to cancel them, the cavalry still turned up. "Everything alright, sir?" one of the guys in the police car enquired.

"It's all good. Just a few lads trying to throw their weight around. It calmed down as quickly as it started, thanks to Higgins here." Higgins was about to correct him when Bob added with authority, "Isn't that right, Higgins?"

"Hurricane?"

"Yes, something and nothing. I radioed it in just in case, but it's all sorted now."

"I tell you what, guys, can you give Higgins a lift back to the station? I'll see you tomorrow; I have a couple of things to sort out in the flat."

"Thanks, sir."

"Thank you, Hurricane, you did well today, son. Your dad would be proud." Higgins gave him a nod before leaving for the station.

Chapter 6 – Detecting a Change

Monday morning announced itself through the gap in the curtains. Bob was up and ready to greet it, pulling the curtains back and allowing the bright winter sunlight to enter the room. After a shave and a shower, he managed to lower the brightness levels by changing into one of his ill-fitting dark grey suits. He performed his usual 'Do I look fat in this suit?' pose in the mirror, concluding that he looked no fatter than yesterday. Whether this was a good or bad sign, he was not sure. He took it as a good one.

After a lighter than normal breakfast, he headed up towards the police station in the hope it would be open early for once. He needn't have bothered, so the coffee shop it was. But there was a bounce in his step today – he was going to enjoy Saltburn and his new job whether the locals liked it or not.

Audrey greeted him. "Skinny latte and a croissant, Bob?"

"Not today, Audrey, just a fresh orange juice and a smile would be nice."

She looked up in surprise at the orange juice request, but as always, she afforded him a smile.

"Is this the new you again, Bob?"

"Yes, you could say that. Tell me, what do you know about Lizzy Scraggs?"

"Lizzy Scraggs? Mmmm, not much. I remember that she took her dog for a walk, Saltburn to Redcar, and I guess she lost track of the time. The last people to see her were her friends, who walked with her back to Marske before returning to Redcar. It was dark by then. Poor girl, nobody ever saw her again. Her dog was found on the beach by her brother, I think. He'd gone out looking for her, and said the dog was all over the place, looking confused. He found the dog's lead in St Germaine's churchyard, overlooking the sea in Marske. Do you know it?"

Bob, who had been frantically writing in his notepad, looked up, realising she had asked him a question.

"Err, not really. Is that all?"

Audrey looked a bit puzzled. She thought that was quite a lot.

"I don't think there is anything more to tell, Bob. She

disappeared into thin air. Everyone was out looking for her. Oh, it was a big tide, one of the biggest for years. And it was a stormy day. My guess is the sea got her. The tide can be scary around here, if you get stuck the wrong side of a sandbank. Before you know it, it's got you."

"That doesn't explain the dog lead," Bob reminded her as he looked back through his notes.

"No, I suppose not. Maybe someone found it and left it on the churchyard wall, or something?"

"I guess so. Thanks, Audrey." As Bob took his orange juice to a table and waited for someone to appear on key duty at the police station, his mind gave him a nudge as a thought drifted past.

Maybe I should offer to do key duty. At least I could then get in at a reasonable time.

Before he had time to weigh up his options, a police uniform appeared in the distance. To Bob's surprise, it was worn by Sergeant Hopkins.

Bob met him at the police station door.

"You not in uniform today, Dicko? It is Dicko, isn't it? The boys have been talking." The sergeant gave Bob an appreciative tap on the back as he fumbled with the keys.

"Yes, Hoppy. If you can't beat 'em, join 'em, I guess. It is Hoppy, isn't it?"

They both laughed, sharing their first moment of mutual respect in three months.

"You have done more than join 'em, Dicko. Hurricane told us all about your heroics, and how you put yourself on the line for him." Hopkins opened the door before continuing, "The thing is…" he left a gap "…you proved you had his back. That's all these lads want, you know."

"I know, Hoppy, I just went about it all the wrong way."

"Come in, Dicko, I have a surprise for you." Hopkins took Bob into the main office, where some storage cabinets had been moved around to make space for his desk. "Ta da!"

"They didn't have to do that."

"I know they didn't." Hopkins's smile spoke volumes. "But they did do it, didn't they?" They both knew it was a sign of acceptance. "Skelly has also pulled Lizzy Scraggs's case file for you from Redcar CID. He said you were interested in reading it. It's on your new desk."

"Thanks, Hoppy."

"Hey, it's not my doing. They're a good lot, Dicko. Just don't piss them off again."

"I wasn't planning to."

The heavy buff-coloured case file had string in a figure-of-eight loop keeping it shut tight against the round cardboard spools that were struggling to hold in the contents. Bob unravelled the string, relieving the pressure. A few pictures fell out; they were of the churchyard where the dog lead had been found, the dog, Lizzy Scraggs and what she had been wearing that day.

This is going to take a while, he thought, but Bob was not short of whiles. He could dedicate all the whiles he needed to the task.

He took out his notepad and noted anything down that he thought would help him; anything that seemed out of place or important enough to remember. He had been on the go for an hour before the rest of the guys came in, then he broke off to thank them for sorting the office out. The atmosphere was different today; the lads in the office offered him coffees and involved him in their conversations. He felt at home for the first time since he'd set foot in Saltburn.

Over the next week, Bob dedicated all his time to finding out what had happened to Lizzy Scraggs, or proving that she could not be found. Either way, he saw it as his mission to absorb everything he could about the case before making enquiries of his own, which would be tricky since six years had passed since her disappearance. He had a large whiteboard put up in his old office cell on which he wrote important facts, people and locations. The problem was, he felt that there was something missing, but as yet he did not know where, when or why it had gone missing.

All cases can be solved. Something must have happened or Lizzy would still be here. The one thing that was clear was Lizzy Scraggs had not been seen or heard from since that stormy day six years ago. Yes, she could well be dead – Bob was not stupid – but how would she have died? Did the sea get her, as Audrey had suggested, or was she taken? Who knew? The only thing Bob did know was that he was thinking and behaving like a detective again. It was like a drug, pulling him in, deeper and deeper. The clues were all there; he just had to look at them from a different angle.

He thought about how Audrey had said someone probably left the dog lead on the churchyard wall, but on the picture, it was on the grass, not the wall. But whereabouts? Bob's mind was analysing the facts.

The dog lead's location might be important, or it might not be, but it's the only lead I've got. Bob smiled as he recognised the pun. He knew he needed to get closer to the detail.

It's time to go see Scraggs, he thought.

Chapter 7 – Where the Hell is Lizzy Scraggs?

Bob knocked on Scraggs's door. There was no immediate answer, so he knocked again. This knock had more purpose and bite to it, suggesting that if Scraggs were in, it would be a good idea to answer. A dog started barking, there was movement inside, then someone answered the door. It was Scraggs.

"I can't believe you're a copper, Bob. You are called Bob, aren't you, or were you lying about that too? Bloody coppers."

"Scraggs, I'm here about Lizzy. I don't have to be, so I suggest you get over the fact you hate coppers. This one is here to help, believe it or not. Have you got anything for me?"

The dog's barking was getting louder in the back of the house.

"Quiet, bloody dog!" The dog obeyed, sort of, his angry bark turning into a menacing growl. "Nothing new. I have tried, believe me, but everything I knew, I told you lot. You even thought it was me for a while, bastards! As if I would hurt Lizzy. You're all the same, you lot."

"Do you want me to send the case back to Redcar, Scraggs? I'm quite happy to do that; I'm working towards my retirement here. It's your call, son." Bob purposely left a gap, allowing for some sort of reflection in Scraggs's brain. "The one thing I need from you is trust."

The dog started barking and snarling again.

"Is that Slaven?"

"Yep, how do you know his name?"

"I've read Lizzy's case file, Scraggs. I've taken in what I can, but I need some help from you."

Scraggs stared at the detective standing at his front door.

"OK, trust, you say? You're on. Anything to find what happened to Lizzy." The dog let out another loud bark, and Scraggs continued, "Bloody idiot, he thinks he's going for a walk. I'm glad you're looking at the case. Nobody seems to give a shit about her anymore, so thanks for that, and I'll tell you what I know if you think it will help."

"How about we take him for a walk? I'm sort of on a diet, so it might do me some good. We can talk while we walk, if you like, and maybe you can take me to the churchyard in Marske?"

"I've done all of this before. What makes you think it will be any different with you?"

"Well, I'm here, aren't I? And I have your sister's case on my desk, so that's got to count for something."

"OK, I'll get his lead."

"No need, son, I have his old one." Bob pulled out the lead he had taken from the evidence and gave it to Scrags.

"Slaven, here, now!"

The dog obeyed instantly. Scraggs went to put the lead on him, but he wriggled away, snarling at his owner.

"Is he always like this?" Bob enquired.

"No. Slaven, sit!" The dog obeyed again, but still fought against the lead, refusing to have it anywhere near him. "I'll get his normal lead, crazy dog."

Bob put the lead back in his jacket pocket as Scraggs headed inside. The dog looked up at Bob's pocket where the lead had been placed, growling again to ensure the man got the message that he was having none of it.

When Scraggs returned, Slaven accepted his normal lead with all the doggy mannerisms of walkie time: tail wagging, bouncing on his hind legs, and jumping up at Scraggs. Then they headed off to the beach, where Slaven was released to enjoy the freedom of the shoreline while the two men ambled towards Marske-by-the-Sea.

"So Slaven, what type of name is that for a dog?"

"You really need to do your Middlesbrough homework, Bob. And I thought you were a detective. Bernie Slaven, Middlesbrough's top goal scorer. Have you had a parmo yet?"

"No, not yet, but I've had a lemon-top. Quite a few, actually."

Scraggs laughed. "There is hope for you yet, DI Dixon."

"So take me back to 12 February 2006. I'm all ears."

The dog was chasing seagulls back and forth with no luck, jumping in and out of the rock pools that had formed as the tide receded. The sea was now on the way back to reclaim them, and Bob could see how easy it would be to end up the wrong side of one of these deep pools. The tide would creep up on you, and you'd be trapped.

"It was a bit of a mad day. I would normally take Slaven out, he was only young then, but this was a day in a million. One of the biggest tides Saltburn has seen, mixed with a north-easterly wind. It's bad for fishermen; they love a sou'wester as it backs the sea down."

Bob looked confused.

"For surfing, it was like a perfect storm." Scraggs stopped as if he were reliving the day. "When the tide turned, it produced some of the biggest and best waves for decades. Coincidentally, we have another big tide tomorrow. It's like a mad, crazy surfer's dream."

Scraggs and Bob continued walking. Slaven was busy swimming back across a large pool, having already got blocked off by the incoming tide.

"So Lizzy took the dog out for me and headed off to Redcar to see her mates. Slaven was with her, and as you have seen, he can be quite protective, so she should have been OK." Scraggs paused again to take a large breath. "Bloody surfing! She would still be here if it wasn't for me and my bloody surfing."

"OK, son, none of this is your fault. What happened next?" Scraggs was getting visibly upset, but Bob's calming tone allowed him to wrestle back some composure.

"We could only surf for a few hours after the tide had turned. It was so big that later that night, it would crash over the sea wall. They even had to sandbag The Ship's doors. Anyway, I finished surfing about three pm and headed off home."

The dog was shaking himself dry next to them after his swim. They continued walking.

"And when did you start to think something was wrong?"

"When it got dark, I suppose. My mam was getting worried, so I grabbed a torch and headed off to the beach. I was about here." He stopped walking. They were more or less in Marske. "Yes, it was here, opposite the black ash path, and it was pouring down." Scraggs pointed out the black path weaving its way onto the beach through a gap in the hills.

"Then what?"

"Slaven came running along the beach and saw me, but he was not his normal self. He was whimpering and whining. He grabbed my jumper and started pulling me towards Marske. I followed him to the graveyard where I found the dog lead on the grassy area next to the steeple of old St Germaine's."

"Can you show me?"

Scraggs pointed at the steeple on the bank top. "There is no church – hasn't been for years – just the ruins and the steeple." Scraggs pointed to another path that led up the sandbank to the churchyard. "There is a path just after Blue Mountain."

"Blue Mountain?" Scraggs pointed to a small, muddy hill. "It's not very blue, or very big. I wouldn't really call it a mountain." Bob looked again, making sure he was looking in the right direction.

"It's been called Blue Mountain since I was a kid, beats me why. I've never really thought about it."

They worked their way past the brown hill masquerading as a much larger and bluer landmark to the path which would take them off the beach. As they approached the churchyard, Slaven got noticeably more nervous and discontented, staying close to his owner. They climbed the path to the cemetery and walked across the grass bank at the top to the opening in the wall. Scraggs placed Slaven back on the lead.

"He won't go in. I've tried before, but whatever happened in there, he's not forgotten it."

"Really?"

"Yes, really. You'll see."

As they entered the churchyard through the gap where a gate probably used to be, the dog was having none of it, snarling and growling, pulling at Scraggs's arm.

"See?" Scraggs pointed to the derelict church's steeple and the grassy area on the foundations where the church itself used to be. "I found the lead over there. Slaven won't come in. I'd better stay with him."

As the dog whimpered again, still refusing to budge, Bob looked at what was left of the church. As he approached the ruins, he looked up at its crumbling walls and the steeple which had stood there for hundreds and hundreds of years.

"So where did you go to, Lizzy Scraggs?" he said out loud, feeling that the question would be better aired in public than fumbling around in his mind.

Slaven was still snarling at the churchyard entrance. "I'll take him for a walk along the top, calm him down a bit," Scraggs shouted. Bob threw up an arm in acknowledgment. He then reset his mind and posed the question again.

"So, Lizzy, what happened to you here?" Bob touched the wall of the church as he made his way round the steeple, looking for inspiration. As he appeared on the other side, the sky got noticeably darker and it started raining. He stood in the centre of the grassy area where the dog lead had been found, getting wet.

He took the dog lead from his pocket. "Come on, Lizzy. Give me something."

The lead started to glow with a fluorescent blue colour in front of Bob's eyes. In shock, he dropped it on the ground and the blueness faded away. Immediately, the sky lightened and the rain stopped.

"What the…?" Bob picked up the lead, which once again let out a blue glow, and the darkness and rain returned. As the sky got darker still and the rain got heavier, the lead appeared to be gaining power. It glowed and fizzed in his hand like it was feeding off the environment.

A movement caught Bob's eye. He instinctively looked to the cemetery wall. A man dressed entirely in black was walking through the gap where Scraggs and Slaven had been, a girl with him. Bob took cover behind the steeple to keep out of sight. Placing the glowing lead back into his pocket, he took up a position where he could see the two figures approaching, but they could not see him.

The man was talking to the girl as they approached, and to Bob's surprise, Slaven was with them. This Slaven was younger than the terrified dog Bob had last seen with Scraggs, but it was unmistakably him, and he was off the lead. Lizzy had the lead in her hands.

Bob cupped his ear to try to eavesdrop on their conversation.

"You should not be out this late on your own, Lizzy. I'll drop you back in Saltburn."

"I didn't realise the time, my mam will kill me."

"We'll have you safe and sound back home soon. My car is parked just over here."

They left the path and walked over to the grassy area next to the steeple, and Bob moved too, taking cover on the other side of the church wall.

"Stand here for me, Lizzy."

"Can we go, Mister? I'm getting wet."

The man took a step back and raised his hands to the sky. A blue glow engulfed Lizzy and the grassy area took on a misty quality, diffusing the blue light outward from Lizzy's body as Bob looked on.

"What the hell?" he said under his breath.

Lizzy looked calm, as if she was in a trance and unable to move. Slaven, who had scuttled ahead, ran back to the church to protect her, barking loudly at the man as he approached. As he jumped up to bite him, the man moved the palm of his hand. Mid-flight, Slaven fell to the ground, helpless and whimpering in pain.

"No!" screamed Lizzy, unable to move.

"Lizzy, you are coming with me. I'm so sorry, but I have to take someone. It's in the rules. You are going on a journey with me – I always have to take one."

Lizzy looked on, a haze of blue emanating from her body through the thickening mist. Bob watched both figures drifting in and out of focus. At times he could see straight through them as if they were transparent, and their voices would fluctuate. It was like watching an old TV with a weak signal. As they more or less disappeared, the signal seemed to pick up, and they would gain clarity once again.

"You have to leave a little magic here, Lizzy, I only need your soul."

Lizzy looked at her dog, helpless on the floor, and then at the dog lead in her hand. Her glowing blue body slowly turned back to normal, with the dog lead absorbing her glow.

Bob left his hiding place behind the wall and ran to help Lizzy. As he approached, he held out his arms to grab her, but flew straight through her body and collided with a gravestone on the other side. Neither Lizzy nor her abductor flinched.

Bob picked himself up and turned to look at them, it dawning on him that he was seeing history. This wasn't the here and now; he had somehow unlocked a projection of the past.

Armed with the knowledge he could not be seen, Bob moved in front of the black-clad man.

"Good girl, Lizzy," the man was saying, "we all have to leave some magic behind. I'm so sorry it's you. I'm so sorry it's anybody."

Lizzy nodded, mesmerised. There was no fight left in her. After the blue light had gone out of her, it was as if she had no need for her body anymore.

Bob eyeballed the black-clad man. As he did so, the stranger raised his hands to the sky. When he lowered them, there was a flash and Lizzy disappeared, the dog lead falling onto the grass. Bob gasped.

"You bastard! I'm going to catch you, arsehole, and I won't stop until I do." Even though the man in front of him was a projection, Bob continued to eyeball him. "You'll screw up, sunshine, and I'll be there when you do."

The man had a skinhead and a distinctive diamond-shaped scar on his cheek, with deeper marks on the corners.

"I don't forget a face, definitely not one as ugly as yours."

The signal to the past was getting weaker now, the man more or less disappearing from view in front of Bob's eyes before regaining form again.

"Why me? Why do you make me do it?" he shouted up at the sky, the rain pouring down on him. "Somebody needs to stop me, please…"

The stranger fell sobbing to his knees, taking out a knife and looking at the blade inches away from Bob's face. He then turned and ran to a gravestone to the left of the churchyard.

"I don't have much time. Think, Stephen, think. THINK!"

Bob followed the stranger to a group of gravestones.

"Which one is it? Not that one. Nope, nope… here it is. Emily Harper." The black-clad stranger took out the knife again and scored under the date on the gravestone, 10 February 1906, underlining the day and month with four or five sharp swipes of the knife. He then circled around the back of the gravestone. Bob watched as he frantically and clumsily scored more of the stone. He then ran to the centre of the grassy area, picked up the dog lead and formed it into an arrow, pointing at the gravestone.

"Come on, coppers, don't let me down. I need you to stop me. I'm done with all this shit. She'll be scared." He then stood up straight and raised his hands as he had done before. His eyes glowing red, he clapped his hands before disappearing into thin air.

As soon as the stranger had vanished, the dog struggled to his feet and staggered his first few steps before running out of the churchyard. The dog lead on the ground disappeared, the daylight returned, the rain stopped, and Bob was left standing alone in the grassy area.

"What the hell was all that about?" He checked the lead was still in his pocket, and it was, but it was no longer glowing. And Bob's hair, which had been flattened to his head by the rain, seemed to have dried instantly.

Bob went back to the grave. The lines the man had scored had been worn over the years, but were still visible through the green, almost fluorescent moss. He noted down the date and Emily's name, then rubbed the back of the gravestone with his hand to make the marks clearer, copying what he could make out into his notebook.

"Did you find anything?"

Bob heard Scraggs shout from the gap in the wall; the dog was still refusing to enter the churchyard. He stood up from behind gravestone.

"No, nothing at all, Scraggs." Bob shrugged for effect before joining Scraggs and Slaven at the churchyard entrance, deciding not to mention a thing about what he had just witnessed. They walked back to Saltburn along the bank tops overlooking the sea, Bob making small talk and reassuring Scraggs that he would do everything he could to find out what had happened to Lizzy. As they approached the pier and funicular, he thanked Scraggs for his time.

"Keep out of trouble, Scraggs."

Scraggs nodded as they said their goodbyes.

"Thanks for doing this, Bob, it means a lot."

Chapter 8 – MMXII P + W B

After Scraggs left, Bob stayed where he was for a while, trying to put things together in his head, baffled by what had just happened in the churchyard. But it had happened; he remembered it all. He gave his head a shake, recalling something Keith had told him and his fellow travellers during his funicular ride.

Bob walked up to the cage-man at the bottom of the funicular. "Bill, isn't it?"

Bill was a thickset man who looked like the fat controller on *Thomas the Tank Engine*, complete with watch on a chain in his pocket, a black three-piece suit and checked shirt. Imagine the stereotypical Victorian train guard, and you would be spot on.

"Yes, I'm Bill."

Bob flashed his warrant card. "DI Bob Dixon from Saltburn nick."

"I know, I remember you from the other day. Did you enjoy Keith's speech at the top? He always winds our passengers up, that one." Bill laughed. "He says it's good for business. Did you know he was a copper like you?"

Bob nodded and tried to get back to the point.

"That's what I wanted to chat about, Bill. Keith said there was a night, thirty or so years ago, where a man and a boy failed to make it to the bottom. He said they disappeared." Bob took out his notepad, which did not go unnoticed.

"And you're investigating that? Are you not very busy?" Bill's broad frame heaved up and down as he let out a chuckle.

"Busy? Believe it or not, not really." Bob joined in with Bill's chuckle, which was lasting longer than he was expecting. "I was going to ask you about it at the time, but you were busy loading the next group, so I never got to hear the end of the story."

"You wouldn't believe me if I told you."

"Try me, I'm intrigued." This Bob said sternly to get the conversation onto a more serious vein. It worked. Bill's chuckling stopped.

"Well, I don't believe in all the crap Keith spouts about ley lines and stuff. I can only tell you what I saw."

"Of course, just stick to the facts." Bob had gone into his evidence-gathering stance, notepad and pencil poised. He liked facts; he could feed off them.

"We had just about closed up for the night. It was raining and there was a big tide, so the sea was lapping up over the sea wall. Even the pier had been closed by the police. We had nobody going up, but the brake-man called a last trip coming down. He told me later that the man had said they had left something in the arcade. It was an old man and a boy. He assumed it was granddad and grandson."

Bill looked at Bob to see if he was following. He was. "Go on."

"We set the cars off, and then I saw a flash of blue and lights bleeding out of the stained-glass windows as the cars crossed. When I opened the cage, there was nobody in it."

"What was the date? Do you remember, by any chance? Roughly?"

"I can give you the exact date. When I opened the car, there was one ticket on the floor which had the outbound punch and a date stamp on it. It was… well, it was… never mind."

"It was what, Bill?"

"You're going to think I'm crazy, but it was giving off a blue light. It was sort of glowing." When Bob did not look surprised, Bill continued, "Look, nobody believes me, but that's why I kept the ticket. That's what I saw. Do you think I'm mad?"

"No, you're not mad, far from it. Where's the ticket now?"

"I'll show you. Keith tells people to ask me to show them when they get down, so I've had it framed. Here." He went into his cabin. Following him in, Bob saw a framed ticket with the date 16 Mar 1980 stamped on it and the punch hole where the word 'out' used to be.

"Thanks, Bill." Bob wrote the date into his notebook. "Can I borrow the ticket?"

Bill opened the case and took it out. "I don't see why not. I'll just put another one in there to back Keith's story up."

"Thanks. Is Keith up there now? I might need a word later."

"Yeah, he's up there. Do you want to ride?"

"I'll walk, Bill, thanks. I've done about three or four miles already today, which is helping my diet. Anyway, I've got a lot of thinking to do, and I have to go to the station first."

"No probs. Nice to have met you, but please keep it quiet about the blue lights stuff. People think I'm crazy as it is."

"Mum's the word. Hey, thanks – you've been a great help."

Bob put the ticket in his wallet and headed up the winding path to the top of the hill and back to the station.

Back in the office, Bob's mind was spinning. He was a man on a mission and it showed. He'd left this morning with one dog lead, which had led him to a series of events he now had to try to piece together. Bob was an intelligent man who could work out the most difficult of puzzles when the evidence was all laid out in front of him. The problem here was that the events he'd witnessed this morning had given him more questions than answers. This was not an episode of *Scooby-Doo*; this was real. He had been there to witness what had happened to Lizzy, and he had to believe what he had seen and take it on face value, or go to see a doctor to find out if he was going mad.

He went into his cell and drew all the facts as he knew them on the board. He drew the church steeple, complete with grassy area, in the middle of the board. Next to it, he drew a square which he filled with bulleted information.

- Lizzy Scraggs's last known position
- Suspect – Stephen, tall, diamond-shaped scar, black overcoat, wants to be caught?
- The dog lead as an arrow
- Gravestone – Emily Harper, died 10 Feb 1906
- Back of grave – MMXII P + W B

Bob's brain was not tuned in to thinking, so he was brain dumping. Thinking would come later. *It's a lot easier to do a jigsaw puzzle when you have all the pieces*, he thought. He did not have all the pieces at the moment, but he was getting them out of the box. Information breeds information. *One thing will lead to another as long as I can see the connection.*

Hopkins popped his head in. "Coffee, Dicko?"

"Not now, Hoppy, just getting things out of my head." It was the first time Hopkins had seen Bob in detective mode since he'd arrived, so he left the DI to it.

Bob drew the position of the grave, and then added a dotted line from the arrow-shaped dog lead.

"Who are the players?" he said out loud to prompt himself as his brain was working on the timeline. "Lizzy was last seen about five-thirty by her friends on the beach in Marske, which must have been near the boats."

Bob drew a picture of a boat, badly, to signify Marske beach, along with another information square. Inside the square, he wrote, *Lizzy last seen alive 17.30pm with friends (Names x 4 in case file)* adding *five mins from church.* He then positioned Scraggs near the black ash path with an information square containing the words *ten minutes from the church, Scraggs found Slaven here, dog agitated.*

"OK, is that it?" he asked himself, surveying his work. *No, hang on, I've missed something.* He swapped his black pen for a blue one. *Strange blue lights* did not seem a sensible thing to write on a board in public view, or even locked away in a cell. Instead, he rubbed *dog lead* and *Lizzy Scraggs* out of the church information square and replaced them in blue. As he did this, he remembered what Bill had said about the funicular. He thought for a second, then spoke out loud.

"OK, let's connect it for now."

He drew the funicular with a square listing the information *Bill the cage-man,* then added *ticket* in blue, before getting the ticket out of his wallet and noting the date: 16 March 1980. Finally, he added *old man and a boy (Stephen?)* to the bottom of his latest list of information.

"Right, that's it. Coffee time, then thinking time." Bob was quite proud of his brain dump. He would let things settle and get comfortable on the board before clicking the thinking switch in his head. It felt good being a detective again.

Bob made a coffee and went to join Hoppy and Skelly in the office.

"Having fun, sir?" Skelly enquired. "She just seemed to disappear. Keith was all over the case for a year or so, but you know how things get further and further back on the priority list. She was probably lost to the sea – big tide that day. The sea is a bugger if you don't respect it."

Bob looked at Skelly, and then at his office cell, sipping his coffee. He'd missed something.

"Yes, I wouldn't call it fun, Skelly, but it's nice to be on a case again."

"Poor girl. Her mother has died now and her brother's a right tearaway."

"Well, I'm just getting things out of my head for now, Skelly. I will go and see Keith, though. I'm sure there'll be a few things he'll know without knowing he knows them."

"He was a good detective, Keith. I'm sure if there was anything to find, he would have found it. That casefile is massive."

Bob agreed. "I know, I've read most of it." He finished off his coffee quickly, eager to get back in the cell he had been trying to get out of for the last three months. Back at the whiteboard, he wrote *big tide* in a new general information box and added *Scraggs – surfing – big surf.* Then he put the pen down and stared at the board, focusing in on the graveyard section. What had happened six years ago was in his mind. He had been so busy keeping all the details locked in, it was the first time he had had time to reflect.

What the hell happened? It rained, it got dark, and somehow something gave me a porthole to the past.

Nobody would believe him if he spouted off about it, except maybe Bill. It did happen, though. He could still see it in his mind as clear as day. Or was it night? Either way, it was clear. He had been given front row seats to a kidnap, or possibly even a murder.

"So, Stephen, what were you trying to tell me?" Bob said as he moved nearer the whiteboard, looking at MMXII P + WB. "Come on, you wouldn't have gone to all that trouble to write it without a reason."

He then looked at the board again, pen poised. Taking the underlined date from Emily Harper's gravestone, he wrote as he talked.

"I don't think you're important, Emily my love, I think he just needed your date." He then looked at the Roman numerals scored onto the back of the grave. "You guys *are* important, though. M, M, X, I, I. Even I can work that out: 2012." Bob wrote 2012 on the whiteboard next to Emily's date. Then he stood back from the board, startled. "That's tomorrow! What's so special about tomorrow, Stephen?"

Bob thought back to Scraggs on the beach, telling him about the massive tide that appeared once every six or seven years or so and the surfing pleasures it would bring with it. He could not connect anything to this directly, but knowing it was too much of a coincidence to have no importance, he wrote on the whiteboard *???* after the *big tide* he had written earlier. The three question marks would remind him to follow this up and confirm it.

Then he turned his attention to the rest of the puzzle on the back of Emily's grave. Staring at the letters, he looked for inspiration.

P + W B. It must mean something.

He tried again, staring harder at the words on the board as if they were in trouble, but the result was the same. Nothing.

What could it mean?

Pulling an 'I'm doing my best to answer that' face, he flicked over to his default setting of logic, looking at the date again.

"So we have a date and a year here. If Stephen is telling me a date, it must be for a reason, but I would expect a place and maybe a time to go with it." Bob wrote *place, P + W, and time, B*. "Well, I guess the 'B' could be an eight. Eight o'clock, maybe?" Imagining how hard it would be to score an eight with a knife, Bob decided that was probably why Stephen had chosen Roman numerals for the date: they were all straight lines.

Clever boy, Stephen.

"Let's say it's an eight, then. OK, so we have a date, tomorrow, and eight o'clock. Well, maybe eight." As he circled this section of the board, his mind agreed with him and ruled the eight in as a good idea. "That leaves P + W, probably P and W."

I'm lost on that *one,* he thought. *It must be a place and he wants us to meet there?*

"Six years ago, Stephen planted evidence to lead someone to him and stop him from taking or maybe killing kids. He wants to meet tomorrow at eight pm, but where?"

Bob was not sure if any of this was right, and he did not have a clue where 'where' was, but the evidence did appear to tell him when, and it was tomorrow.

I need some air, he thought. *I'll go see Keith at the cliff lift. Maybe he can shed some light on where P and W might be.*

It was 2.30pm. As he approached the lift, Bob could see Keith had hoodwinked another group of paying customers with his ripping yarn about the funicular.

"Can I have a word when you're done, Keith?"

"Of course. Just let me get rid of this lot down the hill."

Bob stood to the side, listening to Keith deliver his well-rehearsed speech before corralling the passengers into the funicular car, scared to bits.

"So what's up, Bob? All OK?" Keith said as he kicked off the brake in the central control station hut and the cars slowly reacted to each other and set off on their opposite journeys.

"It's this Lizzy Scraggs case, Keith. Well, your name's all over the file, so I wondered if you could enlighten me on a couple of things."

"No problem. Sad day, that. How can someone just disappear?" Keith was looking straight ahead, attending to his brake applying duties. "Ask away."

"Did anyone report a blue light at Marske churchyard that day?"

"No blue lights, Bob. You must have been listening to Bill down there. He's crazy – still claims he saw blue lights in the funicular car. Old fool."

Bob put his serious face on, which was wasted as Keith was looking at the cars through the hut's window. The sternness of his voice did the trick, though.

"Nothing, Keith? No mention of a blue light?"

"Do you know what? When we did the door-to-door on the houses opposite the churchyard, there was talk of a blue flare going off out at sea. It lit up the houses facing the church for a couple of minutes."

"Did you follow up on it?"

Keith gave him a copper to copper look before turning back to attend to his brake duties as the car approached the upper station.

"What do you think, Bob? Of course I did. I called the lifeboat station in Redcar and there was no report of it. They weren't called out that night, and they would have remembered as it was the biggest tide for years. If anyone did set a flare off, they would not have stood a chance out at sea. We put it down to kids mucking about. They used to nick flares from the engine boxes of the boats on Marske beach."

"Thanks, Keith. One more thing – you know your story about the ley line coming from the sea, up through Marske church to the funicular, and then over Huntcliff?"

"Yes."

"Is that really all bollocks to beef your scary story up?"

"How dare you suggest such a thing?" Keith gave Bob a playful nudge as he applied the brake and brought the car to a halt. "It's all bollocks to me, and I guess it does help my story out, but there is a farmer on the cliff who believes in all that crap. He is the one who told me about the ley line a few years back."

"Really? What's his name?"

"Charles White. He goes by the name of Chalky, and he lives up there." Keith pointed out a farmhouse on the way to the top of Huntcliff as he left the control hut to let out the waiting passengers. "He uses dowsing rods to find water holes for farmers. A whole load of crap, if you ask me. You'll always find water if you drill deep enough."

"OK, thanks. You've been a great help."

"Have I? Are you sure, Bob?"

Bob winked at him. "Of course I'm sure. Are you open tomorrow, Keith?"

"It'll be a mess tomorrow night – big tide again. We will probably run until about six pm, then we'll have to shut down. I doubt we'll have anyone down there anyway, and definitely no one up here who'll want to head down there. The pier will be closed, too. The tide turns two-ish."

"Thanks, Keith. I might come for a ride before six. I want to test out a theory."

"OK, but don't be too late. We'll knock it on the head earlier if we can. They might need help moving all the boats into the park."

"Thanks, Keith. Do you have this Charles White's…" Bob consulted his notebook, "…Chalky's number?"

"No, but they will have it in the office. Everyone knows him."

Bob thanked Keith again as a couple more people joined the queue for the funicular.

"Last thing, Keith: if I said the initials P and W to you, would it ring any bells?"

“P and W? No, nothing springs to mind. Why?”

“Nothing to worry about, I just wondered if anything would jump out at you, that’s all.” Bob had no wish to be banished to the blue-light-crazy-fool farm along with Bill the cage operator and Chalky White the dowsing farmer.

Chapter 9 – Every Holmes Needs a Watson

Bob made his way back to the station and headed straight for his old office. He'd spent months hating that cell, but now it was serving a purpose, he could not wait to be back in it again.

He looked at his whiteboard. There was no doubt about it – he needed help, and he needed local knowledge. He sped off to the kitchen and made himself and Hopkins a coffee.

"Hoppy, I'm deep into the Lizzy Scraggs case and I think I'm getting somewhere."

"Really, Dicko? It's a case so cold that I doubt even you'd be able to warm it up."

"Well, no, not on my own. I think I'm missing out on some local knowledge. It's hard when I'm not from round here to work out where the gaps might be. On my own."

The second 'on my own' did the trick. Hoppy rolled his eyes and looked at his coffee, which he now saw as a bribe.

"Who do you want, Bob? It's not like we are snowed under."

"Skelly was telling me that young Higgins from Redcar is a whizz on computers. I don't really want to be getting files delivered from Redcar every time I need some info."

Hopkins took a sip from his coffee while weighing it all up. Bribe or not, it tasted good.

"What do you think of him, Dicko? He's a bit geeky, but the lads all like him. His dad was a good copper, you know, and he's got a lot to live up too, poor kid."

"He's a Saltburn lad, and he was by my side when it kicked off at The Ship. I like him. I just need another pair of hands and eyes for a bit. It will do him some good to do some detective work like his dad."

"I'll make a call. When do you need him from?"

"Like, yesterday?"

Hopkins had just taken another sip of his coffee, and almost choked on it when he laughed.

"You don't want much, do you? I tell you what, I do have a space over here. We are running one short at the moment, so I'll ring Sergeant Shakespeare at Redcar. Shaky and I go back years. Like you say, it might do the young lad some good, make him come out of his shell a bit. I'll tell him he's on a probationary period over here."

"Out of uniform though, Hoppy. I don't want a uniform walking around with me," Bob added. "Oh, and as a last request, can I have the computer and desk back in the cell?"

"Bloody hell, Dicko, you don't want much. We have just let you out of your bloody cell and you want back in." Hopkins laughed again. "I'll sort it, but you owe me, and more than just a coffee." He picked up the phone. "Shaky? It's been a while, how's Kath?"

Higgins arrived in a white shirt and tie that highlighted his drainpipe figure more than his uniform and protective vest did. He looked like he had turned up for interview practice from school.

"Sir," he said as he walked in.

In London, many years ago, Bob and his partner Frank Cartwright had just started to go after the gangster culture stirring up in the East End when Frank was stabbed. Bob saw Frank die in his arms, unable to stop the bleeding from a knife wound to his femoral artery. Ever since, Bob had blamed himself for not having had his partner's back, even though there was nothing he could have done. And from that day forward, he had never worked with a partner. He couldn't risk going through the pain and blame of it all again. If he absolutely had to work with someone else, he would ask for the biggest, toughest copper on offer.

But Bob did not want Higgins for his brawn. All of the case files he needed were on the computer, and Bob didn't even know how to log on. He needed brains and IT skills, and Higgins had both in abundance.

"Hurricane, I told you I would get you over here. There's your new desk."

"Not sparing on the luxury then, sir? It's in a cell."

"I know, but you'll get used to it. I have." Bob beamed a big smile at his young apprentice. "We need to be out of the way, Hurricane. We have work to do. One thing I do need from you, though."

"What, sir?"

"Trust. I am going to tell you a few things you might find hard to believe, so what happens in this cell, stays in this cell. Deal?"

"I suppose so, sir."

Bob spent the next thirty minutes talking Higgins through the whiteboard. Higgins did not say a word until he had finished.

"Did that really happen, though, sir? Blue lights and all that stuff?"

"Yes, son. I've not gone mad yet, and no, I can't explain it. You don't have to believe me, but you do need to help me chase up on some of it. I can't do it on my own, OK?"

Higgins nodded. "But blue lights and projections? It's like you have been listening to my dad's stories. OK, let's say for now that I believe you. Where do you want me to start? Do you want me to show you on the computer? It's not that hard – have you got a login?"

"Do you know what, son, yes, you can show me. I might not always have you here. I was given a login on my first day; it's in my notebook. Everything is in my notebook sunshine."

Bob pulled up a stool next to Higgins and took out his notebook.

"No, you sit here, sir, and I'll show you."

"I'm not really a computer person, Hurricane." Bob, who normally had confidence in abundance, was abundantly short of confidence where computers were concerned. They were his Kryptonite.

"Every day is a school day, sir." Higgins smiled and vacated the seat, gesturing to his new boss to get comfortable.

Bob was staring at the computer screen, so Higgins started the lesson.

"OK, you have to press Control, Alt and Delete." Bob located the keys on the unfamiliar keyboard, took a deep breath and nervously, with the same finger on his right hand, pressed 'Ctrl' followed by 'Alt', then 'Delete'. Nothing happened.

Higgins laughed out loud. "At the same time, sir. You really are crap at this, aren't you? I thought you were joking." His laugh stopped and he put his serious head back on. "OK, sir, deep breath: Ctrl, Alt and Delete at the same time."

"How? I've only got two hands." Bob located the keys again and thumped them at the same time. Nothing happened.

"When I say at the same time, it's more Ctrl and Alt with your left hand, and then tap Delete."

Bob lost his patience. "Hurricane, I promise I will learn one day. How about you just show me today?" He stood up and left the chair, which had become far too much of a hot seat for him to handle right now, looking like he had escaped from a bear pit. They both laughed, and Bob added, "I'm a quick learner, honest."

"You promise, sir? I'm not your typist, you know. How did you get by in London?"

"Everything is in my notepads, sunshine." Bob tapped his current pad. "Old style, me, remember? If anything needed typing up, the typists did it and printed it out for me. I used to give them a good Christmas tip."

"OK, but you'll have to learn one day. I'm not spending all day typing; I'd rather be back in Redcar, sir. Watch and learn."

Higgins logged on to his account and gave Bob a tour of the case management software and Google before doubling back to the case system.

"So what are we looking for, sir?"

"Missing persons, to start with. Try Lizzy Scraggs."

"You already have that case file, sir, but this is how you would find it on the computer, so I guess it's a good one to show you." All the information Bob had been reading through for the past week or so showed on the search, and Higgins explained how he could double click on the files to open them and print them if required.

"Impressive, Hurricane. How about missing people in general?"

"There will be loads, sir. Anything else to go on?"

"Missing and unsolved. There won't be loads of unsolved cases in this area. Kids go missing all the time, but they normally show up after a day or so."

Higgins put the information into the system and five results were returned.

"The earliest we have on record is 1980 and the latest is Lizzy. Not had one since her." Higgins looked proud of himself before adding, "Unsolved, that is."

"Click on that the oldest one, Stephen John Farrell."

Higgins opened the file and paraphrased it back to Bob. "Reported missing from Redcar 16 March 1980, age twelve, after a row with his dad. His dad owned a pub in Redcar, blah-blah-blah." He scrolled further down. "Never seen again, blah-blah-blah…"

Bob interrupted. "If he was twelve in March 1980, that would make him how old today? About forty-three, forty-four? Did he have a scar on his face?" Bob looked at the board behind him to see he had written the same date against the funicular ticket that Bill had given to him. *I hate coincidences* he thought, trying to give nothing away.

Higgins looked through what little information there was in the case file. "Doesn't say, but there's an old picture." He zoomed in on the blurry old photo of a fresh-faced young boy in school uniform – with no scar.

"I can't tell if that's him, he's too young." Bob put on some reading glasses and moved closer to the screen.

"He's not glowing blue, so probably not." Higgins got a punch on the arm for his jibe, but it was worth it.

"I know what I saw, Hurricane. Was it a big tide that day?"

Higgins turned to Google, and then thought better of it. Not even Google would know about the tide back in the eighties, but the lifeboat station kept all the tide charts.

"They're open twenty-four-seven, and I know the guy who runs it."

"OK, Hurricane, thanks. You're quite good at the computer thing. Can you print off that list of missing people and their dates?"

"I already have. They should be on the printer now, so we can pick them up on our way out."

"Do you have a car?"

"Yes, sir, my car's outside."

"We are trying to remain under the radar. Inconspicuous is the name of the detective game, Hurricane. I don't really want to be showing up in blues and twos."

"Under the radar, you say, sir? Um… OK." Higgins laughed as they left the cell.

Armed with the missing persons list, Bob and Higgins headed for the car park around the back of the station. Higgins pressed the button on his key fob and the four corners of a bright purple Vauxhall Corsa lit up. It had spoilers, fins and bling wherever there was a gap on the bodywork, and the chrome wheels were dazzling in the sunlight.

"You are joking, Hurricane? Inconspicuous, I said."

"It's my pride and joy, sir. You could always get the train."

"No, it's OK, but bloody hell. Talk about pimping up your

wheels." Struggling into the racing bucket seat, Bob shook his head. "This will make me lose a few pounds. Redcar coastguard station, our first port of call, and no speeding."

Higgins's turbo did its best to remain asleep, offering only the occasional disgruntled spit as they crawled out of Saltburn, through Marske, and along the coastal road to Redcar. They parked on the seafront opposite the coastguard station, which was sporting an assortment of aerials and what appeared to be a look-out station on the top of the building.

"We'll have to go through the museum to get up there, sir."

"Museum?" Bob could see the sign proudly announcing that *The Zetland*, the oldest lifeboat in the world, lived here if anybody outside fancied a perusal. As they entered, Higgins gave a nod to the curator, who was showing a group around the large white rowing boat which was the centre of attention. Old pictures of the boat adorned any wall space that was on offer.

Higgins pointed upwards to the curator and received a nod of acceptance without the man breaking his speech to the group. Higgins then showed Bob through the door and they made their way up a winding staircase.

"Hi, Jack," Higgins said as they entered the lookout station. For a young lad, Higgins seemed to know everyone. Having a dad who was the local DI had to have its benefits. Jack stood up and moved away from a bank of computer screens and radar and weather monitors to greet him. "This is DI Dixon from Saltburn nick."

"Pleased to meet you…"

"Bob. It's Bob, Jack, and I'm pleased to meet you, too." They shook hands.

"So, Hurricane, how's your dad getting on? Still scaring people on that cliff lift?" Jack said with a giggle.

"He keeps trying. I remember my dad saying you keep all the tide charts from way back up here – is that right?"

Bob liked how his new partner operated. Higgins was a natural.

"Yes, every chart back to the forties, I think."

Bob took over the conversation. "Great, can you check out a few dates for us, Jack?" He withdrew the folded printout listing the dates of the missing persons from his pocket. Jack walked over to a large bookcase holding the tide tables for each year.

"What year, Bob?"

"The sixteenth of March 1980. I'm guessing it was a big tide?"

Jack took out the 1980 tide table and thumbed his way to March. "Massive. It was a beast – biggest for years, I would guess."

Bob went through the rest of the list. Each date returned the same results – massive tides on all of them.

"Can I ask why?"

Bob laughed. "You can ask, Jack, but I'm not telling you."

"He's just like your dad, Hurricane, giving nothing away." Jack giggled again before adding, "OK, Bob, if you need anything else, let me know."

"Will do. Thanks, you have been a great help."

Chapter 10 – Ley Lines

As Bob struggled back into the seat of the car, which seemed to be easier to get out of than into, he asked Higgins, "Do you know Charles White? Known as Chalky?"

"What, the farmer?"

"Is there another one?"

"Not that I know of. He's a bit mad, sir."

"Well yes, the farmer, then, mad or not. Your dad told me about him and his ley lines. We need to pay him a visit."

"Ley lines?" Higgins started the car and gave it a rev or two out of habit. He got a disgruntled look from his passenger for the day and backed off the throttle.

"Yes, ley lines. Just drive, Hurricane. I'll fill you in on the way."

Having taken the hint, Higgins set off slowly, creeping along Redcar's promenade like he had a dozen eggs in the boot. They went down Saltburn bank and headed up the road past The Ship, climbing the hill before turning up the long, winding dirt track to Chalky's remote farm overlooking Huntcliff. Parking on the enormous drive, they looked up at an even bigger farm house shrouding the driveway in shade.

Bob and Higgins approached the house before knocking on the door. A man in his late sixties opened it. He had bright white hair and a scruffy beard which would have matched his hair had it not been for the yellow nicotine stains around the mouth area.

"Hello, can I help you?"

Bob flashed his warrant card barely long enough for it to be seen. "DI Bob Dixon and Constable Higgins. May I ask you a few questions about ley lines? Apparently, Mr White, you're the expert around these parts, according to Keith who runs the funicular."

"Chalky, please, everyone calls me Chalky."

"OK, Chalky, so what can you tell us about ley lines?"

Chalky was in stereotypical farmer's attire: tweed from head to foot, with a bright yellow and red checked shirt and a matching cravat. He looked like he was about to go out shooting. If people around here thought he was a bit mad, his dress sense wasn't helping to change their opinion.

"I love talking about the ley line, but I don't normally get visitors. Especially ones who want to listen to me ramble on." The man opened the door wider and they followed him into a large, traditional farmhouse kitchen. "Coffee?"

"Do you know what, Mr White… sorry, Chalky? I will. Hurricane?"

Higgins nodded while looking at the array of pictures on the wall. Local landmarks fought for pride of place with some more foreign-looking scenes. Chalky put an old-fashioned kettle on to boil on a large cream-coloured AGA.

"So, what do you want to know? She'll whistle when she's ready."

"Who will?"

Chalky laughed. "The kettle, that's who."

"Oh, do they still do that?" Bob enquired, trying to remember the last time he'd heard a kettle whistle.

"This one does, screams like a good 'un. She always lets me know when she's ready, don't you?" Bob ignored the fact that the man was talking to a kettle as Chalky continued, "OK, what is it you want to know, DI Dixon?"

"Call me Bob, and this is Hurricane." Higgins turned away from the pictures for a second and nodded a welcome in Chalky's direction. Bob left a pause for the names to sink in before continuing. "Hurricane's dad, Keith, said you claim there is a ley line running under the funicular. We just want to know more about it."

"Yes, it runs right through the middle, under the tracks where the cars pass, as far as I can tell."

"How do you know?"

Chalky retrieved a leather-bound notepad from the kitchen drawer.

"Wheeeeeeeeee," the kettle announced to anyone within a half mile radius.

"There she goes, good girl."

Behind Chalky, Higgins gave Bob a look and drew small circles with his finger near his temple.

Chalky took the kettle off the heat and poured out the coffees, placing a bowl of sugar cubes and a spoon on the kitchen top. He then looked at a drawing in his book.

"From what I can work out, it hits land on Marske Beach near the boats, and then heads into the Valley Gardens up Monks Walk before doubling back on itself towards the sea across the headland. I lose it there, but I pick it up again at St Germaine's churchyard. It then seems to head over Blue Mountain and the bank tops to Saltburn, dipping back to the beach occasionally."

Chalky looked up to see if they were still paying attention. They were. Armed with the knowledge he had a captive audience, he continued, "Then, from what I can map out, it goes directly through the centre point of the funicular before heading over towards The Ship, up this path out here, and through my tractor barn, disappearing over Huntcliff where it hits the sea again."

"You mapped all this out?"

Chalky took out a green tin with Golden Virginia embossed in fancy gold letters on the lid and rolled the thinnest of thin cigarettes.

"I've mapped many around the world, but the ones near the sea are my passion. My dad told me about this one, and his dad told him, so we have mapped it for three generations. I should finish the bugger off tomorrow."

He put the cigarette behind his ear like a carpenter would do with a pencil.

"And how do you map it, exactly?" Bob asked.

"It depends on timing and divine intervention."

"Divine intervention?" Bob was starting to lose the thread of the conversation.

"Divining rods, so you could call it divine intervention." Chalky laughed, proud of his joke, before taking two sticks out of the drawer. Each was bent at a 90 degree angle, forming a natural handle. "Like this." Chalky showed Bob and Higgins the correct position in which to hold the divining rods.

"Does it really work, though, Chalky? I thought that was a load of old tosh."

"It only works with the right timing. The coastal ley lines rely on high tides, which is when the lines are nearest the surface. The ones inland take more notice of the moon and solar activity. They are all different, you see. Ours is a tidal ley line, and she's a big bugger, too."

Bob ignored the fact that Chalky seemed to love the ley line as much as he did his kettle.

"I hope to finish mapping the gaps tomorrow. She only shows

herself every six or seven years, which is a right pain. It's took me most of my life to map the gaps left by my dad. She's a right little bugger."

Bob looked over to Higgins, who seemed to be getting bored.

"Do you want to try? The tide is already flowing in, giving her some power. The line runs up this lane, but is more powerful through my barn. Oh, and there is one other thing you need…" Chalky left this sentence hanging in the air as he took two more sets of rods out.

Breaking the silence, which was lasting far too long, Bob posed the question he guessed Chalky was waiting for. "What's that, then, Chalky?"

"It needs a very special ingredient, Bob…" Chalky left another gap and eyeballed his student. "It needs belief. You can find anything you want with dowsing rods; you just have to channel your brain into what it is looking for. Nothing works without belief."

"Belief? Really?" Higgins mocked, shaking his head. If it required belief, he was having none of it. He may as well use knitting needles to find wool.

"Yes, belief, Constable Higgins. You can find water, oil, gold, and more importantly, ancient ley lines if your mind is tuned in. The mind is an amazing thing, if you allow it to be."

"OK, Hurricane and I will give it go. Won't we, Hurricane?"

"Yes, sir, I can't wait."

"Come on, the tide will be turning soon, so we might pick her up."

Chalky had a bounce in his step like he had rubber shoes on as he took his cigarette from behind his ear and lit it.

Bob had been thinking. "Chalky, if I need to believe in a ley line, I need to know what one is. And, I guess, what they do. And maybe why they are there."

Chalky's face contorted to the side and one eye closed as he sucked in what little tobacco lined his cigarette.

"Good questions, Bob. Difficult to answer, though. There are many theories. The coastal ones, it is said, are the oldest of them all. They are meant to be straight lines used for spiritual travel to and from the lost city of Atlantis."

He once again sucked the life out of his cigarette, which was disappearing rapidly in front of their eyes.

"What, the underwater city? The *Man from Atlantis* with Patrick Duffy from Dallas?"

"Who's Patrick Duffy?" asked Higgins.

"Swam like a dolphin," Bob said. Higgins looked at him as if he were stupid. "Don't worry, Hurricane, I'll fill you in later."

Higgins shrugged. "So how come our ley line's not straight, then? You said it goes all over the place."

"It was more or less straight when it was put there. The earth has shifted a lot since, tectonic plates and all that."

"Do you believe in Atlantis, though, Chalky? I thought that was a myth."

"Not sure what I believe, Bob, but there is some energy the ley lines kick out, especially on the high tide, so I guess they must have a reason."

After the two lung-bursting puffs earlier, Chalky's cigarette had nothing left to give. Not that this stopped him trying, closing his eyes to draw in all the nicotine he could from thin air before putting it out of its misery in an already overflowing ashtray.

"OK, Chalky, you have my attention. Can we have a go, then?"

"Of course, follow me." Chalky put on a tweed cap to complete his look. "Remember, it's all about belief. Do you believe, DI Dixon? Constable Higgins?"

Chapter 11 – A Barn Full of Junk?

The walk was longer than it looked. It took twenty minutes or so before they arrived at the barn on the edge of the cliff top, overlooking the sea. Chalky took a large set of keys out of his pocket and unlocked three padlocks, removing their chains before cranking the lock, now free of its restraints, to the horizontal and pulling the bar to allow the barn doors to open slightly. The barn was all beaten up with rotten wooden slats that anyone could peer through, so the padlocks were more for effect than anything. A good kick would have rendered them useless.

Chalky opened the large door and entered, flicking on the lights inside. They came on in stages, making a thumping sound as each bank received an injection of power.

"Wow, look at these beauties," said Bob as the strengthening light allowed him to see a number of tractors, all in pristine condition, on raised plinths. It was like a museum.

Chalky walked over to the first one. "This one is my pride and joy, Bob, a David Brown 1954 Cropmaster." Bob was all over it, giving it the once over, while Chalky looked across to Higgins. The young constable still stood near the door, and Chalky picked up on his lack of enthusiasm – if no enthusiasm whatsoever could be accused of lacking anything. "Are you not into tractors, constable?"

As Bob moved on to the next tractor, Higgins walked over, feeling he should make more of an effort to join in.

"Not really. More of a car man."

"You like Aston Martins, then, I assume?"

Higgins's attention level jumped up several notches. "Oh, I love them. I'll have one, one day."

"Really, which one?"

"Probably a DB9 Coupe. It only came out last year, but I can dream." A smile exploded across Higgins's face at the very thought of it.

Bob rejoined them.

"So you like Aston Martins, but you don't like this tractor. Funny that." Chalky laughed, but neither Bob nor Higgins could spot the humour in the comment. They smiled anyway out of politeness, until Bob came clean.

"What's so funny, Chalky?"

"What do you think the DB stands for, Constable Higgins?"

"The Dog's Bollocks," Higgins answered Chalky, pleased with his own joke.

"You're looking at what it stands for. David Brown owned Aston Martin. He ran the show, so if it wasn't for this little baby," Chalky gave his number one tractor an affectionate tap on its red engine box, "there would be no DB9, 8, 7, or any of them."

"Really?" Higgins looked startled.

"Yes, really. Do you want to see an Aston Martin, Constable Higgins? Are you bored with tractors?"

"What? You have one here?" If enthusiasm was a thermometer, Higgins's mercury had just exploded out of the top.

"Of course, I wouldn't have offered otherwise. Is he always like this, Bob?"

Chalky, with his two pupils for the day in tow, headed to the back of the massive barn, passing all the other tractors, to a car-shaped dustsheet. He threw off the cover as if he were a magician applying some misdirection. But there was no misdirection necessary. Higgins and Bob were presented with the iconic DB5, made famous by James Bond in the film *Goldfinger*.

Higgins stood with his mouth open. Bob helped him out, slowly reconnecting his jaw to the closed mouth position, rescuing him from what could only be described as a gawp.

"WOW! It's beautiful."

The car looked like it had never been driven. The silver sparkled in the roof-lights, which had warmed up to white from the yellow tinge they had been emitting.

"So next time you slag off one of my tractors, Constable Higgins, just remember who made this car. I prefer the tractor myself. I knew David, you know, he was a Yorkshireman. That's how I ended up with her. Anyway, we have come here to spot ley lines, not look at old junk."

Chalky covered up the car and they all moved into the centre of the barn. He took three sets of dowsing rods out of his pocket and handed them a pair each.

"OK, you hold them like this." He dropped the handle into the small hole in the centre of his fist, allowing the rods to move freely on a horizontal plane. "And what is it we need for it to work?"

Bob answered as Higgins was still looking at the cover of the silver Aston Martin. "The tide and a ley line, Chalky."

"And what else?"

"Belief. We have to believe in what we are looking for."

"Correct." Chalky stood in front of Bob. "Do you believe, DI Dixon?"

Bob thought he did and tried not to give any tell-tale signs that he didn't. After the graveyard episode, he had to believe. He was either going mad, or Saltburn had a hidden secret, and believing seemed the least he could do to get answers.

"Yes, I'm looking for ley lines, Chalky. I believe." As he said the words, his mind repeated, *Believe, Bob, believe.*

"And you, Constable Higgins?" Chalky eyeballed him. Higgins did not believe in anything he could not see or hear, but he was willing to play the game.

"Yep, ley lines. I can't wait. I believe."

"OK, lads, here we go. Channel your energy into the rods and walk slowly, scanning the barn. Try to feel where you think you should go and let your body follow."

All three of them set off in different directions and scanned the barn left and right, although Chalky was watching his students more than scanning. Treasure hunting is less fun when you know where the treasure is.

Bob had looped around the front of the barn and back down the right-hand side; Higgins was like a mirror image, hitting the back of the barn, turning and surveying the left-hand side. Bob's mind was hooked into the rods under his control in his hands. As he approached another of Chalky's tractors, a green Massey Ferguson, the rods both flicked inward violently.

"Here, I've got something." As he looked at the rods, his focus left him and the rods reset. Higgins and Chalky ran over. "They both flicked in, promise."

"Really, sir? Are you sure you didn't just force them in?"

Bob started doubting himself. He tried to focus again, but nothing happened.

"I promise, Hurricane, it wasn't me. They just moved in on their own."

Before Higgins could respond, Chalky interrupted.

"Bang on, sir, bang on."

"Really?"

"Yes, really. Belief, Bob, that's all it takes. Now see if you can find where it goes from here."

Bob reset the sticks in his hands. "OK, here goes." He closed his eyes and concentrated, saying, *"Ley lines, ley lines, ley lines,"* over and over in his mind. As he did, the rods again reacted to the forces that were gravitating towards Bob's body. Eyes still closed, he started walking with the rods twitching in his control. He made his way diagonally across the barn to the other wall, then opened his eyes.

"Wow, you can feel it. It grabs hold of you." The rods reset the minute he spoke.

"So there we are, Bob, you have mapped your first ley line. Well done."

Higgins was walking the path Bob had just mapped, not even a flicker on the rods.

"It won't work without belief, Hurricane."

Higgins looked disappointed at having missed out on the fun – if it was fun. He still assumed that Bob had faked it and made a mental note to ask him why in the car.

As Chalky took the rods back from Higgins and tried explaining to him why he'd failed, Bob felt a warmth in his back pocket. Taking out his wallet, he opened it just in time to see the funicular ticket giving out a blue glow. He put it back in a hurry so as not to give anything away. Higgins was not a believer of anything right now, so it was not the time to add more confusion to a pot that was already overflowing.

"Thanks, Chalky, that was quite an experience."

"Bob, have you done this before?" Chalky had the dowsing rods out, retracing his steps. "I barely get a murmur on the rods. That's why I have to wait for the bigger tide tomorrow."

"Beginner's luck, I guess."

"I suppose so. OK, let's head back. Big day tomorrow. Thanks, Bob, I think you've proved I'm not mad."

Bob thought it would take a lot more than his word to clear Chalky from the lunatic asylum. "I still think you're mad; I've just proved I might be mad, too." Heading out of the barn, Bob added, "Can I keep these?" holding his dowsing rods out.

"Of course you can. Nice to see you have the golden touch. Consider them a gift."

"And mine? Can I have mine back?" Higgins added.

"You're joking, aren't ya? They're hard to find, Constable Higgins, so you have to earn them." Chalky took Higgins's rods and placed them into his pocket, then took the keys out to lock up the barn. Bob and Higgins said their goodbyes and left Chalky, heading back down the track to the farmhouse and the car.

As they got in the car, Higgins turned to Bob. "Did you fake it, sir?"

"What type of accusation is that? I hope you don't say that to your girlfriend." Bob laughed, and then carried on. "Of course I didn't fake it. The sticks just moved, all on their own. You need to believe in stuff more, Hurricane. It's not my fault you were crap at it."

They laughed, together this time.

"Drop me back at my flat, Higgins. It's been a long day. Bright and early in the morning – coffee shop at seven o'clock, OK?"

"OK, sir, and I don't have a girlfriend."

"Well when you get one, keep the faking it line to yourself."

The engine of Higgins's car roared and the wheels spat out some pieces of gravel as he sped off, dreaming he was in an Aston Martin DB5.

Chapter 12 – Time and Tide Wait for No Man

Bob slept on and off. His thoughts were racing around his head, chasing each other in a random game of tag, all of them confused. He finally woke up at 5am, and it was one of those awakenings which would not allow him the luxury of a five minute snooze. He had too many things to absorb, and had to be awake and alert to allow his mind to take them all in.

He put on some tracksuit bottoms, a grey sweatshirt and some trainers he'd bought a month ago for his new fit and healthy lifestyle. The fact that he had to put the laces into the trainers was a giveaway that this new lifestyle had not really taken hold yet. At least he looked the part, though.

He resisted a look in the mirror, knowing that it would be the same as yesterday's reflection, and that of the days and months before. It was still dark, but he was determined to go for a run on the beach, giving his mind time to tame his thoughts and line them up into a reasonable order.

The run soon petered out to a jog, then a brisk walk. Before long, it was just a walk, but it felt better than a walk as he was in his gym gear. That had to count for something. Luckily it was a nice day for a walk, brisk or not.

Bob headed over towards The Ship, where he could see signs of activity. As he got closer, he saw sandbags being placed on the pub's side of the sea wall, and some of the boats on the promenade were being moved up to the safety of a grassy area of parkland across the road, as far away from the sea as possible. Bob looked out to sea. At first glance, it did not look that angry, but it was creeping in for the first high tide of the day. A second glance showed a different story as Bob stopped to take a closer look at the breakers. The white horses were on the stampede, joining forces to form bigger stallions to rise high and hammer into the helpless beach.

Bob knew when the tide was flowing. He'd watched it a lot since he had arrived in Saltburn. An ebbing tide looked tranquil, backing off and gently caressing the sand, waving goodbye to the coastline like a long lost friend. A flowing tide had edge, anger and passion. It was like the sea was in a rush to invade and claim the sand ahead of it, the breakers crashing down relentlessly, sweeping aside anything that was stupid enough to get in their way. The flowing tide had no sympathy, just glory and victory.

Bob thought about Scraggs and his surfing mates, looking forward to pitting their wits against that monster. And this was only the starter – they were planning on having the main course. There were two high tides a day, and this was the smaller one. And even this was not due to peak for a couple more hours. The sea would then take a lunch break of sorts when the tide would turn – the locals called this 'slack water'. It was like the eye of a hurricane – a period of calm when the flowing tide would hand over the baton and the ebb would slowly regain control. The sea would then make its way back where it came from, as if retreating from the battle. The white horses would be fed and watered, the troops re-energised, preparing for the next battle. Then the flowing tide would snatch the baton back, eager for the battle to recommence.

Today's battle would be more ferocious and more violent than any for years. The high tide tonight was going to be one of the biggest on record, coupled with a north-easterly wind, which would only anger the elements even more. TV crews were heading to Saltburn to cover the carnage that would unfold, no doubt planning to put a weather presenter next to the sea wall with the waves crashing all over them to make it look as bad as possible. But there would be no pretence required tonight – as bad as possible would be a let off. Everyone was expecting much worse.

Bob had his own plans. The walk had allowed his thoughts to settle and his subconscious mind was gaining control of them, putting them in an orderly queue to be dealt with later. He continued along the road to The Ship, where he could see the grey plumes of tractor smoke and smell the distinct smell of diesel. A crowd of people was helping lift the boats and move them into the park, away from the sea wall.

"Can you give us a hand, mate? We have about twenty to shift." A man beckoned Bob over, and he broke into a light jog to respond to the urgency of the question. Time and tide would wait for no man, especially an overweight one in a pair of trainers.

"Of course, what can I do?"

The tractor was dropping the latest boat off in the park and heading back for more cargo.

"Can you push the wheel back so we can get the next one on balance?" Bob nodded and leant into the boat and started to push. Nothing happened. "You have to wait till we lift it, you stupid bugger."

"Oh, OK. Sorry, I'm not from round here."

"No shit, Sherlock." Bob took this as a compliment. He was a detective, after all. "OK, when I say 'Right', up, lads. RIGHT."

Three men lifted the bow of the boat, with Bob and another volunteer on wheel duty, rolling the wheels back, allowing the boat to balance on the beam.

The man who seemed to be in charge said, "Right, Paul, you get this one's bars hooked up to the tractor and we'll get another balanced." The tractor reversed into positon like a well-oiled machine.

Bob helped get the rest of the boats balanced and shipped off to the park, enjoying the workout. He even offered to join the lifting crew as more willing volunteers arrived to take his rookie job on wheel duty. Bob loved how the community came together. The fishermen needed their boats moved, and every passer-by, whether they were walking their dogs or just out to get a newspaper, dropped everything to help.

"Well done, lads. Right, there is coffee in The Ship, on me. I'm glad we got that lot shifted as the sea's away tonight."

As Bob sat down at one of The Ship's barrels, needing a rest after his exertions, his phone rang in his pocket. It was Higgins.

"Sir, are you OK? I've been waiting twenty minutes."

Bob looked at his watch. It was 7.20am. "Sorry, Hurricane, I've been helping move the boats. The sea's away tonight, you know, son." A couple of the fishermen gave him a look as they eavesdropped. 'The sea's away' sounded strange in a cockney accent. "I'm at The Ship, having a coffee with the lads."

"OK, sir, I'll be down in a bit. Audrey has just sorted me out my second coffee."

"No rush, see you soon."

"Are you not joining us, Ray?" Smithy, the man who had taken charge of moving the boats, was speaking to the tractor driver as Bob ended his phone call with Higgins. Ray had expertly reversed onto all the boats' bars and moved them with minimal fuss.

"No, I'll be alright on my own, Smithy."

Smithy delivered the last of the coffees, then joined Bob. "Silent Man! He's a crazy fool, that one. He can catch bloody fish, mind."

"Silent Man?" Bob enquired. "Why Silent Man?"

"Well, he's not the most talkative. And always fishes on his own. He puts his own boat in, drives his own tractor. He's out before any of us are even up, tells us nothing, and seems to catch fish at will." He cupped his hands around his mouth so Ray could hear him. "Tells us bugger all, do you, Ray?"

"Bugger off, Smithy, I helped move the boats, didn't I."

Bob took a slurp of his coffee, feeling like he was part of the Saltburn fishing community.

"It would have took you lot hours if not. I've seen you drive tractors. Bloody useless, the lot of you."

Bob got the impression Silent Man was not so silent if someone rattled his cage, and Smithy was rattling away.

"Only joking. Thanks, Ray."

Ray gave a wave and turned a little to the side, not wanting to engage with anybody more than he already had.

Bob enquired, "So, Smithy, is he a good fisherman, then?"

Smithy looked over. "Who, Silent Man? Ray?" Bob nodded. "We don't have a clue. He catches fish when there is none to be caught – he's got a net out there right now. He went out this morning. Have you seen it?"

If Ray had already been out, it must have been in the middle of the night. Smithy pointed to the sea, which had been creeping further in, unnoticed. The occasional wave was now smashing into the sea wall and coating some of the barrelled tables near the sea in salty water and foam. Bob gazed seaward and thought how easily Lizzy Scraggs could have been stranded on the other side of a sandbank all those years ago, which was what everyone seemed to think had happened. The tide had stealth; it seemed to creep in every time he had his back turned, like children playing the game 'What's The Time, Mr Wolf?'.

"He's been out in that today?"

"Yes, about four-thirty, he said. He went off through Penny Hole in that mess. He's a madman."

"Penny Hole?"

"Over there, under Huntcliff. It's like a natural harbour. You can get out from there in most weathers, but today, no one else is stupid enough to try." Smithy raised his coffee as if giving Ray a compliment. "The thing is, he will have five or six boxes of cod tomorrow. He did it on the last big tide a few years back, and the one before that. Crazy, maybe, but lucky bastard, too."

"So why don't you put a net out?"

"One, we aren't stupid enough, and two, we have tried. We even followed him and put our nets next to his. We were nearly killed, it was so rough. The day after, our net was ripped to shreds on the rocks. Ray's was laid out perfect and teeming with fish."

There was respect and jealousy rolled into one in Smithy's tone as another couple of fishermen joined in.

"Good lad, Silent Man. He will always have your back if you're stuck. I don't know how he knows where the fish are, though. He must have a sixth sense."

"I've heard he talks to the fish."

"Talks to the fish? I'm sure he's not *that* crazy."

Bob looked over to Silent Man. He was now looking out to sea with his back to them.

"Redcar lifeboat went out once for him on a big tide – a day like today. Someone reported the boat was in trouble. The coxswain claims to this day he could see Ray talking to the sea, hauling his net and speaking to the fish as they came in."

"Mermaids, some say. He has a guardian angel out there, that's for sure." This comment got a few mumbles and grumbles in response, and sparked off two or three conversations which headed in different directions. Smithy brought it all back together.

"Right, that's enough. Mermaids? You'll be telling me the Loch Ness monster is real next."

"My uncle's Scottish and he reckons he's seen it. He used to live near the loch."

"Bloody hell, drink your coffee, you lot. Bloody mermaids, Loch Ness monsters – no wonder people say us lot exaggerate. And we think Ray's lost it." Smithy finished his coffee. "Right, lads, the boats should be OK, but I'll check on them tonight at high tide." He stood up and waved to them all, adding, "See you, Ray," as he left.

Most of the crowd had dispersed. The high tide was more or less here, and although it was menacing, it had to play to nature's rules. It would be a thirty-minute fight through slack water before the tide was reeled back in again.

As Higgins turned up, his car all wet from the sea, which was crashing over the small bridge along the sea front, he flung the door open.

"Sir, you look like Rocky."

Bob looked down at himself. Grey sweat top with plenty of sweat showing through was not the look he was aiming for, although he probably did qualify for the heavyweight division.

He laughed. "Thanks, Hurricane, at least I'm making an effort. Take me to mine first so I can take my Rocky gear off. We have a busy day ahead."

Chapter 13 – Catch a Wave

Back in their cell, Higgins was reading the case file and Bob was staring at the board, looking for inspiration. But inspiration was having none of it.

"So, tonight at eight pm, but where? P and W, P and W, P and W? P and Bloody W? Hurricane, anything?" Bob looked over to his partner, who popped up his head above Lizzy Scraggs's buff coloured case file.

"Nothing yet, sir. I'll let you know if I find anything."

"Keep looking, Hurricane."

Bob bounced up as if inspiration had moved and given away its hiding place. Armed with his pen, he addressed the already over busy whiteboard. He drew a picture of Chalky White's barn on top of Huntcliff, and another of The Ship. This one had a small box by the side of it, containing the words *Silent Man talking about fish*. Bob thought *talking to fish* would be a little too crazy to put on the board, but he knew what he meant. Besides, the board looked crazy enough already.

He then drew the ley line as a blue line trailing through the relevant landmarks, finishing at the barn before disappearing over the top of Huntcliff. He drew Huntcliff in orange due to the lack of brown pens, then stared at his drawing of the east coast, hoping inspiration would be seduced by his artwork.

"Anything yet, Hurricane?"

Higgins looked up, annoyed at another interruption. "Sir, I've read two more pages."

Bob needed a plan. "Right," he said sternly as he wrote TTDT, short for things to do today. "OK, what time is high tide?"

"Quarter to eight tonight, sir."

"So the tide should be high enough at six, then." Bob wrote '6pm funicular' as the first item on his to-do list.

"High enough for what?" said Higgins as intrigue got the better of him.

"To go for a ride on the funbus."

"The funbus? I think you're losing it, sir."

"Well, the funicular. You know what I mean."

"What are you expecting to see, sir?" Higgins stopped reading for a second and looked over to the board where Bob was standing

"I don't know, but I do know what I saw yesterday in the graveyard." He pointed to the graveyard section of his map. "I am hoping for something similar on the funicular," he said as he circled the cliff lift.

"OK, sir, whatever you think." Higgins lifted the file higher to indicate that he was still busy reading, and all the interrupting was not helping him find a P or a W.

The second item Bob added to his list was to revisit the graveyard in Marske at 7.15pm, and lastly he wrote 8pm with a question mark as he was still not sure it was a time. Then he wrote P and W with another question mark. He followed this with Scarface, and Stephen Farrell with a question mark in brackets. This was a bit of a guess, but the clue on the gravestone was written by someone called Stephen. It could be the same Stephen who went missing in the eighties; the age would more or less add up and the date he went missing was the same as the date stamped on the funicular ticket he had in his wallet.

Bob tilted his head to the side and thought. *Do I really have a meeting on my to-do list with someone I don't know, today, maybe at 8pm in a place as yet unknown?* He smiled. In the detective world, this was known as a hunch, and good coppers follow hunches. And Bob was a good copper.

Higgins put the case file down on the table with a thump and a sigh, like he had just finished a good book. "Nothing, sir. Read it cover to cover, but nothing's jumping out. I'm clueless as to what P and W mean. Are you sure you wrote it down properly? My dad was all over this case, he would not have missed anything. I'm quite proud of him, really. He left no stone unturned."

"You should tell him, Hurricane."

"Don't be stupid, sir, he's my dad."

"You know how much I love my notepads, so I won't have written it down wrong. But the graveyard's on my to-do list." Bob pointed at his list. "So we can check on the way to P and W, once we know where it is."

Higgins tried to work out the last sentence. It had a chicken and egg style dilemma about it.

"If we don't know where P and W is, how can we be on the way to…"

Bob interrupted. "If there is nothing in the Lizzy Scraggs case file, after lunch, move on to whatever we have on Stephen Farrell. There might be a clue there." Bob's hunch gave him a nudge. "If it is the same Stephen, that is."

Higgins drummed up what little enthusiasm he could. The Stephen Farrell angle was a longshot, based on a projection Bob saw in a graveyard. "OK, I'll print it out now and have a look after lunch." He followed this with a yawn.

Lunchtime came and went with very little said, Bob staring at his board and making the odd addition, Higgins painstakingly trawling through the Stephen Farrell case.

"Anything, Hurricane?"

"Nothing, sir."

"OK, let's get out of here. The tide is on its way back in. Let's go see what's happening down at the beach."

After parking at the top of the bank, Bob and Higgins opted for the long walk down the snake-like path to the beach. Bob wanted the funicular ride when the tide was stronger; if he was going to see any projections, he wanted a strong signal, and that, he assumed, came with a bigger tide. He might only get one chance.

After ambling down the hill, they made their way onto the pier. As they walked along the old structure, the flowing tide was already on its way back in. The waves were rolling on a huge swell before crashing down beneath them. A couple of surfers who obviously didn't fancy the paddle out to sea passed them with their surfboards under their arms, throwing their boards in the sea and jumping off the pier into the relative calm beyond the breakers.

As Bob and Higgins walked along the pier, the gale blew straight into their faces. The sea looked angry; the wind was plucking water from the tops of the waves and spitting into their faces. The sun was doing it best to pretend it was a nice day, but even that looked like it was soon going to take shelter behind some clouds. It was not going to be pleasant later; they could feel it.

As they approached the pier end, Bob and Higgins saw that there were no fishermen. They had the pier all to themselves. They turned their backs against the wind, watching the surfers trying to stand in the growing power of the storm. A few of them were already giving up. If they caught a wave, they would get the ride of their lives, but catching one was the tricky part.

Bob turned and looked further out to sea. He saw Scraggs in the water with a few others. Were they more experienced or just madder than the rest? Scraggs stood out due to his lack of hair compared to the flowing locks of the rest of the surfing gang. Bob gave him a wave.

The surfers huddled together like seals in wetsuits beyond the breakers, planning their next attempts while looking out to sea for the waves to join forces. Scraggs had clearly spotted his wave – it was a monster. A couple of others looked like they were going to attempt the same wave, but they were overtaken by its sheer power and speed.

Rotating his arms windmill fashion to try to get up to speed as the wave approached, Scraggs was on his own: man versus nature. He masterfully matched the pace of the wave before jumping onto the surfboard in more or less one movement.

The wave had visibly grown and was starting to roll up and gather all of its power ready for its assault on the sandy beach. Scraggs was crouching, perfectly balanced as he headed away from the pier toward Huntcliff, trying to tame the wave. He picked up speed before making a sharp turn off the top of the rolling monster, shooting spray high before turning back towards it. He was then heading for Bob and Higgins in the tube of the wave as it was crashing to his left. It was as if it were chasing him, teasing him, before inevitably taking him and his board with it. But Scraggs was having none of it, leaning back with his hand, putting a finger into the tube ceiling as if to tickle the wave and show it who was in charge. The wave responded and the crashing became more violent.

What a ride, Bob thought, *wow!*

Scraggs was coming straight for them as they ran back along the pier to get a better view. He would have to abort the ride as the pier, with its iron legs and crossed-wire supports, would have him if he continued.

"He'll have to back out now, Hurricane, or he's a goner."

Scraggs had other ideas. You don't wait six years for a wave just to jump off when you have it tamed. He sped up and spotted the gap between the pier legs, pumping the board up and down with his legs.

"Jump, you idiot," Bob cried out as Scraggs approached. He was traversing the wave, which was in no mood for slowing down. Scraggs had to miss the first pier leg, and be through before the wave carried him onto the next. "He's going for it, Hurricane.

Christ, bloody idiot."

Scraggs fizzed under the pier, avoiding the leg by inches. Bob and Higgins ran across the pier as if playing a sped-up version of Poohsticks. They arrived just in time to see Scraggs's board graze the leg on the other side, making an audible twang, Scraggs fighting to keep control as the wave gave in.

Scraggs stood on his board, arms aloft. Bob and Higgins could hear the cheering from the beach.

"Wow, that was close, sir," said Higgins, who had been too on edge to speak. Bob put his hand to his chest, trying to regain some composure and calm down his breathing.

"He's crazy. Bloody idiot could have killed himself."

They started to walk back along the pier to where Scraggs was taking the plaudits from his fellow surfers and well-wishers on the beach near the surfing hut. He had taken on all the North Sea had to offer and won.

Chapter 14 – Owing To the Wind and Tide

Darkness was taking hold. All of the surfers were on shore, and the night was starting to win its battle against the day. Along with the encroaching darkness, the wind had strengthened and the rain was more or less horizontal. The Ship had been the surfers' refuge for the last couple of hours, but even she was ready for a beating. The sea was getting closer and closer, the white tops of the breakers reflecting in the light of the full moon.

Bob looked up at the funicular, and then at his watch. "Right, Hurricane, quarter to six. Let's go see your dad and take a ride." He took Stephen Farrell's ticket out of his wallet and placed it into his jacket pocket.

They walked up the road and negotiated the corkscrew turns of Saltburn's bank. No drivers were stupid enough to be anywhere near the shoreline, so they had the road to themselves, allowing them to take a short cut from the path. The rain was still teeming down, so Bob put his jacket over his head for shelter.

They reached the top of the bank and took a sharp right to find Keith waiting for them at the funicular. He invited them into the brake-man's small hut so he could be heard.

"I hope this is all worth it, Bob. You're the last ride of the day and we're done. It's going to be a mess down there. The pier is already shut and the road's getting blocked off – no one in, no one out."

"I only need one trip, Keith, and then you can be off." Keith pulled the water lever to prime the funicular car with weight for its journey, and Bob added, "Which side did the man and the boy go down all those years ago? Which car were they in?"

"I don't know. Does it matter?"

"Oh, I guess not. Let's just hope it was this one."

"What are you expecting, Bob? My young 'un said you saw something in the graveyard?" Bob gave Higgins a stare. Keith picked up on this and continued, "Well, he believes in you." Bob's stare abated. "Hope you get to see what you're after."

Keith gestured for them to enter the car. Bob opened the door and entered; Higgins started to follow, but Bob stopped him.

"Hurricane, I think I have to do this on my own."

Higgins closed the door.

"Let me know when you're ready, Bob," Keith shouted from the hut before waving to Bill at the bottom.

"Good luck, sir," said Higgins, his voice unsure.

"OK, Keith, give me a minute."

Bob sat in the car listening to the rain pounding the outside, which was quite satisfying. He took the ticket out of his pocket. It was already looking bluer than it had before – maybe it was the light, maybe it wasn't. He slowly looked around the empty car and gave a hand signal through the door window to Keith to release the brake.

As soon as the brake was off, the ticket came alive with energy and started to spit blue sparks. Bob looked down at it, and as he looked up again, he saw he was not alone. First he saw the boy in grey shorts and a white school shirt, although it was tinged with blue. Bob then stood and turned his attention to the man. He was very old and his face had more or less given up on the skin that was attempting to cover it. He looked more haggard than any man Bob had ever seen.

The man turned to the boy, who was alone and scared in the middle of the car.

"You have to leave some magic behind, Stephen. You can feel that, can't you?"

Stephen looked at the funicular ticket in his hand, at the old man, then once again at the ticket. As he did so, he disappeared, and the glowing blue ticket floated to the floor. There was a loud clap and bright blue lights filled the funicular car just as the other car approached. The old man disappeared too, leaving Bob all alone in the car again.

He watched the projection of the ticket fade away, and then he looked at the ticket in his hand. There was another bright flash of light from his ticket, cascading out like a blue fan, engulfing the car, blinding Bob and making him drop the ticket to the floor. He knelt down to pick it up, and as he stood again, he saw the silhouette of a man in the other car, making his way up the lift. The blue lights filled both cars, then they were gone.

Bob made his way safely to the bottom where Bill let him out.

"Did you see what you came for, Bob?" asked Bill, hoping Bob would back up the story he had been carrying around for the past thirty-two years. Bob thought on his feet.

If Bill had seen the lights just then, he would have said.

"No, nothing. Did you see anything outside the cars?"

"Not a sausage."

Bob stood with the cage-man in the hut, keeping dry. Higgins arrived, having run down the snaky path, getting wet.

"Anything, sir?"

"Nothing, Hurricane. Maybe I did dream up the graveyard stuff after all." Bob looked at his ticket, which was doing its best to look like a ticket again. Turning it over, he saw that the 'rtn' portion had been stamped with the same date as the 'out' portion. He quickly put it into his pocket, trying not to draw attention to himself or, more importantly, the ticket.

Higgins's eyes followed the ticket to Bob's pocket and back to his boss's guilty face.

"Well, you win some, you lose some, I guess. Thanks for staying open, Bill. I guess we'll never know who the mystery man and boy were in the car that night."

"No, nor the man who appeared at the top. The car was empty when I sent it on its way, but I saw him talking to the brake-man. He even gave me a wave."

Bob looked at Bill, and then retrieved his notebook from his pocket. "Bill, why have you not mentioned this before?"

Bill looked at him, confused. Higgins's expression doubled the confusion.

"I told you all about it, and you wrote it in that book of yours."

Bob looked at his notes: *Bill said no one got into the car at the bottom, but a man appeared at the top. He waved.*

Bob corrected himself and read the words out loud to confirm to Bill he had not made a mistake. However, Bob was sure he would not have forgotten such an important piece of evidence. He would have put it on his brainstorming board.

Am I going crazy? he thought.

Keith gave them all a wave and headed down to pick them up in his car. Bob took a last look at the anger of the sea, which was an hour or so from high tide and was looking menacing. The wind had done a great job of whisking it up into a storm, and it was not a good idea to be on the coastline right now. The waves were already smashing against the sea wall, leaping into vertical white fountains as they did.

Keith dropped them off at Higgins's car.

"Where to now, sir?" asked Higgins. Bob's mind was racing, again.

"The office, I need to pop into the office."

As soon as they arrived, Bob headed straight for the cell and his brainstorming board. There it was, plain to see.

No one got in the car at the bottom, but a man got out at the top of the funicular. Waved at Bill. Wanted to be seen? If Bob was looking for confirmation that he was going crazy, he'd now got it. He took a couple of deep breaths.

But how? he thought. It would have to wait, though. He had a meeting at 8pm, and the first thing he needed to find out was where. No venue, no meeting.

He looked at the board again, shaking his head. Higgins walked in, towel drying his hair.

"Where to, sir?" he asked again.

"Hurricane, do you think I'm going mad?"

Higgins offered Bob a clean towel he had brought in for him. "If anything, I think you're starting to make more sense, sir." They laughed.

"Marske graveyard," said Bob in response to Higgins's question. They started to walk towards the exit, then Bob ran back into the cell to pick up Slaven's dog lead. "I think I might need you," he said as he caught up with Higgins at the station doors.

Chapter 15 – I'm Sure I've Seen This Film Before

It was pitch dark now. Mother Nature was not having her best day; she seemed to be dazed and confused. There was a sinister feel to the surroundings – the wind was swirling, not sure which way to blow, and the rain was coming down like stair rods, illuminated by cars' headlights. It was relentless.

Bob's mind was racing again. As if the visions he had seen in the funicular were not enough, the fact that he had not remembered key information from Bill the cage-man was bothering him now. He had clearly written it down in his notebook and on his whiteboard, and it was annoying him. He didn't make mistakes. A small mistake could easily be overlooked, but he would need a cherry picker to overlook this one.

The rain had got worse, if that were possible, and Higgins's windscreen wiper blades were struggling to keep up with their duties. They were doing their best, beating out a steady rhythm, but having little to no effect on the visibility.

"Hurricane?"

"Yes, sir?"

"You know your dad's funicular speech?"

"Yes, sir, I should do. I've heard it a million times."

"Does he mention the man going up the lift as well as the old man and the boy who go down?"

"Every time, sir. He says," Higgins put on his dad's scary voice, "'Bill swears to this day that no one got in the lift, but he saw the man get out at the top'." Higgins was getting no reaction to his silly voice, so he finished off the sentence normally. "He tells all the visitors to ask Bill when they get to the bottom."

"Are you sure?"

"Of course I'm sure, sir. I have heard the story enough. Why?"

"Oh, nothing, just trying to make sure I have all the facts, son. That one seems to have passed me by."

They were driving through Marske-by-the-Sea, the rain rolling down the hill, causing spray to cascade out onto the pavement as they approached the roundabout in the village centre. They went straight on and passed another pub called The Ship before turning right to head up St Germaine's Lane to the churchyard.

"Are all the pubs around here called The Ship?"

Higgins laughed. "No, just ours and Marske's, sir."

As if the day could get any worse, a flash of forked lightning dipped its bony white fingers into the sea, followed by a crash of thunder three or four seconds later. As they parked up, Higgins asked, "Are you really going out in that, sir? It's a mess."

"*We*, Hurricane, are *we* really going out in that, and yes, we are."

They got out of the car just as another lightning strike lit up the night sky. The crash of thunder that followed was louder and angrier than the last.

"Have you got a torch, son?"

Higgins leaned back into the car to pop the boot open, which Bob took as a yes.

Retrieving his torch and a coat from the boot, Higgins asked, "What now, sir?"

"Follow me, son." Bob checked he had the dog lead in his pocket before they headed through the graveyard to the gap in the wall where he had seen Stephen and Lizzy enter last time. He wasn't going to miss a word this time – anything could be important. His hair was more or less flattened onto his head. Higgins, choosing not to put the coat on, had it draped over his head like a makeshift umbrella.

They reached the gap in the wall. "Right, we're here, sir. Hope this is all worth it. What now?"

Bob took the dog lead out of his jacket pocket and they both stared at it. Nothing happened. Lightning forked again, making them both jump, and the clap of thunder following this one was deafening. They could smell cordite in the air, as if they'd just enjoyed a huge firework display.

"Jesus, that one was close," Higgins said before refocusing on the lead. "Is something meant to happen, sir?"

As the words tripped out of his mouth, the dog lead started fizzing and sparking, turning blue in front of Bob's eyes.

"See!" Bob exclaimed with a nod of his head. "Now do you believe me?"

"It's just a dog lead, sir, nothing's happening."

"Really? Can't you see that?"

"I think you need to go to see a doctor, sir."

Just then, Slaven the dog and two blue ghost-like figures walked straight through them.

"Follow me, Hurricane, and keep quiet. I need to listen. I'll tell you what's going on."

"If you say so, sir."

They followed Stephen and Lizzy closely enough for Bob to hear their conversation.

"He's saying, 'You'll be OK, Lizzy, we need to get you home to your mam'. She says she's going to be in trouble."

Bob followed the projections to the grassy area of the churchyard. Another lightning bolt hit the church steeple and the bang of thunder made the ground shake beneath them.

"Bloody hell, sir."

"Shh."

As before, Stephen positioned Lizzy in the grassy area. Bob did not need to hide this time; he knew they could not see him, so he could get up close and personal. Lizzy dropped the dog lead, leaving her magic behind, while Bob continued narrating to Higgins.

"Stephen's just stopped the dog in his tracks. Now Lizzy will disappear… there, she's gone." Bob was now ahead of the projection, narrating what was about to happen as he had seen this film before. But still nothing was giving him any idea where P and W was.

"What happens next, sir?"

"He talks to himself, which is why I know he's called Stephen, then he runs off and scores the grave. He then positions the lead and disappears."

Bob was expecting the man to run to the gravestone, but Stephen looked over to it instead.

"No, that's not right. That's not supposed to happen. It's all wrong."

"What's all wrong, sir? What's happening?"

"*Shh*, Hurricane!"

They were standing right in front of Stephen, who was still looking across to the gravestone.

"There is someone else there, Hurricane. Who the hell is that?" A man in a dark overcoat and a flat cap was scoring away at the back of the grave. "He's giving Stephen a wave. Now he's disappeared. They're both gone."

The rain was still beating down, but it had lightened a little, and the thunder and lightning had moved inland.

"We have another player. Who the hell was he? Stephen has an accomplice, but he wasn't there before."

"Any clue on P and W, sir?"

Bob had forgotten all about that; he had been slipped a curveball by the film's new ending. He ran to Emily's grave. The dates were underlined as before. Higgins switched on the torch and looked at the back.

"Sir, you need to see this."

"I've seen it, Hurricane: the date and time and P and W. We've learned nothing and it's seven-thirty already. We need a clue or we're screwed, son."

"Sir, it doesn't say that."

"*What*? But I saw it, Hurricane, with my own eyes. What the…?"

"There's the clue, sir: DIG?" Next to the word dig was an arrow pointing down, but this was not new writing. It was covered in moss and had been there for years.

Bob took a thin slate-like rock from an adjoining plot, and dug. After taking off the grassy layer, he hit something solid and dug around it.

It was a wooden box. "Open it, sir," said Higgins. Bob did so and took out a bubble-wrapped object.

"Do you think it's one of Lizzy's fingers?"

"You've been watching too many films, sunshine. We're not in Hollywood."

"You could have fooled me, sir. Things like this don't happen in Saltburn."

Bob slowly rolled the object out of the bubble wrap, ensuring he did not touch it.

"The bastard's playing with us, Hurricane, but six years is a long time to wait for a cheap gag."

They both stared at the contents of the box. A porcelain pig was dressed up in a police uniform.

"So at least they know we're onto them. Bastards. A pig in uniform, and he's even got a bloody whistle."

"What did you say, sir?"

"I said, he's even got a bloody whistle."

"That's it, sir! The Pig and Whistle."

Bob gave Higgins a confused look. "Pig and Whistle?"

"It's a pub in Redcar, sir, full of porcelain pigs. It's famous for it. It said in the notes that Stephen's dad was a landlord of a pub in Redcar. P and W, sir, eight o'clock, remember?"

"Well done, son! What time is it?"

"Twenty to eight."

Bob wrapped the pig up and carefully put it in its box.

"Let's go. We should still make it."

They looked over towards the road as they were heading back to the car. Another car's headlights were shining out next to Higgins's, and a man was standing by the graveyard wall. As soon as he saw them coming, he got into his car and sped off.

Higgins, who had sprinted ahead, got to his car just as the other vehicle was vanishing out of sight down St Germaine's Lane. Bob caught him up.

"Did you get the registration number, Hurricane?"

"No, sir, it had gone."

They both squeezed their wet bodies into the car.

"The Pig and Whistle, and yes, you can open her up, just this once."

Higgins needed no second invitation. The turbo kicked in, and they were gone.

"Tomorrow, Hurricane, I want you to do door-to-door to see if anyone saw that car. He's playing us. Now, let's go and meet him. See if we can find out what really happened to Lizzy Scraggs."

As Bob said this, his breath steamed up the windows. He could read something in the condensation.

"Hurricane, pull over."

"But, sir, we'll be late. It's quarter to."

"Pull over, *now*!"

Higgins did as he was told, and they both stared at the message: FRANK CARTWRIGHT.

"What does it mean, sir?"

"He was my first partner… the one who was stabbed. That's the lowest of the low, son." Bob felt as if someone had just walked over his late-partner's grave. The least he could do was say his name out loud. "Frank Cartwright, bless his soul. For God's sake, they are really trying to push my buttons, Hurricane. What the hell has Frank got to do with anything?" A tear started to form in the corner of Bob's eye, then he realised something he'd missed.

"Do you have a spare key for this car?"

"Why, sir?"

"That message is written on the *inside*."

Higgins used his sleeve to rub what was left of the fading message off the window, his face a mask of confusion. "But how?"

Bob opted not to answer. This could wait. Now they had an appointment with a madman who knew about Bob's past. Had the London mob been sent up to screw with him? Bob's body tensed, ready for a fight.

"Drive, Hurricane." There was anger in Bob's voice. If someone was trying to push his buttons, this particular button had just hit the jackpot.

Chapter 16 – The Pig and Whistle

They pulled up outside The Pig and Whistle at ten minutes to eight and walked into an empty pub. The landlord, surprised to see anyone out on such an atrocious night, left his stool to attend to his unexpected guests.

"What can I get you, lads?"

"Pint of beer, that one will do." Bob pointed to one of the pumps. "Hurricane?" he added.

"Just an orange juice, sir, I'm driving."

"You coppers, then?" said the landlord.

"Is it that obvious?"

"Unless you're a knight of the realm, which I'm guessing you're not, the only reason he'd be calling you sir would be because you're a copper or a magistrate. I'm guessing copper."

"Very clever. Hurricane, we need to work on this undercover stuff. You have my permission to call me Bob from now on."

"OK, sir." Bob gave Higgins a look and the landlord mustered up a smile.

As the landlord sorted their drinks out, Bob took a look around the bar. As Higgins had described, there were porcelain pigs of all shapes, sizes and professions on display, just like the one they had found in the graveyard.

"Impressive. How many are there?" Bob said, pointing to a shelf full of pigs.

"There's about three hundred down here on display in the bar, and another hundred or so in the cellar and upstairs rooms. I can't move for bloody pigs." The landlord handed over Bob's drink.

"If you don't like them, why keep them?"

"Because they're famous, and we are called The Pig and Whistle. The previous owner started it and we just carried it on. Customers bring them in from their holidays or wherever – they think I like them. I bloody hate the things!"

"Did you know the previous owners?" Bob was good at pulling people into a conversation without them realising.

"Not really, apart from when I bought the place. They moved to the Lake District and took over a pub up there. I think they're both dead now. I've had this place nearly twenty years."

Bob spied a picture on the wall. He'd seen the same picture before while looking over Stephen Farrell's case.

"Is he your son?"

"No, not mine. That's the previous landlord's son. He went missing one day, never seen again. I don't think his parents ever got over it. I promised I would leave it up, and to this day I can't bring myself to take it down."

Bob looked at his watch. It was two minutes to eight, so he thanked the landlord and grabbed a table in the corner. More pigs sat on a rail running around the pub wall.

"So what now, sir?"

"I don't know, son. Wait, I guess, and I meant what I said – when we are out and about, you can call me Bob. You can drop the sir, us being partners and all that."

Higgins smiled. He'd not been called a partner before.

By the time they had finished their drinks, it was five past eight.

"I guess he's not showing, Bob."

"We may as well have one more, just in case." Bob was not holding out much hope. If Stephen, or the mystery man in the graveyard, had planned a meeting six years ago and taken the trouble to give out clues as to when and where, he would not be late.

Going over to the bar for refills, Bob made more small talk with the landlord.

"So, it must have been a shock when he went missing from this pub. Hit the papers, I guess. Was his room upstairs?" Bob was hoping Stephen's old bedroom would be like an untouched shrine. Maybe that was why Stephen wanted to meet him here.

"Oh, he didn't live here. He was in the first Pig and Whistle, a multi-storey car park now. They knocked the original pub down and moved it to here."

"What? The pub was not right here?"

"No, it was next to the train tracks down the road."

"Hurricane, we're moving. Thanks." Bob threw the last word at the landlord as he sped out of the door before turning to Higgins. "You didn't tell me there was another Pig and Whistle."

"I didn't know, sir. Only been one since I can remember."

Bob stopped running, slightly out of breath. "Go back for the car, Hurricane, and I'll see you there."

Bob approached the multi-storey car park just as Higgins got there in the car and threw the door open.

"Sir?"

Bob took a while to answer as he was out of breath and wet again.

"I'll walk up. You keep an eye on anything coming out of here."

"OK."

Bob walked the wrong way up the spiral exit road. The car park seemed to be empty. He saw nothing on the lower floors and headed up to the top. As he made his way round the final bend, he saw a tall man looking out over the wall of the car park.

Bob slowly approached. Without turning round, the man spoke.

"My good friend, Bob Dixon."

"I'm no friend of yours, Stephen…"

"You're late."

"I went to the wrong Pig and Whistle."

The man ignored the comment and continued. "So you're the one who is going to stop me, are you?"

"I will. I've seen what you did to Lizzy Scraggs. Where is she, Stephen?" The taller man turned to face Bob.

"I would never hurt Lizzy! You know that." Stephen's eyes started to flicker red as his anger levels rose. Bob could see the diamond-shaped scar on his face, and he looked older than he had in the projection. Well, he was older – six years older.

"So why do you do it, Stephen? You were taken, so you think you can take other people, is that it?"

Bob took a step closer. Stephen reacted to Bob's movement.

"I wouldn't do that, if I were you. You don't know what I am capable of." Stephen laughed. "Or maybe you want to find out."

"I don't even know you. But I do know you're mad and need some help. Where is Lizzy Scraggs, Stephen? Where did you bury her?"

Again Bob took a step forward.

"I'm warning you, Bob, come nearer and it's all over. Remember we invited you here. Why do you think we did that?"

"We? What crazy fool have you roped into your little game, Stephen?"

Again, Stephen laughed. "You know nothing, Bob. You have

some catching up to do. Do you have your stupid notepad with you?"

Bob checked his jacket. "If you know me so well, you know I have."

"Today I am going to take someone, and you are going to do nothing about it. I have to, you see. You don't know what will happen if I don't, so write this in your notepad."

"I am sure I will remember." Bob wanted to keep his hands in the on-guard position. "What is it you need to tell me? More riddles?"

"You appear to be good at them. It stops on 16 December 2018. I don't know how – we're working on that. We'll be in touch before then." Stephen lowered his head. "We will take Carl as is necessary. I need you to trust me and not to get involved..."

Before he could finish, Bob lunged at him. "You bastard!" Stephen stopped him in his tracks, picking him up one-handed by his jacket. Bob's feet were dangling as Stephen held him effortlessly, staring at him, his eyes like flames. He then threw Bob against the wall, and Bob landed in a heap.

"You do not know how powerful I am. They give me a drug – they make me take one child back with me, and we have chosen Carl. You will see why. I have no choice, or we all die. *All* of us. If I fail, there will be another and another, and then another. Carl will be the last, and you will do nothing to stop it, understand?" Tears were rolling down Stephen's face, extinguishing the flames in his eyes to reveal a peaceful sapphire blue.

He stood on the wall at the top of the car park and looked down at where Bob still lay in a crumpled heap. "Be there in December 2018. We'll tell you how to prepare before then. You're my last hope, Bob Dixon, so don't let me down. This has to stop."

With that, Stephen jumped off the top of the multi-storey car park. Bob hauled himself up just in time to see him land as if he'd jumped from a low step.

"That's got to be a fifty foot drop," Bob muttered. Stephen ran around the corner, and then Bob heard a car engine roar. He was gone.

Bob walked slowly back down to ground level to meet up with Higgins, trying not to rub his arm, hip and the back of his head where he'd crashed into the wall.

"Anything, sir?"

Bob knew there were some things he would have to keep to himself, partner or no partner.

"No, Hurricane, we must have missed him. Did you see anything?"

"Not really, sir," Higgins said with a smile on his face. "It's been a strange day."

"What do you mean, not really?"

"Well, I have seen my dream car today, and you don't see that every day."

Bob looked at his beaming face. "What, an Aston Martin?"

Higgins looked confused. "How do you know I like Aston Martins, sir? But yes, good guess, and a rare one at that – a DB5, sir, like the one off *Goldfinger*. Rare as rocking horse shit, those."

Bob tilted his head to the side. *He saw Chalky's DB5 only yesterday.*

"So you have never seen one before, Hurricane? Are you sure?"

"I think I would remember seeing my dream car, sir."

Bob was good at reading faces and Higgins was telling the truth. It was written all over him.

"That's good you saw one today then. Where did you see it?"

"It was just over there. A man got out. He was looking around for a minute, and then he got back in and sped off. I would have gone over for a look if I hadn't been manning the road for you. I can't believe that nobody showed up, sir."

"Well you win some, you lose some." Bob had Stephen's words running through his head: *Carl will be the last, and you will do nothing to stop it.* The fewer people who knew what he knew right now, the better. Either he was going mad or everyone else was, and he needed to buy some time to evaluate.

"Come on, Hurricane, it's been a long day."

Chapter 17 – If Things Don't Weigh Up, Get New Scales

Bob was up early and out on his morning run, which was turning into a routine – if doing the same thing two days in a row could be classed as a routine. To his amazement, he felt fitter and ran harder than he had done yesterday, not stopping to walk this time, just pounding out a steady rhythm along the pavement, allowing his mind time to think, evaluate and drift through the facts.

After thirty minutes, when he reached the promenade, he sprinted to the pier, giving it everything he had left in the tank. While catching his breath next to the surfers' hut, he took a look up at the stationary funicular. It looked all innocent, as if it was an angelic child who couldn't possibly have anything to hide. But he knew that the funicular had its secrets – he'd seen them with his own eyes.

He slowly headed up the snaking path to the top of the hill. As his breathing stabilised, he took a look towards the sea, and then across to Huntcliff and Chalky's farm, making a mental note to go and see Chalky White.

Bob, who rarely got bothered and was always in control, was bothered and out of control. Too many questions and not enough answers. Nothing made sense; everything was niggling away at him like an impatient woodpecker, tapping at his logic.

How could Higgins not remember *having seen Chalky's Aston Martin? What did Stephen's riddle mean? Who had Stephen roped into his little game as an accomplice, and what was he going to do with a little boy called Carl? Had a boy been taken last night?*

As he stared out over Saltburn, Bob's eyes slid into a neutral gaze, not really focusing on its beauty. He sighed, his breathing slowly returning to normal. His hands were released from the clasped position behind his head and allowed to fall to his side. Just when he thought he was getting somewhere, he seemed to be back to square one. It was like a cruel game of snakes and ladders.

He started to jog slowly back to his apartment to get changed for work, still thinking and planning as he did. The rules appeared to have changed, and he needed to reconfirm everything that had gone on before. This was not normal – he'd seen too much. No longer was he in a box that resembled reality, so thinking outside the box might be the way forward. If this was a game – and he suspected he was being played – it would be hard to win if he was unaware of the rules.

By the time Bob arrived at his apartment, he was more at ease with the projections, his meeting with Stephen and all he had witnessed since he had come to Saltburn, but he knew things happened for a reason. He was at a fork in the road. Either he was going crazy or he had to believe in craziness.

He took a look in the mirror. *Is that a crazy man staring back at me?* he thought. *No, let's ride with the punches. If I saw it, let's say it happened.*

He left his reflection in the mirror, half thinking it might call him back to talk some sense into him. He knew things that other people didn't; he also saw things happen which apparently didn't happen according to others. And Higgins forgetting Chalky's Aston Martin was really bothering him. It had only been two days ago that Higgins had been staring at it in all its glory in the barn. Bob would have to tread carefully, skirting around the edges of the facts, exploring what others thought was true and what he thought was true. The answer would be in the gaps between the two.

Plan formed, he headed to work.

Higgins was in the coffee shop, waiting patiently for the station doors to be unlocked when Bob joined him. Bob opted for the cheery approach, trying to prise information out of Higgins without Higgins knowing he was being questioned.

"Morning, Hurricane, I'll just get myself a coffee, son." Bob ordered his coffee, smiling away at Audrey.

"You're a bit cheery, Bob." Audrey smiled back, giving him a curious look. That was enough to tell Bob he was overdoing the happy routine.

"I've been for a run, Audrey. I think my blood sugar is a bit low."

Audrey placed a sugary doughnut on a plate. "Here, it's on the house. I don't want you flaking out on me."

Bob took his doughnut and coffee and headed back to

Higgins with a toned-down smile.

"So, Hurricane, I bet it was a shock seeing that Aston last night."

"I know, sir, my dream car, that."

"There can't be many of those about. Did you see the driver? Someone famous, maybe?"

"No, it was too dark. He just stood there, looking around."

"Did you get the registration?"

"No, sir. Why, do you think it's important?"

"No, Hurricane, just police perks. We could have looked it up, seen whose it was." Bob knew exactly whose it was and would be heading up to see Chalky – without Higgins – as soon as he could.

Let's see what Higgins does know about our little visit to the barn.

"So, you know Chalky White?" Bob smiled. He did not have a clue where this conversation was heading; he just knew that what he remembered and what Higgins remembered were not aligned.

"Of course, sir. We went up to see him and ask about all that ley line crap a couple of days ago."

Maybe we're not as misaligned as I thought. Bob couldn't really ask about the Aston and the tractors in the barn outright; he would have to tease the information out of Higgins. It would be like trying to find the end of the cling film when the roll has split, hoping that the little pieces will merge and the roll will again be useable.

"Did Chalky give me those dowsing rods? I can't find them anywhere."

"They're in your jacket, sir, I think. That's where you put them. We went out the front of his house, and you *say* you picked up a signal on the little track heading up to a barn."

Bob ignored the emphasis on *say*, knowing that wherever it had happened, Higgins would still believe he'd faked it.

So I located the ley line outside on the track, not in the barn. Really?

Bob needed confirmation, so he added with a laugh, "I wonder what that crazy fool keeps in that barn of his."

He got another look from Audrey, who'd been listening as usual to bits and bobs of their conversation. She had clearly picked up on his false laugh.

"I think you should eat your doughnut, Bob, get your sugars up," she said. Bob took a big bite, nodded to Audrey, and then gestured with a rolling hand signal to Higgins to respond as his mouth was temporarily full of sugary doughnut.

"Big barn that, Hurricane, up on Huntcliff, don't you think?" Bob mumbled with his mouth full when his hand signal had no effect.

"I know, it looks massive from the outside. I've not got a clue what he keeps up there. We only went half way along the track. Sir, are you sure you didn't make those rods move? What with that and the graveyard thing, I think you're going… a bit crazy."

So that proves it. We didn't go into the barn. Bob's mind-notepad was marking all this down and evaluating it. *At least, Higgins didn't go into the barn.* Bob still remembered the inside of the barn as clearly as if he'd seen it yesterday. Or, more accurately, the day before yesterday.

Bob was subconsciously working on his 'I am not mad' alibi. He put on his jokey face and lied.

"I had you for a second with all that projection stuff, didn't I, Hurricane?"

Higgins laughed before rolling his eyes in Bob's direction. "I did think you had flipped, sir, commentating on nothing. Yes, you got me going, I guess. I was about to phone the loony bin." Bob laughed back, keeping it light. "It doesn't explain the porcelain pig and his whistle, or the DIG sign, though."

Bob felt cornered. That would take some explaining away. His latest laugh was of the buying time variety.

"I'll square up with you, Hurricane, I dreamt it – all of it, including the grave – after taking Scraggs up to the churchyard. I know it sounds crazy, but it has helped us find key evidence."

It was the best he could do in the circumstances. Higgins gave him a break.

"Dreamt it, sir? I don't believe in all that stuff, but we found the pig and got Stephen's name, so I guess you should dream up a bit more." Higgins tilted his head and was about to delve deeper, but Bob was rescued from further cross examination by Constable Skelton opening the nick bang on time. Well, bang on time for someone who lived in Guisborough and had an allowance for being late.

It's amazing how easily one load of bollocks can cover up another load of bollocks, Bob thought as they finished their coffees and headed off to the nick.

Chapter 18 – Breaking News

They entered the station to find Constable Skelton fumbling with the TV control in the office.

"Bloody stupid telly." Skelly twisted the remote left and right next to the sensor on the TV, hoping it would help. "Bloody stupid remote." Rolling the batteries at the back of the remote, which were held in place by black tape as the back of the remote was actually missing, he added, "Bloody stupid batteries."

"What's so important, Skelly?" Bob asked as the reluctant TV finally kicked into life.

"Have you not seen the news?"

Both Bob and Higgins shrugged, replying in unison, "What news?" They then exchanged looks, Higgins said, "Jinx" and held out his little finger. Bob ignored it, mainly because he didn't know what jinx meant. Higgins was left hanging, slowly lowering his hand and remembering never to jinx Bob again.

"It's all over the TV. Even the nationals are reporting it, look." Skelly flicked to *BBC Breakfast* where the tickertape at the bottom declared that a boy had been abducted. Doctors had said the child only had a week or so to live, and someone had taken him from a hospice – in Redcar.

"And now we go over to our reporter, Gail Jackson, who is live at Redcar hospice. Gail?"

"All we know at this point is that a man entered the hospice behind me," the reporter, Gail Jackson said, glancing over her shoulder and gesturing with her hand, "by smashing a window, and took a boy. The child had been diagnosed as being in the latter stages of leukaemia. He was in palliative care at the hospice, with his parents staying in an adjoining room."

"Do we know any more details about the boy and whether he requires constant medication?" the breakfast show presenter was asking as Bob thought, *you bastards! It must be Carl.*

"The boy is thought to be Carl Townsend." Bob tried to give nothing away, but he couldn't help clenching his fist in anger. "His parents are expected to make a statement later today, and yes, he was on medication to keep him comfortable. Without it…" a sombre look crossed the reporter's face, "well, one doctor told me… let's just say that he will find it very difficult without it."

"Gail Jackson there reporting from Redcar. We will bring you further developments as soon as we know them."

Skelly turned the TV down manually; he'd already thrown the remote across the table. Bob looked around the room, hearing Stephen's words of warning ringing in his head: "*We will take Carl as is necessary. I need you to trust me and not to get involved.*" But why should he trust a madman? He should go straight to Redcar CID with what he knew.

More memories then echoed through his mind: "*They make me take one child back with me, and we have chosen Carl. You will see why. I have no choice, or we all die. All of us. If I fail, there will be another and another, and then another. Carl will be the last, and you will do nothing to stop it.*" Bob remembered how the tears had rolled down Stephen's face.

"That's so sad, Skelly. I guess Redcar CID will be all over it?" Bob played it as coolly as he could. He'd already fed Higgins a whole heap of lies to stop the lad thinking he was mad, so maybe some things were best kept quiet. Pandora's Box needed to stay shut for now, but Bob had the keys and could open it whenever he wished. He needed to know more about what he was dealing with before peering inside, though.

For the first time since he'd taken the mysterious ride on the funicular yesterday, Bob had a look at his brainstorming board. Things had changed. He knew this from the Aston Martin episode with Higgins, but what else? Not much, it seemed, apart from the mystery man who got out at the top of the funicular on the day Stephen went missing. Bob felt relieved that even though he may have lost some of his marbles, he had others still in his grasp, but he also knew that the writing on the back of the grave had changed. He'd seen it with his own eyes, but the Roman numerals were still proudly looking at him from the board. How? He had been there last night. The grave had shown no sign of Roman numerals, or a P + W.

He amended this section of the board with DIG and an arrow.

Bob left Chalky's barn on the board. There was no mention of the Aston Martin, so there seemed no reason to take it down. He did add the farmhouse, though, and the track where Higgins had said Bob had located the ley line.

Bob was looking at the farmhouse picture as Higgins walked in, balancing a tray holding two coffees in one hand and carrying a box he had brought in from the car in the other. Higgins looked at the board, not missing a trick.

"I'm glad you rubbed off that riddle from the back of the grave, sir. DIG was a much easier clue than the P and W stuff, although it did add up with The Pig and Whistle. Who do you think planted it?" Higgins placed the box on the table.

"I don't know, son. Redcar will be busy today with what has just happened, but can you get it checked for prints? You never know."

"I will do, sir. What's next then?"

Bob gave him a look and sighed. "Do you know what, Hurricane, I'm not sure. You might have to go back to Redcar, especially with what's going on. It will be teeming with press. Maybe we'll pick this up again once it all dies down." He shuffled uneasily in his chair. Even he did not know why he'd said this.

"But, sir, don't you think they're connected?" Higgins pointed to the board, especially the words 'high tide'.

"Maybe we're being played. After all, Stephen failed to show, and the pig? Maybe we just stumbled on a joke meant for someone else."

Higgins thought better of questioning Bob. His boss was acting strangely, but Higgins knew there was a reason for everything Bob did.

"Hurricane, you've been a great help and I'll get you back the minute things die down a little in Redcar."

Higgins put his head down. "Are you sending me back, sir? But why? I think we're onto something – there are too many coincidences."

"Hurricane, as much as I love having you around, Redcar needs you right now. Sergeant Hopkins said you have to go back."

They both knew this was a lie. The news had only just broken about Carl Townsend and Hoppy was not even in yet.

"Is this about your ex-partner, sir? Frank?" Higgins looked straight at Bob with a furrowed brow.

"Hurricane, whoever is setting us up knows how to get to me. He wrote Frank's name on the inside of your car. I've lost one partner and I'm not losing another one, son." Bob thought of Frank and looked over to the young fresh-faced constable; he was not going to put Higgins in any danger. "I just think we need to cool off for a bit. People I left behind in London would not think twice about… Well, you know."

"OK, sir, I get it. I'll put this in for prints. What about doing door-to-door at the graveyard?" Higgins picked up the porcelain pig, still in its box.

"Leave the door-to-door to me." Bob had no intention of knocking on one door, never mind many. He was going to back off, as Stephen had ordered.

"I've really enjoyed working with you, sir."

"You too, Hurricane. You'll make a great detective one day, just like your dad."

Higgins left with the box under his arm, stomping out like a stroppy teenager. Bob called him back.

"Hurricane, see what you can find out about the Carl Townsend kid," he said, sensing he had upset the young man and dangling a carrot. Feeling useful again, Higgins turned his face upside down and managed a smile. If he were a dog, he would probably have been chasing his tail right now.

"Will do, sir."

"And Hurricane? Be careful. The guys who were after me in London won't hold back, son, so keep your eyes and ears open."

Higgins nodded and left the room with more purpose than he'd had a few seconds earlier.

Bob went and told Sergeant Hopkins the news that he'd offered Higgins back to Redcar and gave Higgins a glowing reference for his help over the last couple of days. Hoppy was grateful for the offer – he'd already offered a couple of lads to help.

Bob was not going to get involved, but that did not mean he wouldn't keep himself informed. Having Higgins on the other side of the fence, doing his eavesdropping for him, made perfect sense. Technically, he *was* backing off; he was just leaving another player in the game.

Part Two – Time in a Bottle

Chapter 19 – Chalky's Junk Yard

Bob was on his own again. *Just the way I liked it,* he thought as he was walking past The Ship and up the steep hill, heading for Chalky's farm. It was the type of hill that required him to put his hands on his knees and push his legs down to combat the gradient. He did miss Higgins for the rides everywhere, but he also missed his banter. In the short time they'd worked together, Bob had become very fond of his new partner.

It was the right thing to do.

Bob stopped half way up the hill and looked over Saltburn in all its splendour. It was a picturesque village, full of character and charm. Bob had heard people describe Saltburn as quaint, but quaint did not do it justice. It was much better than quaint – if quaint was the second division, Saltburn was the Premier League. Bob had fallen in love with the place and its people.

He looked over at the pier and the surfers like black dots in the sea beneath it. "Wow," he said, "absolutely beautiful."

Leaning forward, Bob continued. *Well, my diet has well and truly started now,* he thought as he powered up the road and onto the track that led to Chalky's farmhouse. As he approached the farmhouse, he could see a tractor snorting out plumes of grey diesel in one of the fields to the right. He assumed it was Chalky White driving it, as he had never seen a Mrs White.

The farmhouse looked a lot more spick and definitely a lot more span than it had a couple of days ago. It was like it'd had all its worn-out edges straightened and the white bits looked whiter, as if the house knew it had guests coming and was looking its Sunday best for the visit. Bob could not put his finger on what was different; it just was.

Out the back, he spied bits and bobs of what used to be working machinery in a less than well-made corrugated lean-to, which was just about managing to live up to its name. The corrugated roof was orange with rust, and the wooden legs were bowing with the weight it had carried over the years.

Bob got closer to see the lean-to also housed three battered and rusty tractors. *It couldn't be, could it?* Bob's thoughts were interrupted by an engine doing its best to creep up behind him, and failing miserably. Tractors were not very good at creeping.

The engine stopped. "Hands up or I'll shoot you, you little bugger!" Bob put his hands up "Turn around slowly." Bob obliged and turned to face Chalky, who lowered his gun the second he caught sight of his face. "Sorry, Bob, you can't be too careful around here." He broke the gun over his knee to ensure it had lost all of its menace. "I managed to map the rest of her.." He waved his hands in a downward direction to indicate that Bob's hands no longer needed to be raised. Bob had forgotten they were still up.

"What?" Having had two barrels pointing at his head a few seconds ago, Bob had not quite caught up with the conversation.

"The ley line. Big tide yesterday. I managed to fill in all the gaps."

Bob's brain, realising a decision between fight and flight was no longer required, allowed his adrenaline to stabilise.

"Oh, the ley line, of course. That's good to hear, Chalky."

"That's what you came for, right?"

It wasn't. Bob had come to look in the barn, although that might not be necessary now. He turned to look at the David Brown tractor, which had clearly been rusting away in its makeshift shelter for years. Higgins had said that they hadn't gone into the barn two days ago, so he had to tread carefully to fathom out the truth. Or, at least, Chalky's version of it.

"Shame to see a good tractor end up this way. A David Brown, isn't it? Looks like a 1954 Cropmaster, if I'm not mistaken?"

"It sure is, Bob. I didn't know you liked tractors?"

"I love tractors, Chalky. Shame this one's a little the worse for wear. I bet it was the star of your farm back in the day?"

"She was until her engine packed up. Worked her to the bone, that one. She owes me nothing. She's more or less family, she is."

"Family? I'm surprised you don't keep her in that big barn of yours on the cliff top." Bob gestured casually towards the barn with his arm. "Look at her engine – some power in there. Phew, what a beauty."

"I had her in there for a while, Bob, but then I was made an offer that changed my life." Bob knew more than anyone that things change. They were changing right in front of his eyes. "I guess you could say I found my guardian angel."

"Guardian angel?"

"I was offered a handsome sum for the barn years ago, and I still get a monthly allowance as it's on my land."

"Really, Chalky, from who?" Bob stepped away from the tractor to join him.

"The thing is, Bob, I don't know. The money is paid in every month, and apart from the odd murmur up there and a few workmen on my land when they built a separate access track at the back, I've not seen or heard a squeak for over twenty years. Hey, don't get me wrong, I had plans. I was going to have a shrine to my favourite tractors and stuff, but things change. It was an offer I could not refuse."

Bob was tinkering with questions in his mind, ensuring they were sharp enough to burst a balloon before being released into the outside world. He had to find a way into the Aston Martin story. As they walked back to the house, his mind settled on one, hoping it would lead Chalky to give him the answers he needed without drawing to much attention to itself.

"Chalky, I was told once that the DB in Aston Martin, like James Bond's DB5, stood for David Brown, like the tractors. What a load of crap that must be."

BANG! The metaphorical balloon exploded. "It's not a load of crap, Bob. Not many people know, though. He was my mate, David Brown, and it *is* the same guy. Fine Yorkshireman, you know."

"Really?"

"You mentioned the DB5 – the Aston Martin in *Goldfinger*." Chalky opened the door to the farmhouse kitchen and made his way to his whistling friend, filling her with water and giving her a chance to warm up her vocal cords ready to deliver two cups of tea.

"Iconic car, that one."

Chalky was busy rolling an impossibly thin cigarette from his Golden Virginia tin. "Yes, that very one – the DB5 – I used to have one, you know." He gave Bob a proud smile. Bob did know, but he still put on his best startled face.

"You had a DB5? Wow, where is it now?"

"Sold it with the barn. The estate agent said it had to be part of the deal. Look, you won't believe what I got paid for that rickety old barn. I had to let her go."

Wheeeeeee!

"Oh, she's ready. Always lets me know when she's ready, don't you?" Chalky was talking to the kettle again. Bob ignored it and got the conversation back on track.

"Estate agent? So you never met the man who bought the barn?"

Chalky lit his cigarette and took a couple of drags that reduced its length by half. Bob thought he'd be better off trying to smoke the match. It would last longer.

"Nope, never met him. He bought the barn and it was all done by a London estate agent. They said their client needed to keep it quiet, and for what I got paid, I thought it was the least I could do." Chalky poured two cups of tea and offered one to Bob, who was looking around the kitchen. Everything inside the house looked newer than it had done two days ago, just like the outside. It was as if Chalky had gone up a notch in the social class.

Bob sipped his tea. "Mmmm, I needed that, Chalky. They really must have paid you handsomely, then."

"I shouldn't really tell you, Bob, but I get ten thousand a month for that rickety old barn, and I got fifty times that up front. It's always paid on time, no questions asked. Anyway, enough of all this. Let's get down to what you came here for: our ley line friend."

Bob had already got what he'd come for, but he played along anyway. There were no new surprises about the ley line – it was exactly where Bob thought it should be. Two cups of tea later, he thanked Chalky and left, reflecting on their conversation all the way back down the bank to Saltburn.

Chapter 20 – Conflicting Information

It was 3pm by the time Bob reached the bottom of the hill, where The Ship was waiting for him. The walk had made him thirsty and he needed reflection time with beer and his notepad.

All was quiet and calm. No one was sitting outside the pub, and the sea was flat, exhausted by its tantrum the previous day. Bob's mind was like a washing machine of information with an extra spin cycle for good measure. He needed it to settle so he could separate the colours from the whites. What was true now, compared with what had been masquerading as the truth last week? This couldn't be the London gangs playing games with him. They were capable of lots of things, but not changing the past. And the past seemed to have changed. Either that or his memory was flawed.

Bob bought a beer from the bar and made his way to one of the many barrel-style tables outside. He had his pick, so he chose the one overlooking the sea wall, placed his beer down and looked out to sea, giving the washing machine in his brain time to stop spinning. Taking out his notepad, ignoring what he'd written before, he turned to the blank pages at the back, writing the heading *Conflicts*. He had a simple plan: think about what still appeared to be the same versus what he knew had changed.

This was a strange task. He'd been there when the events that had changed had happened, hadn't he? Well, he thought he'd been there, but now, at the same locations, subtle differences had taken place. If there had only been one inconsistency, he would have brushed it off his shoulder like an annoying wasp, but he seemed to have a wasps' nest that had been hit by a stick buzzing around his head.

Higgins, Keith, Chalky, and even the cage operator, Bill, now seemed to have a different account of the truth, but what puzzled Bob more than anything were the things he'd apparently done himself. He had written different things in his book to the events as he remembered them. What the hell was going on? Writing a list of the things that were out of kilter seemed like a good idea. At the very least, it would be something to show his therapist once he finally went insane.

Bob's list was coming along nicely, and his beer was just about done. He'd noted the writing on the grave that had changed, the mystery man going up in the funicular when Stephen and the old man were going down, the Aston Martin in the barn, the tractors – all the things that were not adding up. And talking of things that weren't adding up, he was about to encounter another.

"I took the liberty of ordering you a beer, Bob." A deep, velvety voice rumbled from behind him and a shudder went down Bob's spine. He'd have known that booming voice anywhere.

He turned to see a man in a wheelchair with a tray, presenting two beers. "Frank?" Bob's eyes welled up. "Frank, is that you? But you're... you're..."

Frank interrupted him as the word seemed to be stuck in Bob's throat.

"Dead? Ha-ha, he said you might say that." Bob stood, still in shock, and took the tray from his former partner before shaking his hand and hugging him. "Do I look dead, Bob?"

"But how, Frank? I was there."

Frank wheeled his chair nearer to the table where Bob had placed the beers and picked one up. "All in good time. Are you joining me for a beer? I've come all this way."

"All this way, Frank?"

"June and I drove up from Cornwall yesterday, we got here late last night." Frank pointed to his wife, who was standing in the car park next to a car that had been adapted for a wheelchair. Bob then saw Frank's left leg – well, he saw where Frank's left leg should have been.

Frank picked up on this. "Bob, if it hadn't been for you, I would be dead. I lost my leg, yes, but I have seen my kids grow up. We even have six grandkids. I would have seen none of that without you." Frank held his glass up to honour his former partner.

"Frank, what do you mean? I saw you die in my arms."

Rather than questioning Bob, Frank looked like he had been expecting this response.

"So, what do you remember, Bob?" Frank smiled. "Take me through it, bit by bit."

Bob took a deep breath, still in shock, and tried to regain

some sort of focus. His mind flashed back to 1993.

"We were in a disused warehouse in London's docks. We'd had a tip-off that an assignment of drugs was going to be delivered that day."

He looked at Frank, who nodded to confirm he was on the right page.

"Bastards set us up. Informer turned out to be one of them."

"I know, Frank. I put him away after you'd…"

"Carry on – the warehouse."

"Well, we entered together through the door. The informer had said it would be open, and all was well up to that point." Bob looked at Frank again. "But you know all this, Frank."

"Carry on," Frank said, raising his eyebrows as if expecting a lightbulb moment.

"Well, I took the right-hand side and you went down the left. That's when they jumped you. I heard you shout and ran to your side."

Bob put his head down as his memory was heading towards a point he did not care to consider. Frank assured him it was OK to carry on.

"Then what?"

"You know what, Frank. Do I have to live through that again? I've never forgiven myself."

"I'd like to know what you remember. So far we seem to be aligned."

"Well…" Bob took a deep breath. "You had been stabbed in your upper leg and were bleeding a lot. I found out later they had cut your femoral artery. Why did I listen to you, Frank?"

"Go on."

"Well, I started to take off my belt to put a tourniquet onto your left leg." Bob looked at Frank in the wheelchair, a flimsy trouser leg flapping where his left leg should have been. "You told me which door they had gone through and to chase them to get a registration number. Stupidly, I listened to you. I got their car registration, and I have put them all away over the last twenty years, but by the time I came back, you were dying. You died in my arms, Frank." This was said on autopilot. Bob had relived this memory so many times, it did not require any effort.

"Close your eyes, Bob, and tell me exactly what happened when you got back to me."

"I have just told you."

"No, you haven't. You have told me without trying to remember." Frank's deep voice cut through the wind, which was just starting to whip up as the tide was about to turn. "Close your eyes and tell me what you *really* remember."

"I ran back to you and you were still breathing. I sat with you, your head pulled into my chest. I could see how much blood you had lost, Frank. Then I saw it…"

Bob opened his eyes for a second, before closing them again to regain the memory.

"Saw what?" Frank asked.

"There was a tourniquet on your leg. Someone had put a brown belt tightly around your leg, Frank"

Frank smiled. "He said you would remember."

"Who said? Who was it who saved you?"

"Let's just say someone was looking over me that day, shall we? The less you know, the better."

Bob felt hurt by this. "Frank, I am over the moon you're OK, but you have to give me something. I am going crazy here."

"It seems to me, Bob, that if you concentrate, you can see what really happened. I need to ask you a favour. Do you know why I came to see you?"

Bob shrugged his shoulders. "To throw some more crazy into the crazy pot I have cooking in my head?"

Frank laughed. "Maybe. The man who saved me told me I had to move away. That's why June and I ended up in Cornwall. He also said that he was taking a big risk changing things, so we had to cut all ties. He made me promise before he applied the belt to my leg."

Bob was not trying to work any of this out; he was trying to absorb as much as he could. He gave Frank the universal go-on hand signal, not wanting to break Frank's flow.

"I agreed, which is why I have never been in touch since. You tried, Bob – you tried to contact me, but I had to completely shut you out."

"But why would you agree to that, Frank? And why would he make you do that?"

"He was changing the past, and one thing can lead to another if you're not too careful."

Bob was more confused than ever. "So why can you contact

me now?"

"Think of a dual carriageway when it goes into one lane. Let's just say you are off the dual carriageway and there is only one path from now on." This did not make sense to Bob, but it seemed to be a speech Frank had rehearsed, so he let it lie. "He said when he applied the belt to my leg that I would have to return the favour many years later and that he would be in touch. He gave me this."

Frank took a bag from the back of his chair and handed Bob a box from within. It looked like the same box as the one that had contained the pig in the graveyard. Bob opened the box and started to laugh. Inside was a porcelain pig in a suit, holding a clipboard. The pig had 'Tax Man' written on his hat. There was also a note, which Bob opened and read out loud.

"*Frank Cartwright, I am collecting my debt. All taxes need to be paid. I saved your life, so you owe me this.*"

Bob looked up at Frank. "Go on, read the rest," Frank boomed.

"*I need you to visit a small village, Saltburn-by-the-Sea. I have booked you a room in the Marine. I need you to personally deliver a message to your old friend, Bob Dixon. Get him to remember what happened to you. You have to ask him to remember. He may think you are dead… sorry about that. I am hopeful he will come around to you being alive again.*"

Bob looked up at Frank again, and then continued without another prompt.

"*Tell him that he is no longer on a dual carriageway and there is only one road from now on, which is why it is safe for you to see him. The past has a way of playing with you.* That's the speech you have just given me. Do you even understand it, Frank?"

"Not really, but I guess it must be important."

Bob continued reading. "*If he remembers why you are alive and well, give him this pig and the other note.*" Bob looked at Frank. "Other note?"

Frank took a note labelled *Bob Dixon* out of his pocket. "Bob, I only remember being saved. I have no recollection of dying. The first I knew of that was the note I received last week. Look, I can't pretend to know what's going on, but I can thank you from June and me for everything you have done."

Frank gave June a wave and she headed over. Bob was thinking, *leaving my partner for dead is not really a just cause for thanks.*

"The note is for you and you only. There was another note

delivered to our room this afternoon, explaining that you would be in Saltburn, walking down the hill, quite possibly going to the pub. Good luck, Bob."

June had joined them both by this time, and she gave Bob a hug.

"It's been a long time, Bob, thanks for everything."

Bob returned the hug with interest. It was great to see Frank a lot less dead than he'd been the last time Bob had had the pleasure of his company. Bob then walked Frank and June back to their car and bade them farewell with a smile, waving as they drove away.

Taking out his notepad, he added to his conflicts list: *Frank Cartwright, alive and well.*

Chapter 21 – La Note

Bob tapped the note in his pocket and took a slow walk to the pier, thinking about Frank. The memory of Frank dying in his arms had more or less evaporated as the new memory took hold. Even the blame he had suffered over the years was diminishing. He could still picture Frank dying, but that now felt more like a dream. The reality had kicked in that Frank was alive and well and living in Cornwall. Bob even remembered the anger he'd felt when Frank refused to take his calls, after they had been partners for years.

Why would *he do that?*

He knew now that Frank had been warned off and didn't want to jeopardise the second chance he had been given with his wife and kids. Upsetting Bob must have been a small price to pay to see his family grow.

Bob made his way up the steps and past the arcade, which was emitting arcade-type noises, trying to lure in passers-by to spend their hard-earned cash on the many games it had to offer. He stepped onto the pier, but apart from a couple of dog walkers, he had it to himself. The tide was a long way out, meaning the pier was high and dry with no water lapping around its legs. As a result, no fishermen were there.

Bob made himself comfortable on a bench half way along the Victorian structure, looking back at the funicular where the cars were crossing half way up the grassy bank. He took out the note, looking at his name typed on the front in a bold typeface and underlined: ***Bob Dixon***. Taking a deep breath, he opened the sealed envelope, ignoring the fact that there might be important fingerprints on it. Policing didn't seem important right now; nobody would believe what had gone on with him so far, anyway. Besides, whoever was masterminding this was too clever to make mistakes, or if he had, he'd made them on purpose.

The letter was triple folded. Bob opened it up and read it silently.

Bob, if you are reading this, you know *Frank is alive and well. I saved him many years ago, and you owe me.*

Bob stopped and looked around. It seemed very presumptuous of the mysterious stranger to assume that he owed anybody anything. Frank was alive and Bob was thankful for that, but it was Frank who owed the stranger, and from what Frank had just told Bob, he was a fully paid up member of the debts settled club.

Bob continued reading, having scratched that patronising itch.

I know you won't think you owe me right now.

Damn right, Bob thought as his anger grew.

Some things have changed, Bob, but they needed to. Frank was a risk, but I had to do it. Everything else has happened for a reason – you will see.

You need to trust me and back off the Townsend case. Stephen told you we will be in touch in 2018. We are working on how to stop this and need your help.'

Bob hated being told what to do, and he was certainly not in the mood for taking orders from a madman. His head was already shaking, disagreeing with everything he was reading.

I have some errands I need you to run before then. In fact, I have a shopping list for you. I know how much you like shopping, Bob, ha-ha.

Bob did not see the humour at all. His anger went up a notch; his buttons were being pressed again.

The instructions are in your apartment. I know you like puzzles, Dodgy Dicko. You need to trust me.

It was signed *A friend.*

P.S. Do you speak French, Bob? S'il vous plaît tournez la page …

Bob picked up on the Dodgy Dicko. It had to be someone from the police office in London, maybe someone in the force whom the East End gangs had corrupted. He looked out to the water, which was slowly heading back towards the pier.

Why should I help a crazy fool like you? he thought. *And do I speak French? Of course not, you madman, what type of question is that?* Bob's blood was boiling. He'd been hoping the note would make sense; his mind was overloaded, and this was making things worse.

Do I speak bloody French? he thought again, concentrating on the words a little more this time. It was as if the words translated themselves in front of him on the page. *What the hell is going on?*

Bob read the words out loud in a perfect French accent, "*S'il vous plaît tournez la page,*" then repeated them in English, "Please turn over. But how has this happened? I can't speak French."

A couple walking their dog looked over to him. "Are you alright, mate? Are you talking to us?"

"Oh… no, just thinking out loud. Sorry, guys."

"OK, no probs, mate."

As the couple and their dog walked off, it dawned on Bob that he could trust no one. Whoever was masterminding the situation seemed to have them all like puppets on a string.

He turned the note over. Looking around to ensure the coast was clear, wanting to hear his new French accent again, he read out the back of the note.

"*Vous devriez me faire confiance, Bob Dixon. Comment pourrais-je peut-être savoir que vous parlez français*? You need to trust me, Bob Dixon. How could I possibly know you speak French?"

How the hell am I doing this?

Still in shock at his new skill, Bob thought on his feet. *OK, instructions in the apartment. Shopping list, you say? You have my attention, madman, so let's follow your lead for a bit, see where you're heading with all this.*

He placed the note back into his pocket and took out his notepad, adding *Apparently, I speak French* to his list of conflicts. Then he headed back to his apartment. Maybe the only way to get to the bottom of things was to trust, or at least be seen to be trusting, who or whatever was leading him down the garden path. After all, he was not going to find all the answers on his own. And if you head down the garden path, more often than not, there's a garden at the end of it. Maybe all the answers would be there.

Bob opened the door of his apartment, saying, "*Je vais vous suivre pour l'instant, voir où vous m'emmenez,*" checking he could still speak French. He smiled before repeating in English, "I'll follow you for now, see where you are taking me."

There was another pig. Bob ignored the fact that someone had broken into his apartment – he'd assumed they must be good at breaking and entering after the writing had appeared on the inside of Higgins's locked car. This time the pig was holding a fishing rod with a little fish on the end. There was a typed note folded over the pig.

Shhhhhhh – 5am tomorrow, don't be late. He doesn't know you're coming, so you need to stow away. You know how much he likes company.

"A fishing pig who doesn't like company? That can only be Silent Man. And he doesn't know I'm coming. That will be fun."

Bob lay on the bed and read all the notes again, but before long his mind had sent him to sleep. Too much information can make your brain crash, and Bob's needed rebooting.

Bob awoke at 4.15am.

"Shit," he said, looking at his alarm and then his watch. The notes were on the floor, so he picked up the last of them and looked at the fishing pig. "OK, Ray, let's see what you have got for me."

Bob put on some jeans, a tee-shirt and a jumper, which was the best fishing attire he had in his wardrobe. He finished his outfit off with his trainers, which would have to do due to the lack of anything more appropriate. By 4.30am he was making haste to the boats parked outside The Ship. He would have to take care not to be seen – Ray liked his own company, not anyone else's.

As he approached the boats, rather than walk in full sight across the road, he jumped off the promenade onto the beach. The six-foot drop would keep him out of sight. As he got nearer the boats, he could hear a tractor snorting and saw its lights through the gloom.

It must be Ray, he thought. *No one else would be up and out this early, and if they were, there would be crew chatting and making a noise.*

As he made his way towards the boat park, he could see Ray hooking the bars of his boat onto the tractor. As the tractor and coupled boat made their way down the slipway and onto the beach, Bob took the opportunity to crouch down behind the stern of the boat, out of sight of the tractor's silent driver.

The sea was quite rough, so Ray was going to head for Penny Hole. At least, Bob guessed they would be heading there. Bob took a look to his left as he ran along, crouched over. In fact, the sea looked *very* rough. What the hell was he doing? The only time he'd been out to sea was to the Channel Islands on holiday as a kid, and all he remembered was being seasick.

As Ray reached the launching area, he swung the tractor into the sea and back out again, bringing the boat level ready to reverse her in. As he did this, Bob had no option but to wade ankle deep into the North Sea, his body straightening up for a second as the cold water bit through his trainers and socks.

Here goes nothing, he thought as he jumped onto the beam and into the boat while Ray was tending to the winch hook on the wheel opposite, readying it for his return. Bob leaped forward into the canvas dodger: a green tent-like device in the bow of the coble, held up by diagonal poles. He covered himself with some yellow waterproofs and a blue fishing box. It was Bob's first attempt at stowing away, and he thought it had gone quite well so far. The plan was to wait in hiding and reveal himself when they were so far out that Silent Man would have no choice but to take him along too.

After leaving the boat bobbing up and down in the calmness of the shallows, Ray dropped the tractor behind the high waterline to ensure it was safe from the incoming tide in a few hours' time. He then ran back in his waders and jumped on the boat.

He had been fishing long enough to recognise when he was not alone.

"I hope you don't think that I don't know you're here."

Bob let out a "Shit" under his breath.

"I don't know who you are, and I don't really care. All I know is that I want you off my fucking boat, NOW!"

Bob jumped out of hiding, lifting the lid off the engine, which was situated where his legs had been. There was a tool box inside, and he looked frantically for a knife. Fishermen always had knives, right? Wrong – no knife.

Now what? he thought, and then he spotted it. *Bingo.*

Bob pointed a bright orange flare gun directly at Ray, and the Silent Man was silent all of a sudden.

"You're taking me fishing, Ray, whether you like it or not." Bob's hand was remarkably steady as the boat drifted further out, nearer to the cliff wall and the quiet pool of Penny Hole.

"You're bluffing," Ray said and took a step forward.

"Don't, Ray, I'll use it. I mean it." Bob sounded convincing enough as he gripped the gun tightly, re-aiming it at Ray's head for effect.

"Bob, isn't it? The copper?"

He might be silent, but he can still listen, Bob thought.

"I know you're bluffing. Only a fool would point a flare gun with no canister inside."

Bob's menace melted as Ray took another couple of steps forward and gestured for the gun. Bob loosened his grip, allowing the gun to loop around his finger before dropping it into Ray's hand.

"You could have just asked if you wanted to go fishing."

Deflated, Bob remembered the note telling him he needed to stow away. "I thought you would have told me to sod off."

"I would have done, so you thought you would commandeer my boat instead?"

Ray raised the gun and pointed it at Bob's head, allowing the muzzle to nestle onto his forehead.

"But you said it wasn't loaded."

"That's because you were pointing it at me."

"Is it loaded?"

"I can't remember. Shall we find out?"

Bob was now sweating.

"Answer me a couple of questions."

"OK, fire away."

"Bad choice of words."

"*Ask* away."

The Silent Man smiled at Bob as they drifted further out to sea and nearer to Huntcliff's rock face.

"The rocks, Ray."

Ray ignored him. "One – why are you on my boat?"

"I received a message saying I had to be on your boat today."

"Mmmm, did you now?" Ray's eyes and the gun were fixed on Bob's forehead. "Two – if I do take you, will you do as you're told?"

"Yes, I promise." Bob didn't know what was more dangerous: the rapidly approaching rocks or the mad fisherman pointing a gun at him.

"Three – if you ever point a loaded gun at me again, I will kill you. Do you understand?"

"Loaded?"

"What do you think? Three… two…"

Bob closed his eyes.

"One."

Ray pointed the gun at the cliff wall. BANG! The flare exploded in an orange plume. Bob gulped.

Five yards from the cliff face and its treacherous rocks, Ray masterfully kicked the gear into reverse. He backed away from the rocks and over the breakers before spinning the boat around with little effort and locking the tiller onto a course. He then turned towards Bob, who was sitting there like a naughty schoolboy who had been caught cheating in an exam.

"Put these on, it's choppy out there." Ray handed Bob the yellow oilskins and thigh-length fishing waders he had been hiding under earlier.

"How come you brought spares?" Bob said as he took off his trainers and put on some dry socks, also provided by Ray.

The Silent Man smiled. "Because I knew you were coming. Someone told me." Ray winked at Bob before heading back to the tiller and making a steering adjustment, consulting his compass.

That went well, Bob thought, *just as I planned.*

Chapter 22 – The Magic of the Sea

Bob's stomach was doing somersaults. The horizon was dipping in and out of vision as the swells lifted the boat up and down. As Bob turned a pale green colour, the Silent Man let out a bark of laughter.

"How are you feeling, Bob?"

Another swell lifted the boat again as Ray gestured to Bob. "The anchor, throw her over."

Bob managed to get to the anchor, which was lodged between two pins protruding up from the gunnels. A roller sat just before where the green dodger started. He threw the anchor over the side and watched the line run out over the metal rollers, then retook his seat.

It was quiet with the engine off. The anchor took hold and the boat flicked round 180 degrees. Bob, who had been sitting on the seaward side of the boat feeling ill, could now see land, and immediately he felt a little better. The smell of diesel fumes and the old fish heads staring up at him from a basket took their toll, though.

Bob's head flew over the side of the boat and he threw up yellow fluid.

"Get it up, DI Dixon, always nice to have ground bait. Helps the fishing." Silent Man laughed again.

The boat was now slowly easing up and down with the swell. Bob gave the fish some more yellow bile-flavoured bait.

"You should have had strawberry jam sandwiches this morning, Bob."

Bob's head was on the gunnel, resting on his arms, and he raised it momentarily. "Does that stop you being sick?"

Ray laughed yet again. "No, but at least it tastes nicer on the way up." He poured a cup of tea from a flask he had taken out of his bag and handed it to his crew member for the day. "Here, sip this. It has sugar in, should sort you out."

"Thanks, Ray." Bob hugged the mug like his new best friend.

"And look at the land. When you can't see the horizon, your brain refuses to believe you are moving."

Bob did as ordered, and to his surprise, it worked.

"So what now, Ray?" He took another slurp of his sugary tea and sat up straighter.

"We'll do some yucking for pot bait."

Ray handed him a rod.

"Yucking?"

"Yes, fishing with rods. That's what we call it up here: yucking. There's some mussels in that tub. Bait up your two bottom hooks, through the heart and the tongue. That's through the white bit and loop back through the black bit, like this." Ray took a mussel out of the tub and baited one of Bob's hooks. "The bait will fly off otherwise. Got it?"

"Got it, Ray, thanks." Now Bob was busy, he forgot all about being ill. He baited up the other hook as ordered and let his sinker take the line to the bottom.

"When you hit the bottom, take a couple of reels up and keep bouncing off the bottom. We're after whiting or sea hens for pot bait, but you never know. We're on the rock edge, church on tip, so we might hit the odd cod if we are lucky."

It was very quiet when Ray stopped speaking. The only sound was the water occasionally lapping against the anchored boat.

"Church on tip?"

"You have a lot to learn, Bob. Landmarks. That's how we know where we are out here. Marske's big church steeple is on the tip."

"The tip of what?" Bob looked over to Marske and could see the big church in the centre of the village. It did not seem to be on the tip of anything.

"The tip – the rubbish dump. The church steeple is on the tip."

"I can't see the tip."

"Oh, it's not there anymore."

Bob looked confused. "So your mark is a church steeple on something that isn't there anymore?"

"Yes, but everyone knows church on tip."

Bob was about to question further when Ray had a bite.

"I'm in!" he declared as his fiberglass rod started kicking and bending violently. "It's a cod." Bob could see a flash of white underbelly as Ray lifted the fish in. "Not joining in the fun, Bob? A five-pound cod, that. Come on, buck your ideas up. We need some pot bait." Ray winked at him and threw the fish into the box before re-baiting for round two.

Bob then felt his rod kick. "I've got one, I think."

"Get it in, Bob."

Bob reeled in a weird looking fish. It was more rounded than the cod and a lot smaller. He looked disappointed, until Ray put him at ease.

"That's what we came here for – pot bait. It's a sea hen, or pouting as they are more commonly known."

Bob took the hook out and put the fish in the box. There were scales everywhere.

"Messy, scaly buggers. Lobsters like them, though."

After an hour of catching whiting, the odd cod and lots of sea hens, they had enough to bait up the lobster pots. Bob was feeling better. When you're occupied and busy, feeling ill is the last thing on your mind, and Bob was enjoying his fishing trip.

"I'd like to do this more often, Ray."

"Ask next time rather than taking my boat at gunpoint. Come on, reel in. Let's see if we have any crabs or lobsters in the pots."

Bob reeled in as ordered, then he turned to Ray.

"Ray?"

"Bob?"

"You said you knew I was coming today. How?"

"Some things should be left where they are."

Bob thought back to the clue left in his room with the fishing pig. *You need to stow away. You know how much he likes company.* Why would the note say this if the writer was going to go and tell Ray about his little escapade anyway? It did not make sense. If he was being played, was there more than one player?

"Anchor please, Bob. You know what? I'm quite enjoying having a crew member."

Bob pulled up the anchor, which took a lot more effort than he had imagined. He basically had to pull the boat along until the anchor lost its hold on the sea bed. No wonder Silent Man liked having a crew member, because being a crew member was hard work. He was sweating buckets and panting for air.

Once the anchor made it safely on board, Ray powered the engine up and Bob immediately started to feel ill again. The boat was rolling and climbing over the swells as they headed further out into the North Sea. He threw up again, which Ray found hilarious.

"Bloody land lover," he shouted above the noise of the

engine, before consulting his compass and steering a course north-north-eastward, heading for the waiting crab pots.

The Silent Man finally slowed the boat to a stop and turned off the engine. Apart from the cries of a few seagulls that had been following them in the hope of some castaway fish guts, it was quiet.

"Do you know why you're here, Bob?" Ray asked as he poured another cup of sweet tea from his healing flask. Bob immediately felt better, maybe because of the tea, maybe because the boat was not moving under engine power.

"Not really. I received a note saying I had to stow away on your boat this morning."

Ray smiled and patted him on the back of his bright yellow waterproofs. "I think you're about to find out." Bob saw an opportunity to probe for more information and probed away.

"Do you know why I'm here, Ray? What's the big secret?"

Ray gave a smile which eclipsed his previous one.

"All I was told was to bring you out to the pots and make you haul them in, so I guess we're about to find out, together."

"Who told you?"

Ray looked around to make sure no one was listening, which seemed an odd thing to do in the North Sea, two miles away from anything. He lowered his voice to a whisper, which was just as odd.

"Do you think I'm crazy?"

Bob did think he was a little crazy. After all, Ray had pointed a flare gun at his head. But this was counterbalanced by the fact he had done the same to Ray minutes before.

He settled on, "Of course not," and added a laugh for good effect.

"Have you heard them say I talk to the fish, Bob?"

Bob had not been expecting this. "I might have heard that. What a load of old tosh." Bob laughed again; Ray did not join in.

"After the big tide every six or seven years, I come and get my crab pots. Do you know how many lobsters and crabs I normally get in the whole beat of ten pots?"

Bob was not an expert, so he shrugged and had a guess.

"Twenty?"

"Ten pots and twenty crabs and lobsters? Who's the crazy one now? More like five or six, max."

"And your point is?"

"What if I were to tell you that each of these pots will be

crammed full of crabs and lobsters today? What would you say about that?"

Bob's logical mind kicked in. "I would say that you catch more crabs and lobsters after a really big tide."

"Ha-ha, you ask the boys in The Ship what they catch today. They won't even have their pots out in such a tide – they would be trashed. Mine won't be."

Bob was still struggling to see the point, so he brought the conversation back a step or two.

"So do you talk to fish, Ray, like they say?"

Ray again looked around for earwiggers.

"He has told me I'm allowed to tell you, but you must say nothing to nobody, understand?"

Bob nodded. "Who told you?"

"He's called Stephen. We have been friends for over twenty years now. He visits me every high tide and makes sure all my nets and pots are full by way of thanks."

Bob's eyebrows rose. "Stephen, you say? Really?"

"Yes, really. Why, do you know him?" Ray looked confused. "How can you know him?"

"It might be a different Stephen. Tell me about your Stephen."

"I went out fishing through Penny Hole. It was a rough one and a massive tide, twenty odd years ago. It was really early in the morning. I approached the dan for my nets and could see the flag and float moving around. I thought I must have a basking shark or even an orca caught up in it. The dan was moving far too much for a seal or any of the dolphins or other sharks we get around here."

Bob did not follow what a dan was, but his eyes were fixed on Ray's. He stored it in the 'probably not important' list in his mind.

"Go on."

"Even the net hauler was struggling with the weight. The boat keeled over to the side. I thought we were going over – the gunnels were level with the sea, so I turned off the hauler and looked down at the net, which was visible beneath the surface. It was beautiful, Bob – nature can be a wonderful thing."

Ray looked up and smiled, reliving the memory in front of Bob's eyes.

"Then what, Ray?"

Ray snapped out of his daydream and looked around again. "I

cut the line – I cut the net away. I could not take such beauty from the sea. It was not my place. As fishermen, we take what we need, and anything over that lives to fight another day.

"After I'd cut the net, I saw whatever was caught up unravel itself. It was actually two of the beautiful things I have ever seen: luminous blue on top with white underbellies."

Ray looked over at Bob to see if he was receiving a 'you're mad' stare. He wasn't, so he continued.

"One was bigger than the other. To my surprise, the bigger of the two headed to the surface. I wasn't scared, Bob, just thankful I had cut the line."

"Then what, Ray?"

"He breached the surface and stared at me. He had powerful tail gills, but he looked human, too. My net had done him some damage. Though he smiled, I could see where the diagonal knots on the net had marked his face. He had blood all over his face."

"How did you know he was a he?"

"He spoke to me, Bob. He told me that he would be for ever grateful and that he would look after me. And he has. He fills my nets with fish and my pots with crabs and lobsters."

"A mermaid?"

"A merman, at least."

"How do you know he's called Stephen?"

"He comes to see me. The day before the monster tide when I'm putting out the nets and pots, we have a chat. When the lifeboat crew came for me, thinking I was in trouble, they saw me talking to the sea. That's why all the lads in The Ship think I'm mad. Do you think I'm mad, Bob?"

"Far from it, Ray, I think I may have met your Stephen. So if you are mad, we both are."

"But you've never been out fishing before. How have you met him?"

"I may have met him on the land." He left a pause to gauge Ray's reaction. "I guess we both have a secret to keep."

"Thanks, Bob. I've carried this by myself for over twenty years, now I feel liberated." Ray's smile spoke volumes as he patted Bob on the back. "Now let's go and see what fruits the sea has for us in those pots."

Chapter 23 – Fruits de la Mer

Ray smiled, he knew what was coming. "According to my instructions, you need to haul the pots in. Have you seen one of these before?" Ray pointed to an hourglass-shaped hunk of metal on a stand near where Bob had hauled up the anchor.

"I'd never been in a fishing boat until I stowed away on this one, Ray, so that will be a no."

"It's a pot hauler. It helps you pull up ropes with heavy things on the end, like pots."

"Or like anchors?" Bob gave him a stern look at the thought of having expended so much effort earlier pulling up what felt like the bottom of the sea.

Ray laughed. "Yes, like anchors, too, but it's more fun doing it the old-fashioned way sometimes. Character building, don't you think?"

Bob just about saw the joke, rubbing his back for effect.

"This is important, Bob. You don't want to end up like me." Ray turned over his hand to show that his middle finger was missing. Bob looked on in shock. "Only joking, but it grabbed your attention." Ray straightened his finger back into view. "But if you are going to lose a finger today, it will be in a minute, so listen carefully."

Bob stretched out his fingers and looked at them, doing as he was told for their sake. Ray explained how the pot hauler worked and how to catch the dan, which Bob now knew was a marker with a float on the bottom and a flag pole on top. The coloured flags told everyone which pots were whose.

"What stops other fishermen pulling up your pots and throwing them back?"

Ray eyed Bob up and down.

"We may slag each other off, we may laugh and joke, and people may even say I'm mad because I talk to fish, but one thing us fishermen have is respect for each other's catches. I have pulled other people's pots in before, but only when they have asked me to. It's a bit like when we all moved the boats together. It's a hard life, so why would we make it harder?"

In a way, Bob wished he'd never asked, but he welcomed the

answer nonetheless, and the passion that came with it. He was now primed and ready and knew what he had to do.

Ray pointed out the yellow and blue flagged dan to the port side of the boat. The engine fired up again, but this time Bob did not feel ill. He was too busy and had too many things to remember.

They looped around the dan so it was on starboard, where the pot hauler was situated, as they approached. Bob hooked the submerged line with the gaff – a fishing hook on a long pole, lifted in the dan and threw it to the back of the dodger as instructed by Ray. He then looped the rope once, then twice around the pot hauler, ensuring his fingers were clear before laying the line out across the rollers. He looked over to Ray and got a thumbs up.

So far, so good, he thought.

Ray was on the tiller at the stern, ticking the boat along to make the hauler's job a little easier. Bob, concentrating for all he was worth, was feeding the rope into a neat circle as it reeled smoothly off the spool of the hauler. His other job right now, if that were not enough, was to keep an eye on the first pot coming up from the sea bed. Missing this and not putting the hauler out of gear in time would be a disaster.

The leader of the first crab pot was visible. Bob kicked the helping hand out of gear and again followed the orders Ray had given him earlier, pulling the pot in by hand. Ray joined him and helped lift the heavily weighted pot into the boat. It was bursting at the seams with lobsters and crabs.

"Wow," Bob shouted above the engine noise.

Ray tied off the rope to the remaining pots on one of the metal pins next to the roller on the boat's gunnels. As he did so, the boat leant over to the starboard side because of the weight. Ray ordered Bob to the other side of the boat for balance, and Bob obeyed immediately, remembering the 'do exactly as you are told' speech from earlier. It worked. The lean felt less menacing and the boat levelled off.

Ray went to work, opening the side door of the pot and dispensing the five enormous crabs and four even bigger lobsters into separate wicker baskets. There was a tennis-sized blue ball left in the pot.

"I guess this is for you," he said and winked as he threw it into the fish-box which contained the bait they'd caught earlier. After baiting up the pot to send it on its next voyage, Ray stacked it near the coiled rope. The first one out would be last one back in.

OK, off we go again, Bob thought, looping the rope around the hauler and kicking it into gear for four or five seconds until the next pot was in view. Again, it was full of crabs and lobsters, and another blue ball. It did occur to Bob that Ray was not playing fair with the sea. He obviously had a guardian angel – or rather, a guardian merman.

After all ten pots had been emptied, and three baskets of lobsters, fours baskets of crabs and ten blue balls were safely on board, Bob could no longer see the front of the boat for stacked crab pots. Next was the bit Bob was concerned about. The task was simple: the dan which had marked the end of the pots when they'd hauled them in would now be the starting point for launching them back. Bob would have to throw all of the pots into the sea in turn, in reverse order, at full speed. Losing a finger was the least of his worries. If he got his foot looped around the coil of rope or leader, he could get dragged overboard. And throwing the pots back in the wrong order would also come with its consequences, causing a tangled mess of ropes, pots, and probably a bollocking from Ray.

Concentrate, Bob said to himself, giving Ray the thumbs up.

The boat kicked into gear at full speed and the dan was sent on its way, Bob following the line which was disappearing from its coil. The first pot went over, followed by the next and the next. There only seemed to be two or three seconds between each. Watching his feet, which had been hit a couple of times by the rope, Bob threw the last pot. After the line had been laid, allowing the pots to descend to the sea bed, the dan followed to mark the end of the pots for tomorrow.

He looked over at Ray, who gave him another thumbs up and wheeled the boat around to head for home. Bob looked at the catch they had made together, feeling proud. He had really enjoyed the day. He then took a look at the fish box. All the fish had been used as bait, apart from half a dozen or so cod, which had been gutted and were staring back at him. And then there were ten blue balls, their stare seeming more intense than the bog-eyed fish. The balls each had letters marked on them.

Goodie, another one of your bloody games.

Right now was not the time to look at them. That time would come. After his conversation with Ray, Bob knew strange things had happened out here at sea, and he knew what Ray had said had been the truth. It had taken a lot for the Silent Man to share those memories. He couldn't have faked the emotion and relief that finally he had someone he could share his secrets with.

Bob joined Ray on the tiller and was allowed to steer them home. He could see people on the end of the pier, waving at them as they passed, so he waved back. He also saw the surfers and wondered if Scraggs was among them. It had already been a good day and it was only eleven o'clock.

Ray took over steering duties to land the boat, but not through Penny Hole. He thought Bob might enjoy riding the surf back to land on Saltburn's sandy beach – which he did.

"Hold her there, Bob, I'll get the tractor."

The boat took little holding as it was in slack water; it was going nowhere. Bob looked around, and it was then that he saw it – and him.

The DB5, complete with its owner, was too far away to make out clearly. The stranger looked like a thin man of normal height, wearing a flat cap and a black overcoat. He raised two fingers to his brow in the way of a salute before getting in the car, driving towards the pier and up Saltburn's corkscrew of a bank.

Bob's thoughts started racing again. *He wanted me to see him. He was waiting for me. He wants me to know that he is in control. Hmm, we'll see about that.*

After they had put the boat back in the park and Bob had helped his skipper get the catch of the day into the trailer behind the tractor, Ray shook his hand and passed over a bag containing the blue balls, a couple of crabs and a lobster.

"Thanks, Bob. Thanks for listening. It's our secret, remember? Oh, and you did well today. If I ever need a crew member, I'll give you a shout."

"Thanks, Ray. Mum's the word, promise."

They released their grip on each other's hands.

"Stephen told me you're a good man and you are going to help. I hope you find what you're looking for in that bag."

"Me too, and thanks for today. What do I do with the crabs and lobster?"

"Eat them or sell them. The chef in The Ship will give you a few quid, I'm sure. You've earned them. I always look after my crew – that's why I fish alone. I'm a greedy bastard."

They shared a laugh and went their separate ways.

Chapter 24 – A Suspect?

If life hadn't been complicated enough before, the last few hours had complicated the complications that had been doing fine on their own. Bob sold his crabs and lobster to The Ship, getting a free pint and twenty-five quid for his troubles. He guessed that was well under the going rate, but taking them home and having them crawling round his bath did not seem like a viable alternative.

The phone buzzed in his pocket. It was Higgins.

"Sir, where have you been? I need to speak to you."

"I've been fishing, sunshine, with Silent Man. I'm at The Ship having a well-earned beer."

"Silent Man fishes with nobody." Higgins left a gap, expecting an answer, but all he got was more gap, so he filled it himself. "Right, stay there, sir, we need to talk."

The phone went dead abruptly. Bob stared at it for a second, thinking that hanging up was a bit rude, before tying a bow in his carrier bag to keep his mysterious blue balls out of sight. Still nothing made sense, and the last thing he needed was someone else questioning his nothingness. He placed the bag under his seat, hoping it would not draw attention to itself.

Higgins must have been phoning from Saltburn nick as it only seemed like seconds later that Bob saw his bright purple car creeping down the bank and heading into The Ship's car park. Higgins ran across in uniform.

"Sir, sir…"

Bob stood up and held his hand out. "Calm down, Hurricane, catch your breath, son. Do you want a drink?" Higgins put his hand to his chest to catch what breath he could before speaking.

"No, sit down, sir, I have a few things I need to tell you."

"It'll wait till after a drink, though, eh?"

"No, it can't, sir. I mean it." Bob took the hint and sat down again, shuffling his bag further under his seat with his leg.

"OK, Hurricane, what's all the fuss about? Is it about the kid who has been taken from the hospice?"

"I'll tell you about that in a minute. It's the pig, sir. We found fingerprints all over it and they have a perfect match."

"Well done, son, now we're getting somewhere. I didn't expect him to make a mistake, though. Who is the little sod? Do we know him?"

"It's you, sir. Perfect match, a hundred per cent."

"But how, Hurricane? You were there. I used the bubble wrap to touch it and covered it back up. I might have left one print on it, but all over it?"

"I know, sir. I need to ask you a question."

"Fire away."

"And you need to answer me honestly, or you're on your own." Bob nodded. "Did you plant the box, sir, with the pig and everything?" Bob took a large breath, ready to defend himself, but Higgins raised his hand in an 'I'm not finished' manner. "I never saw the lettering you said was on the back of the grave; all I saw was the word 'dig', and then we found a box. You could have planted that. The projection or dream or whatever it was could all be a load of old crap, as far as I'm concerned. Was it all you, sir?"

Bob was shocked. He had to think, fast. "What do you think, Hurricane?" Answering a question with a question is a stalling tactic coppers have used for years. Luckily for Bob, Higgins had not been on the planet for that many years.

"The evidence, sir, you told me to look at the evidence."

"Well, what if I'm being framed? Anyone could have got my prints off my door handle, or anywhere."

Higgins thought for a second. "I told the forensic guys you must have touched it. I think they bought it. They are snowed under with what's happening in Redcar anyway."

"Thanks, Hurricane. Someone has it in for me, you know."

Higgins nodded. "It doesn't explain the pig and the gravestone markings, though, sir."

Bob laughed. "OK, I'll come clean." Bob felt like Jerry the mouse, pinned in the corner of a dark alley by Tom the cat with no escape plan or handily placed garden rake for Tom to stumble onto. "I had to tell you something. I told you before that I dreamt the whole thing – the blue projections, the gravestone." His voice lowered. "There were markings on the back of Emily's grave, though. I was right about that, and they were scored years ago, so maybe there is something in my dream. Who knows?

"But was it a dream?"

Bob kept his voice calm and steady to sound convincing.

What he was telling Higgins was some distance away from the truth, but the truth would seem too farfetched to the young man.

"Yes, I dreamt it, Hurricane, and when we went to the churchyard, I just relayed the dream to you."

Higgins was thinking. Bob's convincing style was winning him over, but he still needed the i's and t's attending to with their dots and crosses.

"OK, sir, if that's what happened, how come you said the story changed in the graveyard and there was another man?"

Bob needed to change the subject. His tone lifted from agreeable to 'I don't have time for this crap'.

"Oh, I don't really know what I remember, Hurricane. Do you remember all of your dreams?"

"No."

"Well, there we are, then." Bob had won the game of cat and mouse. Jerry was no longer cornered, and Tom was left not really knowing how he'd escaped – again. "So, tell me what you know about the Carl Townsend case. I bet it's been a busy night?"

Higgins sat up straighter and took out his notebook.

"Carl Townsend is a very sick boy. I can't believe that anyone would take a kid, let alone one who only has days to live." Bob listened intently. "From what I've managed to glean from the CID lads in Redcar, Carl settled down about six-ish on Friday night and went to sleep. His parents went to have a coffee in the communal area of the hospice.

"That's when Carl was taken. His abductor broke a window with a rock, opened the window, climbed straight in, and carried him out through the front door of the hospice, in full view of everyone. I've seen the CCTV, sir."

"Have you got a copy for me to look at?"

"No need, it will be all over the TV. There's a press conference at noon, and they are releasing the footage."

Bob looked at his watch. *How come it's not even twelve o'clock yet?* He'd been up for hours.

"That's in five minutes."

"There's a TV in the pub, I'll ask them to put it on."

Higgins headed off, and Bob retrieved his carrier bag from under his seat before following. The pub landlady turned the volume up on the BBC news just in time for Redcar's DCI to start speaking. Bob recognised him from one of his visits to Redcar to have a look around.

"My name is Detective Chief Inspector Gordon Fisher. Thank you all for coming in at this difficult time." He eyeballed the press room before continuing. "I have a statement I would like to read out from the parents of Carl Townsend. Following that, we have some CCTV footage of the abduction to show you. I will then take any questions."

The room fell silent, apart from the click and whirr of the press photographers. The buzz of anticipation was palpable – this was a big story, and the world's media had hooked into it.

The short statement from the parents said how devastated they were as a family, that Carl would be in grave danger if he did not receive his medication, and if anyone had any information, they should come forward. Bob recognised all the trademark points within the statement which told him that the police had more or less written it for Carl's parents to try to get a reaction from whoever had taken their little boy.

Following the statement, the DCI gestured towards a widescreen TV on a stand. "We are releasing this CCTV footage in a bid to identify the man seen carrying Carl from the hospice. We would urge him to come forward so we can eliminate him from our enquiries."

The footage was grainy, but Bob and Higgins could see a man wearing a cap, a scarf covering the lower half of his face. Bob was just thinking that he did not look tall enough to be Stephen when the footage paused as the man looked directly into the camera. There was no scar on his face.

Bob moved towards the TV. The man had black gloves on and was covered up enough not to give much away, but his eyes were familiar.

But how? Have I met him?

The camera panned back to the DCI, who showed two more stills of the boy being carried out of the hospice in the man's arms.

"This man broke in and entered through the window of Carl's room in the hospice. He left with the child through the main reception area and departed through a gap that had been cut into the fence. We don't have details of any vehicle he may have been using, but we really do need to speak to this man and eliminate him from our enquiries."

"*Eliminate him from our enquiries?*" Bob laughed. "Guilty as sin, I would say. Why do we always say that, Hurricane?"

Bob had Stephen Farrell's voice echoing in his head: "*They make me take one child back with me and we have chosen Carl. You will see why. I have no choice, or we all die. All of us. If I fail, there will be another and another, and then another.*"

"I guess they have to say that until they're sure it's definitely him. What do you think, sir?"

Bob snapped out of his daze.

"Well, I think he's been caught red-handed, and he is one sick individual. There is not much to go on though, son. You can't see much on the CCTV, can you? So he left through a gap in the fence, with no known car or van. I think he's covered his tracks very well. A sicko, yes, but also a real pro. That's what makes him dangerous."

"That's what I thought. Sick bastard, taking a seriously ill boy. I agree, sir, that there's nothing much to go on, which I guess is why they released the CCTV film, trying to flush him out."

"Keep me posted, Hurricane. You're my undercover agent, remember? And mum's the word, son." Bob tapped his nose to emphasise his words.

"Will do, sir."

Higgins got up to leave. Bob called him back.

"Hurricane?"

"Sir?"

"Watch your back, son, and keep your eyes peeled." If it was the London lot behind all the strange goings on, he didn't want to lose another partner. Although technically, he had never lost the first one. Still, better to be safe than sorry.

"I will, sir."

As Higgins left, Bob waited for the landlady to go down into the cellar before grabbing the Sky remote and rewinding the live TV. He pressed pause when he got to the point he wanted to see again. The man on the screen was looking directly up at the CCTV.

"You wanted to be seen, didn't you? Otherwise you would have left the way you came in. Why would you do that?" Bob took a closer look, getting a chair to stand on and putting on his reading glasses. "I have seen you before, sunshine. Where have I seen those eyes?" His brain was not answering him. He would leave it for now, but he made a mental note to try to remember.

He pressed back-up on the remote and cleared the TV to live.

The national weather presenter was declaring a pleasant day for tomorrow. As Bob went to replace the remote on the bar, he took a hard look at it.

When did I become all techy? He had never had Sky or used a remote before. He even struggled with a video recorder, never mind rewinding live TV. *Well, I'm now fluent in French. I guess I've been learning more than just new languages in my spare time.*

Bob had a lot of working out to do, but it could wait. When the landlady returned from the cellar, he ordered scampi, chips and peas, and devoured it. He couldn't think on an empty stomach, and he was going to require a lot of thinking.

After his lunch, he headed off to his apartment with his catch from this morning: a load of blue balls. This was another thing that had been sent to test him and would probably make no sense and drive him crazy. But he liked a challenge.

Chapter 25 – Websites, Puzzles and Treasure

Bob emptied the carrier bag of blue balls onto the floor of his apartment and arranged them letter side up. Most balls had two letters on one side and a number on the reverse. One of the balls, rather than having two letters, had the letter N and a full stop.

Well, that's a start, he thought as he placed that ball at the end, assuming the full stop meant what it normally meant. He was wary of trusting anything right now, even a full stop. Still, he had nothing else to go on.

Ten balls in total. They must spell out something. His mind was working on the conundrum. The numbers on the reverse could wait until he was stuck. He thought of the TV programme *Countdown* where the brainbox contestants seemed to work out the puzzle in seconds. Twenty minutes in, he guessed just staring was not going to help. He had to get in among the balls.

One ball had XO written on it. *Let's start with you,* he thought, realising not many words contain an X. He randomly tried a few balls next to his chosen letters with no success, then the logic of *Countdown* hit him.

"What can it not be? Let's get rid of some."

He eliminated all the combinations of letters that did not end in a vowel. TH, ND and CB were all discarded, along with the N and full stop, which he was still relying on to finish the sentence off properly. This left five balls ending in vowels. He tried them in turn, starting with the nearest to him.

"GI," he said. "Gi-xo? No, you're a goner, it can't be that." As he threw the ball to join the other contenders which had failed in round one, he then eliminated the MA, thinking ma-xo was hardly going to complete a word. LE also went by the wayside. He had a couple of choices left, FI and DI, when it hit him. As he placed the DI ball next to the XO ball, he grabbed the N ball with the full stop.

"Bingo! D-I-X-O-N." He placed the three balls in a row.

OK, so he had the end of the message, and confirmed that whoever had planted the balls in the crab pots had meant the message for him. Deep inside, Bob had already known this, but at least it had refocused his attention.

He grabbed all of the remaining blue balls.

"Ding-ding, round two," he said. He liked games, and had to assume that whoever was playing him knew this, too. It was a good way of grabbing his attention – coming straight out and telling him what was going on would not have worked. He would have been doubtful and sceptical. Forcing him to work things out fused the conclusion into his psyche. It was like he had earned it; it would build trust, and both he and his nemesis knew it.

Round two consisted of completing his name with the CB-OB. He brought all the balls back into the game for round three, which was harder, but after a process of elimination and some guesswork, he completed the puzzle.

FI-ND-LE-MA-GI-CB-OB-DI-XO-N.

Bob looked at the balls he had positioned in the final order and aired the phrase out loud a couple of times.

"Find le magic, Bob Dixon. *Le* magic? Hmm." He assumed the 'le' was to link back to his new French language skills. It was known in the detective trade as a convincer – making something that seemed unlikely convincing, moving it to the 'beyond any doubt' category. A convincer was something he would use when he had a hunch and his bosses needed to give him permission to act upon it. He smiled. It was overkill in this situation, but he accepted it for what it was.

He knows me better than I thought.

He thought about Stephen in the graveyard, and the old man and young Stephen in the funicular. Both of the projections had talked of leaving the magic behind, and Bob had the dog lead from Lizzy Scraggs and the funicular ticket from the young Stephen. What other magic did he need to find?

"Find le magic," he said, throwing a convincer at himself. "That has to be it. Find the magic the kids have left behind."

But how? What are the objects?

He remembered visiting the coastguard station and seeing the list of children who had gone missing every time there was a high tide. *Were they all taken? All of them?*

Where would he start? Some of the children had gone missing years ago. He had a list of their names, yes, but finding objects with no clues as to what they were would be impossible. Well, almost impossible, anyway.

He sat on the sofa in a daze, allowing his thoughts to wash over him in waves, not really taking them in. His mind was full to the brim with facts, some real, some which had been proved to be fake. Different thoughts were trying to have their say, and he was exhausted.

He then snapped out of it. "The numbers!"

The blue balls were in a neat line on the worn rug in his front room, proudly announcing the riddle they had been hiding. He read it out loud one more time.

"Find le magic, Bob Dixon." Turning each ball 180 degrees, he slowly cycled through the numbers on the reverse of them.

Here we go again. Oh, he likes to play games with me, he thought as the balls revealed another cryptic assortment, which meant he would have to expend more brain power.

"So what do we have here?" He looked at the numbered message on the balls.

23x3. 13 01 07 09 03 02 15 02 04

"Twenty-three times three, what's that mean?" He looked up to the ceiling, which seems to be the place to look when working out sums. "OK, that's sixty-nine." He added the rest of the numbers to his sixty-nine, and after a few seconds announced, "One hundred and twenty-five?" He again looked up at the ceiling, and then down at the balls.

"One hundred and twenty-five what? It can't be that. What am I missing? Come on, Bob, think!" He then noticed the full stop after the 23x3. "What are you doing there at the front? I thought we'd established that full stops come at the end of a sentence, not in the middle." He started reeling through the alphabet, counting with his fingers. "A, B, C, D, E, F…" Half way through, he made a mental note to work back from Z for larger numbers, smiling as he continued.

"So T is twenty, U is twenty-one, V twenty-two, meaning twenty-three is W. Multiply that by three and we get WWW, and that's where the full stop comes in. Mmm, very clever. WWW dot." He grabbed a pen and paper and aligned the letters of the alphabet next to their sequential numbers. Armed with the code, he wrote on his pad as he deciphered each letter, then read the complete message.

"WWW dot magic Bob D. The Bob D is Bob Dixon, I assume. It's missing its dot com or dot co dot uk, or whatever they have, though."

Bob settled back in his chair and added his codebreaking solutions to his trusty notepad. Before long, his mind exhausted from the puzzles and his body tired from his early morning fishing excursion, he was asleep.

Bob awoke with a start. For a second, he didn't know where he was. He needed time to allow his mind to assess his surroundings and remind him of his earlier code-breaking exploits.

He stretched out his arms, letting out a wide-mouthed yawn that he kept for really tired occasions.

"I need the internet," he said, looking at the balls on the floor and his notepad.

It was then that he caught a whiff of what could only be described as a fishy smell. Instinctively checking his armpits and smelling his jumper, and being the only human in the room, he concluded it was him. He headed for the shower.

All cleaned up, he chose a pair of jeans that he had struggled to get into a couple of days ago, surprised to find they now fitted perfectly. Looking at his watch, he saw it was 6.30pm.

"Where can I get the internet thingy at this time?" He remembered having seen computer terminals in a library when he was on a case down south. Having no better ideas to do battle with, he headed off in the direction of Saltburn's library.

The lights were on in the library, which was a good sign, but when he tried the door, it was locked. It did not stop him trying two more times, though. Having almost rattled the door off its hinges, he turned on his heels and started to walk back into the town centre.

"Can I help you?" A soft voice drifted over his shoulder, along with the sweet scent of perfume. He turned. And that was the first time Bob saw her. She was beautiful, with flowing blonde locks and sapphire blue eyes.

"I said, can I help you?" This time her voice had the restless edge of one who preferred not to be repeating herself.

"Oh sorry, I thought the library was open."

"Is that why you nearly took the door off its hinges?" She opened the door and checked it was still working, testing it after its rough treatment.

"Sorry, I just thought I would make sure it really was locked."

"Unfortunately for you, we are not open. Although if you like reading, I am reading to some people in our book club. Would you like to join us?" She smiled and leaned her head to the side, making it more of a plea than an invitation. Bob looked over her shoulder into the library to see three people sitting on chairs.

Do three people warrant being called a club? he thought.

"Sorry, I didn't get your name," she said.

"Bob, it's Bob Dixon. And yours?" Bob stepped back to the library entrance and held out his hand.

"Pleased to meet you, Bob Dixon, I'm Beth, chief librarian. So do you read? When you're in between cases?" She smiled again, neatly letting Bob know that she recognised his name.

There was a shout from inside the library, one of the book club members checking Beth was OK. She turned and gave them the thumbs up.

"I'll be back in a sec, guys. So do you read, then, Bob Dixon? Is that why you're here?"

"I've not read a book for years. Not since school, I reckon."

"So you've either found yourself loving books all of a sudden, or you've decided to visit a library – practically breaking in – for something else. Either way, things come at a cost. So what's it going to be, Bob Dixon? Are you off to the pub for a beer and loneliness?" She pointed towards the village centre. "Or do you want to discover what you have been missing all these years? Books are an escape into a wonderful world of fantasy, intrigue, and even love. A book will never judge you. You look like you might have been judged enough."

Beth using his full name all the time should have been annoying Bob by now, but she had a way with words, and her voice could melt candle wax. It drew him in. He got the impression that if she read a restaurant menu, he would be mesmerised by it.

"So, do you want to head for the tavern, or do you fancy a trip in here with my shipmates to see how the crew of the

Hispaniola are getting on? Billy Bones, Jim Hawkins, Long John Silver and all?" Her voice changed to that of a hearty pirate. "What yer say ter that, Bob Dix-ahn."

Her smile was infectious, and Bob beamed one of his best in her direction.

"We've just started *Treasure Island.* Who's with me? Are you with me, Bob Dixon?" She opened the door wide. "We can talk about what you came here for afterwards, unless you have got a better offer?"

Bob did not have another offer, and even if he had, it would have taken something on the extreme end of offers to top the one Beth had just made him.

"Arrrr, oim in."

He got a stare from Beth and her book club members as they walked through the door.

"Best leave the pirating to me, or at least practise a bit before attempting to speak like a pirate in my presence again." Bob saw the group put their heads down and titter, and he joined in.

"OK, this is our new book club member, Mr Bob Dixon. He'll be joining us until we have finished *Treasure Island.*"

They all made their introductions.

"What page are we on?" Bob picked up the book that was lying on his seat.

"Page two, Bob. Are there any objections to us starting again?" The group accepted en masse. "OK, here we go." Beth put on some glasses and added, "Sorry, I meant here we go *again.* Part 1: 'The Old Buccaneer', Chapter 1: 'The Old Sea-dog at the Admiral Benbow'." She looked over her glasses. The book club members were all following, seduced by the beautiful words drifting into their ears. "'*Squire Trelawney, Doctor Livesey, and the rest of these gentlemen having asked me to write down the whole particulars about Treasure Island, from the beginning to the end…*'"

Part one was coming to a close. Beth had lived and breathed every word like the book was part of her. She became the characters and was totally immersed in the story. Bob felt privileged to be sharing *Treasure Island* not only with Beth, but also with the book club members. He was in awe of her talent; he had taken his eyes off his own pages and had been following her instead.

"Now, was that better than a couple of pints in the pub, Bob?" The question did not require an answer. "OK, you lot, same time next week. And if anyone missing tonight wants to be here, make sure they catch up to the end of Part One. See you all next Sunday."

Everybody shared hugs and kisses and headed their separate ways, until only Bob and Beth were left.

"Right, what was so important that you nearly took our library door off by its hinges?"

He ignored the question.

"Thank you, Beth, I really enjoyed that. You are a lovely reader, especially with all the voices. I didn't know books could be so powerful."

"Anyone who doesn't read books is missing out on one of life's treats."

"Well, you are now preaching to the converted, and sorry about the door. I needed to go online and I thought you might have some computers here."

"We have, and a deal's a deal." She moved over to a bank of PCs.

"Not tonight, though, I'm done in. It can wait. I do have one question, though."

"Which is?"

"How did you know who I was?"

She laughed. "You're a friend of my mother's. She talks about you all the time."

"Talks about me all the time?" Bob racked his brain for a talkative soul he might know. His brain did not take much racking – there was only one candidate. "Audrey is your mum?"

"Yes, she's my mam, and I apologise for anything she may have said or done since you met her. You can't pick your mam, you know."

They both smiled and their eyes met for the briefest of seconds – just long enough for it to be noticeable.

"Are you sure you don't want the internet tonight? It's not a problem, although I'm surprised you need to use it here. Surely you have computers in the cop shop?"

"I want to be away from prying eyes."

"Is it about that boy from Redcar? Sad state of affairs, that is. Some nasty people about, you know."

"No, just looking into something, that's all."

"Sorry, I shouldn't have delved into your business. That's my mother coming out in me. I'll be on duty in the morning if you want to pop by. There is a PC against the window you can use all private like." Her smile once again lit up the room. "As long as you're not looking at porn."

"Porn? Really?"

"Ha-ha, only joking. I'll reserve it for you. Anyway, the firewall won't let you on a porn site." She gave him a wink. "About eleven-ish, shall we say?"

"Yes, eleven will be fine."

"OK, sling your hook, I'll see you tomorrow. Oh, and make sure you read *Treasure Island* again before the reading next week. We have a question and answer session on what we have read so far – how the characters felt, where the plot is heading, that kind of stuff. I'm really glad you enjoyed it, Bob. Books are such an escape for me."

"I loved it, and I'll be here, a bit earlier next time to save your door a hammering."

"See you tomorrow, Bob, and thanks."

"For what?"

"Just thanks. It's nice to have someone my own age to read to for once. I love our members, but it's good to see a new face. So it's six-thirty pm next week and eleven o clock tomorrow morning."

Beth had a spark to her. She clearly knew her own mind, which was sharp as his, and she was so beautiful. What was there not to admire? And Bob was admiring away.

Resisting a cheeky 'Aye, aye, Captain' after his failed pirate impersonation earlier, Bob settled on, "I will be here on time, I promise." As he left the library, Beth waved, and then locked the door behind him.

Bob afforded himself a look back at the library as he walked away. *That went well,* he thought. Blue balls, websites and puzzles were far from his mind. He had just had a dose of reality, and it was a welcome break from the weird events that had been going on around him.

Chapter 26 – A Fork in the Road

Bob woke up and went out on his morning run, which was becoming well and truly cemented into his new lifestyle. He felt fitter and ran further than he had on his last run, and after his shower, he was struggling to find a suit that was not hanging off him.

But how? I've only just started on my diet.

There were now so many things that didn't make sense, he decided that wasting thinking time on why he had lost so much weight and was miles fitter than he had been a few days ago was just that – a waste of time. It was the least of his worries right now, if it could even be called a worry. Maybe it was a hidden benefit of going crazy.

He manage to find some trousers that just about fitted, but the jacket looked like he had borrowed it from Herman Munster.

Let's go casual today, he thought and grabbed some grey chinos, a black polo shirt and a thin jumper. He assessed his new look in the mirror. He was still on the chubby side, but not in the same ball park as last week.

"Looking good, Bob," he said in his cheeriest voice. Today was going to be a good day. It was going to be a connecting day. All the loose ends were looking for partners. Yes, he had been told to back off the Townsend case, and he had to a degree, although he still had Higgins keeping tabs on it, but whoever was playing him must know him well enough to know he would never back off completely. Besides, he had other things bothering him. The internet would shed some light with a bit of luck.

Before going to the library, he would head to the office. He had not made it in yesterday, so he planned to see what was going down with the lads. But before that, he would pop in to see Audrey in the coffee shop, maybe find out whether he had made a good impression on her daughter last night. When he went for his morning coffee, Audrey would surely 'accidentally' tell him.

As he entered the coffee shop, the sweet chimes from above the door hadn't even finished announcing his arrival before Audrey delivered her opening gambit.

"I didn't have you down as a big reader, Bob."

"Can you at least let me put my order in first, Audrey?"

"I guessed it would be your usual." She gave him a skinny latte and a fresh orange juice. "Croissant?"

"Not today, thanks. On a diet, remember?"

"But you've lost loads of weight, Bob. Don't lose too much – our Beth is not keen on the skinny types." She gave him the croissant anyway. "On the house. So, what do you think?"

"I haven't tried it yet, but they're normally nice."

"No, about Beth!"

"I know what you mean, I'm joking. Look, I fancied a walk out, saw the light on in the library, so Beth invited me to join the reading group. And do you know what? I loved it."

"What did she read to you? She's a lovely reader is my Beth."

Audrey's daughter did not need building up in Bob's eyes. She was quite capable of making an impression without her mother's help.

"I told her about you, Bob. She might be a bit more wary of you next time you meet – she's way out of your league, and I told her that…"

"*Treasure Island* is the book she read, seeing as you asked." Bob cut into the conversation before Audrey got into full flow. "And there is a character in it that reminds me of you."

"Really? Is there a fair maid…" she flicked her hair back in a mildly seductive manner, "…who maybe stowed away on the ship so the handsome young pirates could fight for her hand?"

"Nope." Bob left it there and grabbed his coffee and orange juice, moving them to a table before returning for his croissant.

"Who then?" she said, disappointed that Bob had more or less ignored her seductiveness.

"Captain Flint, Audrey."

"What, I remind you of a stinky, scabby old pirate captain?"

"No, he's not the captain, he's Long John Silver's parrot, and he never knows when to shut the hell up."

Bob ran off with his food before Audrey could aim a tea towel in his direction.

Well, she said nothing bad about what Beth thought of me. Maybe there is hope for me yet.

"A parrot? You cheeky bugger, Bob."

Although he knew Audrey liked the verbal jousting, and also liked him, Bob was relieved when another customer saved him from further cross examination. Sitting at his table, looking at the police station and waiting for the keys – or, to be more accurate, a policeman attached to some keys – he had a lot of thinking time. He took out his notebook and read from the front all that had taken place since he started investigating Lizzy Scraggs's disappearance. He then flicked the book around to read the back, which claimed that lots of what he had just read never happened. The metaphorical breadknife had cut its way through the past and left a mess on the kitchen top. There were too many crumbs. What was happening was not of the world he had lived in up to now. He was trying to put a finger on the crossroads – the point at which his two pasts had converged to form into one future – but it wasn't that simple. The dual carriageway had narrowed to one lane now and the future only had one path, but when did the two lanes end?

Then it hit him.

"It had to be then," he said quietly to himself, circling a passage in his notebook. "No question, things changed from when I rode in the funicular on that cow of a night. The first change I encountered was Bill mentioning the man waving at him from the top of the funicular." He looked up to the ceiling to question his logic, but when nothing came back to prove him wrong, he wrote *FORK IN THE ROAD* in the front and back of the book.

Happy with his work, Bob looked up and saw some keys approaching the police station door, attached to Sergeant Hopkins. He finished up his coffee, said his goodbyes to Audrey, and crossed the road to the station.

"Morning, Hoppy." Sergeant Hopkins was already inside, unlocking filing cabinets and turning on computers and lights. "Coffee?"

"I'd love one, Dicko. I'll be with you in a minute, just finishing opening up."

Bob headed for the kitchen area and prepared the mugs, having a mental word with himself.

OK, Bob, remember to play it cool. Play it all down. Nothing to see here.

He knew Hoppy would ask him what he thought about the Townsend case. Hoppy was also aware of bits and bobs about the Scraggs case, and had heard Bob and Higgins discussing high tides and their visit to the coastguard station. If Bob was going to back off the Townsend case as Stephen had ordered, he would have to do it from today. Showing an interest would mean he was involved to a certain extent, but not caring at all would look strange. He had to balance the 'giving a shit' see-saw and find other ways of being busy that were not related to Carl Townsend or Lizzy Scraggs.

Bob decided he would bring the subject up and control the conversation. "Here you go, Hoppy. So what's that Townsend case all about? Sad for the lad and his family."

"Yes, I could have done with you yesterday, Bob, we were snowed under." Hoppy took a sip of his coffee. "I mean, you decide to go out on a fishing trip on one of our busiest days of the year."

"Bloody Hurricane!"

"Don't go blaming your partner, Bob. For some reason, he seems to have your back. I had a lovely lobster in The Ship last night with my wife. The chef said you caught it."

"Sorry, Hoppy."

"Bloody sorry? Lucky for you my wife loves lobster and she asked me to thank you."

"Tell her no problem, I'll let her know when I get some more."

Hoppy laughed. "OK, well, I hope you enjoyed your day off. To be honest, I think you deserved one. So, the Townsend case. I've got every officer I have working round the clock on this one – Redcar is snowed under. So I need a favour."

Bob was expecting *the CID in Redcar want your help*. How would he manage to get out of this one?

"What, you want me to help CID in Redcar? Well…"

Hoppy held up his hand and stopped Bob, as if the DI was singing the wrong song on an *X Factor* audition.

"Don't flatter yourself, Bob, they're far too proud to ask. I was going to ask if you would go on the beat for a week or so around here, cover for the lads who are over in Redcar."

"Oh, of course, Hoppy. I have an appointment from eleven until twelve. I'll go put my uniform on after that."

"You'll be out on your own, mind. I just need some presence in the town. You know what these villages are like – even though that poor lad has been taken, it won't be long before people start moaning about no police presence and all that."

"Is there any progress on the Townsend case?" Bob's backing off skills were not the best.

"Not that I know of. The CCTV didn't flush anyone out, so I

think they're at a dead end over in Redcar. Poor kid, not long to live. Who would do such a thing?"

"Beats me, Hoppy."

The other Saltburn lads started arriving before most of them headed off to Redcar. Bob and Hoppy watched the latest BBC news, which had nothing new to say. The 'update' just showed the CCTV footage again and pleaded for anyone with information to come forward. The plea smacked of desperation.

Bob took a seat in his cell of an office, pulling the heavy door closed. He needed some time alone to reflect. It was all well and good unearthing new evidence that threw the past into doubt, but it was another thing believing it. The facts had washed over him like a tsunami, some clinging on to anything they could grab hold of, others being washed away with the tidal wave.

The problem he was facing now was that the new facts, like Frank Cartwright being alive and well, had taken hold, and Bob was struggling to remember the past any other way. The past as he knew it last week seemed more like a dream. He could no longer picture Frank dying in his arms, but he could remember his old partner going off in an ambulance. He could also remember calling Frank over and over again, and the anger he'd felt when Frank had blanked him, not letting him help out, and moved away to Cornwall.

He remembered Frank explaining, "*Think of a dual carriageway when it goes into one lane. Let's just say you are off the dual carriageway and there is only one path from now on.*" But what had brought the carriageways together? Bob looked at his notes from the café: *FORK IN THE ROAD*. So the funicular ride had been when the past had changed, but why then? And why did it all come back together?

Bob opened his desk and took out two painkillers. Whatever was happening to him was taking its toll – it wasn't not every day that you discovered everything you had lived through could all have been a lie. However, he was still a copper, and he had been transferred to Saltburn, so he was guessing whoever was responsible for his pasts diverging had tried keeping most details the same. Frank Cartwright was a risk – the mystery man who'd saved him had said so himself in his note.

Bob took a couple of deep breaths, looking up at his board. *Mmm, you're a bit behind, sunshine.* He drew a picture of a pig with *tax man* written in a box – that was all he needed. Writing that Frank Cartwright was suddenly alive and well did not seem like a good idea, and he knew what the pig meant.

He added a picture of the lean-to at Chalky's farm and a badly drawn tractor, then he moved on to the barn. Writing *Rented, 500k plus 10k a month* in the adjacent box, he made a mental note to check out Chalky's story at some point – who would pay that kind of money for a battered old barn? It could wait, though; he had a date with a computer in the library.

"Bloody hate computers," he muttered, getting to his feet.

His headache had eased off as if his brain had just needed resetting. It knew now where it stood. The past had changed, yes, but acceptance was half the battle, and so half the battle had been won. For today, at least.

Bob headed off to say bye to Hoppy, promising to be back in uniform later to cover the afternoon shift, and then made his way to Saltburn library.

Chapter 27 – Jeux sans Frontières

Bob entered the library and made his way to the reception where Beth was attending to an old lady. He had spent an hour yesterday listening to her read, but he had also been following the words in his book, so this was his first proper chance to look at her without seeming stalkerish.

She had her blonde hair tied back and was wearing a yellow frock, very much in the mould of sweet Sandy in *Grease* before she was sewn into her skin-tight black trousers. If Bob had a type, it would definitely be the sweet Sandy rather than the one at the funfair.

Beth stamped the books and handed them to the old lady.

"OK, Mrs Green, you have until a week on Monday to get them back. Here is your library card."

Mrs Green thanked her and went on her way. Beth spotted Bob and immediately looked at her watch.

"I'm actually early, if you're trying to put me on the naughty step before we even start."

Beth had made it clear last night that she liked to control things.

"Yes, I can see that, Mr Dixon."

Bob was a bit upset. Mr Dixon sounded far too formal, so he tried to lighten the mood.

"Please, Beth, it's Bob, and thank you so much for last night. I didn't know how much fun reading could be."

He smiled; it worked.

"Thanks for stopping by, Bob. *Treasure Island* is a great book by a great author – Robert Louis Stevenson is one of my favourites. Some say *Kidnapped* is better than *Treasure Island*, but I'm not so sure. My favourite of his is *The Strange Case of Dr Jekyll and Mr Hyde.*"

"I didn't know he wrote that."

"Have you read it?" Beth's voice went up a tone or two in surprise, or maybe anticipation.

"No, but I have seen the film. Michael Caine, I think." Beth's voice returned to normal, which Bob took as a sign of disappointment. "I'll put it on my to-do list, though. I'm too busy enjoying *Treasure Island* at the moment."

"It's a TBR list. Every reader should have one."

"TBR?"

"To be read – a list of what you are going to read. The problem is, if you're anything like me, it will take a hundred years to read all the books on it." She smiled, and then laughed. "Right, Bob Dixon, you now have a TBR. *Treasure Island* is your current book, and after that I think you should read *Jekyll and Hyde*. Deal?"

Beth had a way of making the cards fall in her favour without appearing too bossy. Bob was like putty in her hands.

"I guess so. Deal."

"I'm glad that's sorted. OK, the internet is five pounds for the hour, and I have booked you the computer in the corner by the window, as I promised, so you can do your private browsing." She emphasised the words *private browsing* and winked at him.

"It's nothing dodgy."

"Mmmm, whatever."

Bob started going red for no apparent reason. She let him off the hook as she could see him squirming.

"I'm only playing with you, Bob. Do you need a hand, or are you OK with computers?"

Bob did need a hand and was not OK with computers, so the question should have been easy to answer, but pride and not knowing where the blue ball website would lead him made it otherwise.

"No, I'll be fine." This he said with all the confidence of a trembling dog who had been left out all night in the rain.

"OK, so you press Ctrl, Alt and Delete. Here are your log-in details. Give me a shout if you're struggling."

"I will." He smiled the kind of smile that said, "*I won't*".

He sat down at the PC and thought about his one and only computer lesson with Higgins where he'd thumped all the keys at once. He held Ctrl and Alt down together with his left hand, then pressed Delete. To his surprise, a screen appeared, asking for his log-in details.

"OK, thanks for that Hurricane. Now here goes nothing."

He opened the piece of paper Beth had given him. It had a username, a password, and then she had written her name with a kiss underneath. Bob looked over at Beth, who was attending to another customer.

Maybe she gives kisses out to all the customers. Or maybe she doesn't.

He smiled. "OK, concentrate."

Using one finger, Bob eventually entered his username. After fumbling around with the mouse, which seemed to be moving far too fast for his liking, he managed to click into the password box. As he typed the password, asterisks appeared, which he remembered from having logged on to the police computer in London. He took a deep breath and clicked on log in.

"Bingo!" he said as the desktop appeared.

There were only three icons on the desktop. After eliminating My Computer and a bin shaped object, he clicked on Internet Explorer. Nothing happened.

He looked at Beth, and she looked back, knowing only pride was stopping him from calling her over.

He clicked on the Internet Explorer icon again. It highlighted itself in a different colour, but nothing happened. Bob clicked once more, but realised that if he kept doing the same thing, the same thing would happen.

Beth walked across to put him out of his misery.

"Bob, I am here to help, it's my job."

"Not that good on these things, Beth."

"What is it you're trying to do?"

"Well, I'm trying to open the internet, but every time I click on the bloody stupid thing, it does nothing. Look."

He clicked and then clicked again. The internet opened.

"See, you've done it, with no help from me."

Bob looked at the computer, annoyed that Mr Google had not seen fit to make an appearance earlier.

"But how? Why did it work when you were stood near it?"

"It's called a double click."

"A double what?"

"A double click. Look, click once – single click – on the red cross in the top right. That will close the internet."

"But I've only just opened it."

She laughed. "And you will open it again, Bob, but the next time, you will know how. The reason it opened this time was that you lost your temper."

"And how does this thing know I lost my temper."

"You kept clicking on the internet icon, and accidently double clicked."

"Did I lose my temper?" He looked back at her as she stood behind him

"Yes, you did, and I don't like men who lose their temper. It's not a great quality, Bob."

Bob looked ashamed. "I don't normally. I am the calmest person you'll ever meet. It's just, well… me and computers have a hate-hate relationship."

"That's because you let them control you. With a little knowledge, you can control them. This time, click twice. You do this to open anything, really: documents, programs and icons. So point and think click-click in your head."

Bob pointed, thought *click-click*, and his fingers did the rest on the mouse. "Well, that's easy. Why did no one ever tell me that?" To be fair, Higgins probably had told him that, but maybe Bob hadn't wanted to listen to him.

"Probably because you never asked." She gave him a quizzical look which he could feel burning a hole in the back of his head. Without turning round, he acknowledged it.

"I know, I know, thanks, Beth. I think I'll be OK from here. I will shout you if I'm stuck, I promise."

"Is it worth me asking what you're looking for? I might be able to help."

"You can ask, but I can't tell you. It's official police business."

"OK, you know where I will be. You have forty-five minutes left, but I will extend it seeing as you have just got in. Happy surfing, Bob, hope you find what you're after."

Surfing? thought Bob. *I'm not Scraggs!*

"How do I type in a web address? One of those www things?"

"You single click on the address bar here, and it will go blue." It did just that as Bob followed Beth's instructions. "You then type www dot whatever dot com or dot co dot uk."

Bob got his notepad out. "Thanks. I promise I won't get angry anymore."

"I know you won't. Just calm down and let things come to you. We all have to learn at some point." She patted his shoulder and left him to his own devices.

OK, Bob, nice and calm. He typed in the web address from his notepad, *www.magicbobd,* added *.com* and pressed enter… *'404 page not found'*. A few minutes ago, this would have provoked an outburst, but nice and calm was the name of the game now. Logic kicked in and Bob's mind processed his options.

Well if it's not dot com, let's try dot co dot uk. Maybe that will get me in.

Bob slowly and deliberately tapped www.magicbobd.co.uk into the address bar, pressed enter…

"Bingo!" he said again as the screen changed colour. There in front of him was another log-in page, asking for his username and password. A button said, "*Listen for instructions*" with a picture of some headphones. Bob took the headphones from a white mannequin to the right of the monitor, placed them on his head and pressed the button.

"Hello there! I hope you have got your headphones on, or I will be wasting my time. Please press the *I can hear you* button on the screen now if you can hear me."

The voice was high-pitched and sounded like a TV presenter talking to small children. Bob clicked on the *I can hear you* button as ordered.

"That's absolutely fine and dandy. Hello, I'm Felix the Magic Pig." An animated pig appeared on the screen and waved at him. "It's rude not to wave back." Bob ignored the waving pig, waiting for his next instructions. "Are we not in the waving mood? I don't think you know how much trouble you're in. I would wave, if I was you."

Bob was trying not to get angry, but his annoyed levels were rising.

"I don't know why I bother. Wave, Bob Dixon, or the deal is off."

He knows my name, Bob thought, *and he knows I'm not waving. Can he see me?*

The pig came closer as if to tap on the monitor.

"OK, we are crashing in three, two…"

Bob waved at the pig.

"Oooh, that was a close one. It's all about trust, Bob, so don't fuck with me."

Bob looked around. Nobody was watching him.

It must have known I was not going to wave. It's just a recording – calm down. Now, what's next?

"So, I guess you're thinking, *How do I log in?* Luckily for you, I'm here to help. I have taken the liberty of creating you a username and password. I know I'm just a pig, but I'm a magic one. Your username is…"

The pig used a magic wand to make a drum appear, which he started to play. The drum roll went on annoyingly long.

"Oh, my arms are killing me! Make it stop!"

After a further minute, it finally did stop. "Your username is bob underscore dixon. Write it down, you never know when you might need it" The drums were gone and the pig was holding a scroll with bob_dixon written on it. "You got it, Bob? Type yes in the box. Heeeeeere's the box."

A message box appeared underneath the pig, who was dancing around, very proud of his work. Bob typed yes and pressed enter, more to stop the pig dancing and move things along than because he wanted to comply.

"Great! I think we're a team, but I know what you're thinking. Yes, I can read minds. You're thinking..." the pig came close to the screen and cupped a trotter to his mouth, as if he was sharing a secret "...you're thinking, *what the hell is an underscore?* I know we can't all be the next Charles Babbage or Alan Turing. And you don't want to ask our lovely assistant. Beth has helped enough, don't you think? Oh, she's a hot one. If I wasn't a pig and all that... I think she has the hots for you, though, Bob."

Bob looked around again. In the library, there was one old lady browsing through some books and Beth on the computer behind the counter.

"The thing is, Bob, you could not speak French a week ago, so maybe you're better on computers than you think. I reckon you know fine well what an underscore is, you just haven't bothered remembering yet. Do you want to play a game to help you remember?"

Bob was very tempted to say no. He seemed to be taking far too many orders from an annoying farmyard animation.

He typed *OK*.

"I love games, and I know you do, too. OK, what's so special about this sentence? The quick brown fox jumped over the lazy dog. Any ideas?"

Bob typed *no* in the message box.

"Are you suuuuuuuure, Bobby?"

Bob typed *yes*.

"OK, I'll tell you. The quick brown fox jumped over the lazy dog is a sentence in the English language that contains all the letters of the alphabet, which means it's good for..."

Felix's drums appeared again.

"Only joking, I know it's annoying." Felix made the drums go away. "Typing practice. You see, Bob, like I know you can now speak French, I also know you can type seventy-five words a minute. So ten words should be a doddle."

Bob looked at the keyboard. *Seventy-five words a minute? Fat chance.*

"To make it easy, I will put the words above the box. It's soooo exciting. Ready? Three, two one – go!"

Bob typed the sentence letter by letter with one finger. Felix the pig had a big stopwatch and was shaking his head, but Bob was not watching the pig as he was focusing on the keyboard. After *lazy dog*, he pressed enter.

Music played through the headphones. Bob recognised it as being from the old Boot Hill arcade game from the 80s, where animated cowboys would lose on a quick draw game. The screen even showed Bob's name on a gravestone.

"Now we are lucky that was just a practice, Bob Dixon, and you have three lives. Your target this time is thirty seconds. That should be a doddle for a touch typist like you."

The pig again came to the front of the screen.

"Psssst, I'm on your side here, Bob. Maybe close your eyes and let the keys find themselves. You're thinking too hard, Billybob. Remember how you could read French? You just let it happen. Same here. Let it flow – just sayin' and all that. OK, we go in three, two, one."

Bob closed his eyes. His hands adopted the home position on the keyboard and he started. *The quick brown fox…* it was not lightning quick, but it was smooth and getting faster …lazy dog. He pressed enter.

The Boot Hill music rang out again and another gravestone appeared on the hillside.

"So close, Bobsicle, thirty-three seconds. Did you feel it? DID YA?"

Bob had felt it. He didn't know how, but his fingers had seemed to find the keys by themselves.

"I'm not sure if you're taking this seriously, Bob. It's important you remember things – lots of people are relying on you. This is not a game, and I for one am disappointed. Should we up the stakes?"

Bob had had enough. *Stop playing with me, what the hell do you want?* he typed in the box.

"There is no need for all that aggression! You have a split personality, like Dr Jekyll and Mr Hyde. It's a good book – you should read it sometime."

Bob looked over at Beth. *How did Felix know we spoke about that? He must have bugged the library; he's listening.* He then looked back at the screen.

The pig was holding up a gravestone. It said, *Beth Mathews, fifteen seconds or she dies.*

Bob looked over at Beth again. A red laser spot was aimed at her forehead.

"Fifteen seconds, Bob. How much do you want to remember? Three…"

Bob's palms were sweating. He looked behind him, through the window. A man was in the street, pointing a rifle straight at Beth.

"Two…."

Bob turned back to the computer. He had one second. It was too late – he would not be able to get to her in time.

"One – go!"

Bob closed his eyes as before. *The quick brown fox jumped over the lazy dog.* He pressed enter.

The light on Beth's head was gone. Felix was mopping his brow.

"That was a close one, Bobbideebob, fourteen seconds. See, you can remember when you try."

Bob turned around; the marksman had gone.

I'll get you, you bastard, he typed speedily into the message box. Then a big typewriter fell on the pig's head and a gravestone appeared on Boot Hill saying, *RIP Felix the Magic Pig.* A different voice sounded in Bob's ear, distorted as if to hide its owner's identity.

"Well done, Bob. Sorry I had to put you through that, but there are things I need you to remember. She would have come to no harm – the gun was not loaded."

Bob typed, *why should I believe you?*

"All in good time, Bob. We need your help more than you will ever know. When you log in, you will see a file. You need to put this file onto a memory stick, which is sellotaped under the table you are sitting at. I am guessing that if you can now type, you will have unlocked many other computer skills you did not know you had. This website will then be deleted."

Bob felt under the table and located the memory stick.

"You have your username, and your password is RIPFelix, as I know how fond you were of him. And lastly, Bob, thank you for trusting us. You need to back off the Townsend and Scraggs cases publicly. I can't stop you keeping tabs on them, but from a distance, please."

Bob listened, trying not to miss anything.

"There are some instructions on the memory stick, keep it safe, there are things you have to do when we next get in touch in 2018. Keep out of trouble. Oh, and you might want to pick up your library card. Beth should have it for you."

Why should I trust anyone who has just had a gun pointed at Beth's head? But as Bob navigated through the computer's file system, logged on and transferred the file with ease, he knew that remembering skills he had forgotten he had was crucial to the plan – whatever the plan was.

Bob logged out and made his way to the desk where Beth was still working away, unaware of her life having been in danger moments earlier.

"Beth, are you OK?"

She picked up on the concern in his voice. "Why, shouldn't I be?"

He could hardly say, "Your brains were about to be blown to bits."

"Just checking you're OK, that's all. Also, I believe I have a library card to pick up."

She looked at him. "When did you join? I deal with all the joiners and can't remember you filling out a form."

Bob kept silent, not really knowing what to say. Her stare demanded an answer.

"Can you check? I have been told there is one ready for me."

"Are you playing games with me?" She looked him up, and to her surprise, there was a Bob Dixon in the system. "It's a replacement card, Bob. Why didn't you say?"

He would have said if he'd known. He laughed as casually as he could.

"Sorry, Beth, I thought you knew."

That was close, he thought.

"I thought you had just moved here? Mam says October last year."

"Yes, October time, that's right. What of it?"

"Are all coppers good liars, Mr Dixon?"

Mr Dixon? That was not good.

"Why do you ask?"

"This replacement card is yours right enough, but you're a lot younger in the picture." She handed the card over. "You joined this library fifteen years ago, Bob. Why would a London copper be a member here, in my library?"

Bob was all out of lies. They were doing him no good anyway.

"I can explain."

"Try me."

"Let me put that another way. I can explain, but not now. Beth… what have I been reading?"

She looked at him like he was a crazed fool. "You don't know what you have been reading?"

"Would I have asked if I knew?"

She printed a list of his reading history. There were over 200 books on it, most of them ancient folk tales about fabled cities and mermaids, along with medical books on the effects of cannabis oils and the healing qualities of herbs. An eclectic mix. Bob could speak French, was now a whizz on computers, and he was guessing he had read all the books on his list already. But would he have to read them, or at least part of them, again to remember?

"You said you had not read a book for years when I met you yesterday. Why would you say that?"

Bob thought on his feet.

"Fiction, I meant. These are research books I have read for work."

The minute his latest lie tripped out of his mouth, he wished he could take it back. Even he would not believe it.

"You have been taking books out of my library for fifteen years and I have never seen you before. You have basically read half the bloody library."

Bob had nowhere to run, nor was he in the mood for running.

He was becoming very fond of Beth.

"OK, let me come clean with you, Beth, but not here. How about I take you for a meal, and I'll try to explain what is going on?"

"What? You lie to me, and then try to take me out?"

"I'll explain everything, honest."

"OK, you can take me out next week after book club. That's if you turn up. Or were you lying about that too?"

"No, I would not miss it for the world. Right, that's a deal. I'll book somewhere in town."

She looked him up and down. His hair had flopped over his eyes and he did look sorry. And she thought he was kind of cute.

"Right, but no more lies. Promise!"

"Promise."

Beth gave him his new library card and the printout of the books he had been reading, before shaking her head and heading off to the room behind reception. Bob let out a sigh and looked at the list of books. He did not recognise one of them.

Chapter 28 – Playing Fair Doesn't Get You There

Bob spent the afternoon walking for miles in his uniform, around the town and on the beach, getting noticed. Lots of people stopped for a chat, and in quiet moments he would sit on a bench on the prom or the pier, looking at his notes or the list of books he had supposedly read.

There were some loose ends not directly connected to the Scraggs or Townsend case that he had been far too busy to follow up, and the first concerned Chalky's barn. It had been bugging him ever since he had seen the rusty tractor in the lean-to and found out how much Chalky had sold the barn for, and how much he was still getting a month. What would anyone want with a knackered old barn? Bob was going to find out, but he needed back up. Time to bring in his partner Constable Higgins for an undercover mission.

Bob headed back to the office to hand in his radio and jacket, then called Higgins. He arranged to meet the young constable in The Ship at 9pm, and asked Higgins to come on foot and wear dark clothing.

Bob could see Higgins waiting outside The Ship for him as he got nearer the pub.

"Hi, sir, this is all very exciting. Are we on a stakeout? My mam's done me a flask."

"A flask?"

"Yep, she said it would be cold tonight. Always did my dad a flask when he was on a stakeout. It's Bovril."

"How many stakeouts have you been on, Hurricane?"

"This is my first, sir."

"No shit! A bloody flask? Anyway, we're not staking anywhere out; we're going to be breaking in."

"Isn't that illegal, sir?"

"What do you think? Are you in or out, Hurricane? Your choice."

"I'm in, sir. Should I leave the flask behind the bar?"

"No, you may as well bring it now. I quite like Bovril." Bob gave one of his trademark playful punches to Higgins's arm.

"So are you going to tell me where we are breaking in to and why?"

"I'll tell you on the way up to Chalky's farm."

They set off up the hill under torchlight.

"I want to know what is in that big barn, Hurricane. I know for a fact that Chalky sold it for a lot of money years ago and is still getting a fair amount each month for it. Why would anyone pay that much for a knackered old barn? It doesn't add up, and I don't like things that don't add up."

"Why are you so bothered, sir? What's it in connection with?"

Bob could hardly tell Higgins that the last time he'd been in the barn, it had been full of tractors and a priceless Aston Martin, because apparently it didn't happen.

"Let's just say Carl Townsend, Lizzy Scraggs, and maybe others have been taken, and there is a big barn nearby that nobody has looked in for years. They could be in there for all we know."

"Do you really think they could be in there?"

"Well, I want to find out that they're not. Torch off, Hurricane." Bob was whispering. "Not this entrance – Chalky might see us." They could see the lights on in Chalky's farmhouse. "There is private access to the barn further up the road."

Bob and Higgins crept a mile up the road and saw the entrance, which was guarded by a security camera sweeping left and right. They were tight against the hedge, crouching down to remain out of view. Up ahead, there was a six-foot metal gate. A pad on which to type in a pin-code was attached to a post on the road to allow the gate to be opened by a car driver. It looked ultra-modern, in stark contrast to the barn.

Why would you need such security? Bob thought. He called Higgins in closer.

"Right, son, you first. Wait until the camera has swept past and heads off the other way. I'll count you in… three, two, one, GO!"

Higgins climbed the six-foot gate in seconds and landed on the other side, crouching down out of sight behind the hedge just as the camera started its sweep back.

"I'm over, sir, now your turn."

"Bloody hell, Hurricane, what are you like? Bloody Spiderman?"

"I used to do some rock climbing, sir."

Bob sighed and looked at the camera, which seemed to be sweeping more quickly now it was his turn. Then he looked at the fence and waited for the camera to sweep past. And waited.

"Sir, you can do it. It's only six foot. Just plan where you're going to put your feet, and once you're on the top, jump. I'll catch you."

"I'm not sure, Hurricane, we're not all comic superheroes." How had he got himself into this? Bob looked at his heavy frame – yes, he'd lost weight, but he was still more Fatman than Batman.

OK, here we go. The camera was sweeping back to the right.

"Make sure you help me down the other side, son."

The camera finished its right hand sweep and started off in the other direction. *Here goes nothing.*

Bob leapt into action. Half way up the fence, he grabbed the wire mesh with his hands and powered up with his legs to get a hand hold on the top. His hand slipped as the camera swept as far to the left as it was going to go, but he managed to save himself.

"Come on, sir, you can do it."

Bob pushed again with his legs, grabbed the top of the fence and hauled himself onto it. Whether he jumped or fell he wasn't sure, but either way he ended up on the other side. He more or less landed on Higgins, who broke his fall.

They both scrambled on all fours to the sanctuary of the hedge as the camera completed its return sweep.

"Well, you got over, sir. I don't think you'd get many style marks, but you got over."

Higgins got another playful punch to his arm for his lip.

"Shut it, Hurricane."

They crept up the side of the road, trying to use whatever shelter they could from the hedgerow. Eventually they reached the back of the barn and carefully made their way around to the far side so they could not be seen. Chalky's house was a good twenty minutes down the road, but Bob had already had two barrels pointed at his head by the friendly local farmer and was taking no risks, especially with Higgins under his charge.

"What now, sir?"

It was dark, so Bob turned his torch over and switched on a

red beam, shining it onto the barn doors.

"No, no, no! That's not right. This door used to have holes all over it – you could see through."

"It still does have, sir. It's all rotten wood."

Bob put the butt of his pencil torch through one of the gaps in the wood and tapped. *Tang, tang, taaaaang.*

"It's metal, Hurricane. Why would someone build a metal barn inside a wooden one?"

The three padlocks that Chalky had unlocked were no longer in place. Bob shone the torch on the place where they had been and found a wooden hatch. He opened it to see another electronic keypad. As his hand hovered near the panel, it lit up with a green colour and a female voice spoke.

"Fingerprint recognition required."

"Sir, I think we are out of our league. Fingerprint recognition? What's in this place?" Higgins was a brave lad, but this was all a bit too Jason Bourne for his liking.

"I'm not so sure." Bob placed his finger on the panel.

"Scanning… please wait. Robert Dixon, welcome back, sir."

The metal doors, along with the fake wooden front, opened smoothly to let them in. As they entered, the doors closed just as smoothly, and they heard the lock engage behind them. Then they could not hear a sound.

Bob shone his torch behind him and saw light switches to the left of where they had been before. He clicked the switches and the lights clicked on in banks, beaming a dull yellow as they warmed up.

This is the place, he thought. *I remember the lights.* He looked up. The roof was still good old-fashioned wood, although there was metal meshing lining it to stop anyone from entering that way. As the lights took hold, Bob and Higgins could see the barn in all its glory.

There was nothing in there, apart from one table and two chairs at the far end. Due to the lack of furniture, their attention was drawn to what little there was.

"What were you expecting, sir?"

"Well, more than nothing, son." They took a seat next to the table. "I wasn't sure what to expect, but an empty barn? He obviously needed it at some point."

"He, sir?"

"You know, the man off the CCTV. If he is hiding Carl, this would be perfect, but it doesn't add up."

Bob was thinking he was too late. *Something must have happened here. Maybe I was followed. Maybe he saw me talking to Chalky. He certainly spotted me tending the boat after my fishing trip with Silent Man. Whatever or whoever was here is not here anymore.*

"Sir, Bovril?"

"Go on then, Hurricane, I'd love one."

"We'll have to share – you only get one mug thing."

"That's fine, sunshine, we'll share it."

"Sir, have you been here before?" Higgins handed him the Bovril.

Now that's a tricky one. Bob had a few responses lined up, like "*Yes, and so have you*", but he opted for the old answering a question with a question trick.

"What makes you think that, son?" Bob stood up and leaned against the metal wall where the table was situated, still wondering why someone would go to the trouble of securing the barn if all it held was a bit of old furniture. The place looked smaller than he remembered, although the lack of tractors and James Bond cars made it look empty and forlorn.

"Why did the fingerprint detector let you in? And when it did, it said your name, sir, and welcomed you back."

Higgins joined Bob, feeling the coldness of the metal walls seep through his clothes.

"Look, Hurricane, there is a lot of strange stuff going on right now, and I can't explain much of it. I thought this barn would give me some answers, not more questions." He gave Higgins the mug back. Higgins bailed him out just when he was about to come clean. Covering the old past with the new past was wearing him out.

"I guess they could have put your prints on the system, like they did on the pig, sir."

"I guess so. Someone has got it in for me good and proper. Come on, let's get out of here."

Bob took a last look at the barn, killed the lights, and then pressed the green button which opened the doors for their exit.

As the doors closed behind them, Higgins shouted, "Sir, the flask!" He was standing there with a more or less empty mug of Bovril, but no flask.

"Where is it?"

"I left it on the table, sir."

"Hurricane, what are you?" Bob shook his head.

"A doyle, sir."

Bob looked at him and shone the red light in his face. "What on earth is a doyle?"

"Like a dick, sir, but a dopey one."

"Hurricane, you're not a dick, but yes, you might be a doyle. But you trust me and that counts for a lot, son." Bob grabbed hold of Higgins's shoulders and eyeballed him. Higgins had had his back since he'd first met him. "It's not a problem, we'll just go back in and get it. What would your mum say if you didn't take your flask back?"

Bob opened the entrance panel. *"Fingerprint recognition required."* He placed his finger on the scanner. *"Scanning… please wait. Access denied, Robert Dixon, access denied."*

"What's going on, sir?"

"I don't know. He must know we're here. Let's go – run!"

The adrenaline kicked in and they fled down the hill to the gate. Higgins helped Bob up and over before scaling the fence himself. They'd just left the small driveway onto the relative safety of the road when a car's headlights aimed straight at them, blinding them. The engine roared, and Bob threw Higgins into the ditch, jumping in after him.

"Bloody hell, sir, that was close," Higgins shouted, picking his face out of the mud at the bottom of the ditch. Bob was already up and had clocked the back of the car that had nearly run them down.

It was an Aston Martin DB5.

"He can't have seen us, as we're wearing black and all, sir. Bloody hell."

Bob thought differently. Someone knew they would be there; it was like a shot across the bows. He had been told to back off and was doing nothing of the sort. His nemesis had had Beth in a marksman's crosshairs, and now Higgins had nearly been caught in a hit and run, and all in the same day. Maybe it was time to listen and do as he had been told before someone got hurt.

He looked again at Higgins. The constable was just a kid – Bob couldn't put him in any more danger. If this had been a game, it had now got serious, and it wasn't going to end well unless Bob followed the rules.

OK, let's play it your way, he thought as he pulled Higgins out of the ditch and took him for a well-earned beer in The Ship.

Part Three – The Tide is High

Chapter 29 – Wake Up, Little Piggy

Saltburn was good for Bob. He had moved in with Beth, and together they'd set up a missing persons group that met each week in the library. Scraggs, who had mellowed over the years and grown up into a pleasant young man, and the Townsend family, were among those who attended and found solace in each other's company.

Bob had read all the books on his already read list, and Beth had read most of them too. He'd then taken her out with the dowsing rods when the tide was high enough, which had led to Chalky accompanying them on a few far-flung excursions, mapping some of the more well-known ley lines around the world. It appeared that Saltburn-by-the-Sea was not the only place from which people disappeared whenever there was a big tide near a coastal ley line. Beth had even started writing a book on the subject – it was her life's ambition to be a published author.

George 'Hurricane' Higgins had been through training and was now a detective constable in Redcar, following in his dad's footsteps. Bob met up with him once a week in The Ship. Bob had also became good friends with Silent Man and would occasionally go fishing with him, helping him to do the pots or haul the nets, or joining him for a spot of yucking with rods. Surfing had passed Bob by, but he had tried a parmo, which was probably one of the nicest things he had ever tasted. But at two thousand calories a shot, it was limited to special occasions.

Long gone were the memories of projections and mysterious funicular rides. Life was good.

It was now June 2018.

Bob was busy tending the front garden of the house he shared with Beth near the golf course; Beth, who was the green-fingered one in the household, was at the library, working. It was Saltburn in Bloom week, and anyone who had a garden was expected to make it look its best for when the Britain in Bloom judges were shown around. Everyone in Beth and Bob's road had been helping each other with the floral displays and general gardening upkeep – one bad garden would mean the trophy would be going elsewhere. Scattered around the village were replicas of landmarks such as the pier, funicular, fishing boats and steam trains full of flowers.

It was a nice day, and the back garden looked like the perfect place for a gin and tonic accompanied by a good book in the sunshine. It was Bob's day off and all his work was done for the day. G&T poured, he headed out to the patio.

And that was when he saw it in the centre of the lawn.

A porcelain pig lay asleep in his bed with a real alarm clock next to him. As Bob stepped onto the lawn, the alarm went off. He guessed this was to grab his attention – just in case he had not already spotted the pig.

Along with the pig was a note. Bob was not fazed – he had been waiting a long time for this. Like a sleeper in a film now being brought back into the action, Bob was needed again. He did not know what for, but he would rather be doing stuff than waiting for stuff to do.

He had told Beth this day would come. In fact, he had shared everything that had happened six years earlier with her, and they kept the other pigs on top of the kitchen units as a reminder. Bob looked at his watch; he could wait until Beth got home from work. Nothing was going to happen behind her back; they would open the note together. He'd been waiting six years, so two more hours would not kill anyone – hopefully.

Beth got in just after 4pm, and Bob met her at the door with a kiss.

"I've been woken up, Beth." He made his way through to the kitchen and pointed to the pig and the envelope. ***Wake up, little piggy*** was typed on the front in bold type. "It came with a free alarm clock," Bob added, trying to take the edge off the situation.

Beth looked at him in anticipation. "Have you read it?"

"Of course not, I've been waiting for you."

"Do you think you'll be called back into the fun and games?"

"I don't know. Only one way to find out."

He slowly opened the envelope. There was a card inside.

Tick-tock.

PW – Felixisdead

PS Hello, Beth, welcome to the madhouse.

A friend.

"Password for what?" Beth looked up at him. "He knows I'm on the scene, so he must have been keeping tabs on us." She gave him a playful hug. "We *are* in this together, Bob. Who is Felix?"

"It's the password for that old memory stick, and Felix was the annoying pig on the website the day I used the internet at your place. You know, the day… the rifle, red dot and all. I remembered how to type and saved your life."

"That's right, so you say."

"Look, get over it, Beth! I *did* save your life and you owe me big style." They both laughed. "OK, the memory stick is in my laptop case. I'll go and get it."

Bob was back in the blink of an eye, booting up his laptop.

"It's so exciting." Beth clapped her hands together, feeling like she was in a Bond film.

"Beth, this is real life. This man is dangerous. He's already tried to kill two people, you and Higgins, never mind all the kids who have gone missing, so we need to focus. Just calm down a touch."

Beth snapped out of her Hollywood moment. "So, what do you think?"

"Not got a Scooby."

"Eh?"

"I've not got a clue Beth, the high tide is not until December, so I guess he has a few things he wants doing before then."

"My thoughts too."

Bob placed the memory stick into the USB port. As it had many years before, a box appeared on the monitor asking for a password. Bob obliged and typed Felixisdead.

Something was loading…

Bob recognised the disguised voice as being the same as the one that had spoken to him after he'd dropped the typewriter on Felix the Magic Pig to send him to Boot Hill – the same man who'd been responsible for pointing a rifle at Beth's head. Bob's anger grew; he would never forgive him for that, even if the gun hadn't been loaded.

"Hello, Bob, have you missed me?"

Beth picked up his body language. "Bob, listen, we need to take this in. Concentrate, remember?"

"Beth, get your phone out and record this in case the website wipes itself."

As Beth took her iPhone out, the computer-generated voice spoke again. "Beth, you're a clever girl, so put your phone away. If you record this on your phone, the deal is off."

Bob looked at Beth and gestured for her to put the phone back in her pocket.

"The video must have launched a web page. He's streaming to us live, watching and listening to us. Bastard!" He looked at the webcam on the monitor lid. It was not on.

How can he see us? Then Bob saw the pig on the kitchen table.

"It's a Trojan horse! Let's see what you're like without eyes. I'll play your silly games, but you don't play fair." Bob threw a towel over the sleeping pig.

"No need to spoil the fun, Bob." The monitor showed the tea towel blocking the camera's view. "I have more." The view of them then cleared, coming from above the kitchen units.

"You going to blind all the pigs, Bob? I had to protect my asset. You're the only chance these kids have got."

Bob left the other pigs with their cameras engaged.

"I've waited six years, so I hope you have a plan."

Beth put her arms around Bob. If the mystery man was watching, she was going to show him that they were in this together.

"Bob, listen carefully. First, thank you for backing off the Scraggs and Townsend cases. I needed to let it all calm down. Carl Townsend would be dead by now because of his leukaemia – that's why we chose him. Lizzy Scraggs… I couldn't stop that. We just didn't know enough, we weren't ready."

"Ready for what?"

"I have been working with Stephen for years now. He is ready to stop and we do have a plan to bring the kids back. You have read what I've read, and more. I will be in touch nearer the time."

"So why now? Why contact us now?"

"You will find some names on this memory stick, names and objects. Every child had to leave some magic behind, you know that. We think that is the key to bringing them back."

"OK, I'm listening. Go on."

"Some of the families are members of your library support group, some are not. You already have Lizzy's dog lead and Stephen's funicular ticket. You have to locate the rest."

"How do you know what the objects are?" Bob was calmer

and starting to believe what he was being told. How else would the mystery man know about the ticket and the lead?

"Stephen took them, Bob, we both know that. He wants to stop. He has given me a list of items for all of them."

"All of them? The list of missing people Higgins and I found went back to 1980, when Stephen himself went missing. Are there more?"

There was a pause.

"Look, you have been straight with me, Bob, so I will be straight with you. They go back hundreds of years, but we are only bringing the ones back that Stephen has taken; we can't help the ones before that."

Bob was shocked.

"I have said too much. You look after the objects and I will be in touch and explain everything. Trust me."

Bob had heard enough. For the first time, things seemed to be adding up.

"OK, I'll get what I can. How do I contact you?"

"I'll be in touch. And Beth – look after him for me."

She looked up at the three pigs staring back at her as Bob replied.

"OK, you have a deal."

The screen picture of the kitchen disappeared and a Word document replaced it.

"Open it, Bob. Those poor kids! At least we know they're still alive."

"I don't think they're kids anymore. Beth… thanks for believing in me."

"Bob, I have always believed in you, from the day you tried breaking my library door."

Bob smiled as he double clicked the file. There were names from Carl Townsend all the way back to Stephen Farrell. He and Beth knew some of the parents, who attended the library group they ran. There was an object listed against each name.

"What are we meant to do, Beth, just ask for the objects, if the parents even have them?"

"I don't know, but leave it with me, and let me have a think."

Beth was good at thinking, and often her thoughts gave his mind the help it needed to weigh things up. Bob may have been the one with the ideas, but it was Beth who provided the inspiration to help them form.

Chapter 30 – The Objects of Their Desires

If there was one thing that Beth had in abundance, it was drive. She was the reason the book club was thriving – with over fifty active members, it was growing every week. At least twenty would turn up for each reading, many just listeners, others, like Bob, enjoying the performing side of it, too.

Bob could not remember a day without books since he had met Beth. Not only had she filled a big gap in his life, she'd also introduced him to a whole new world of pirates, dragons and mystical creatures. Authors were bigger than rock stars in the book group's eyes – they didn't care for the Rolling Stones or Ed Sheeran, but they did care for a good author. And Beth had managed to get a few semi-famous local authors to come along as guest speakers. She had a way of making things happen, and most authors loved the chance to talk about their books. Beth asked, and they came.

The 'Our Hearts Will Never Stop Looking' missing persons group was the same. It had been Bob's idea so he could keep tabs on the Townsend and Scraggs families, but Beth had been the one who'd made it happen. Beth had an infectious nature about her – when she said things, people listened. Bob would not have got the group off the ground on his own; Beth could take all the credit for that. In fact, it had grown so strong that other missing persons groups around the UK were now joining forces with its members.

Armed with the list of missing people and their magic objects, Beth was in the library. She had already rung Bob and was waiting for him; she'd had an idea that she needed to run past him for tonight's meeting with the group.

Bob entered the library, which was only a short walk from the police station. Beth spotted him and asked her young trainee to cover the desk while she took him to the far end of the library and kissed him on the cheek.

"Bob, I have had an idea how to get the magic items." Her eyes sparkled, as they always did when she was hatching a plan. "OK, after I have read last week's minutes and covered a few admin issues, you're up with your police update from around the country. Then I am going to have a discussion with the group."

The plan was for everyone to sit in a circle and discuss an object they still possessed that had a close connection to their missing family member. They would be encouraged to bring the object in to the next meeting, along with their favourite picture of their loved one, and share it with the group. The object and the picture would then be put on display in a glass cabinet for six months to raise awareness.

Beth was waiting for a reaction. She got one.

"Beth, you're a bloody genius." Bob added, "So simple, getting them to bring the objects to us voluntarily. That's why I love you." He gave her a kiss, holding her face with both hands. The kiss would have been described in the olden days as a smacker. "But what about all those people who didn't go missing on a big tide, and what about Stephen and Lizzy? We already have their magic objects: the dog lead and the ticket."

"Will it hurt, Bob? All the parents and friends will benefit from it." She took out the list. "Six years ago, Carl was taken. His object was a PlayStation Portable, which went everywhere with him. It was the only thing that went missing from the hospital bed, apart from Carl himself, and it was found in the valley gardens in Marske. Remember? You looked it up on the police computer."

"I did, Beth, so I would expect the police in Redcar would still have it, or the parents if they were given it back."

"Before Carl, Lizzy left a dog lead. Before her was John Green – his family will be here tonight, they always are. He left the book, *The Lion, The Witch and The Wardrobe,* which was found and handed back to the family, so I'm sure they will still have it.

"Then it gets harder: Harriet Hall, St Christopher. There is nothing about her in the records, and we don't know where her parents are, apart from the fact they emigrated to Australia, so I'm out of ideas on that one. Thomas Hawthorn's Rubik's cube from 1987 is a long shot, but you know what his mother's like. She's obsessive and still lives in the same house. It wouldn't surprise me if his room has remained untouched and the cube is sitting on the chest of drawers in there. What do you think?"

"Well, it's worth a shot. Let's see what comes up tonight."

Later that day, Bob entered the room as everyone was grabbing a coffee before the meeting started. Beth was talking to Scraggs who, along with his wife, had helped get the group off the ground. His wife was a nurse and always attended when she was off duty, so Bob assumed she was working as she was not there.

Scraggs was still a big Middlesbrough fan, but strictly home games now as his son was only three. Slaven had died a few years back, but Scraggs and his wife now had another dog called Bamford. Unfortunately for Scraggs, Patrick Bamford had just left Boro and signed for Leeds. Scraggs was telling Beth that he was seriously thinking about renaming the dog, not fancying shouting the name of a Leeds player out on Saltburn beach.

Bob caught Beth's eye to save her.

"Well, here goes nothing, Bob," she said, coming over to join him. "Let's see what magic we can unearth." She looked at the thirty people in the room, spanning the decades. Many had little in common, apart from one thing. They had built quite a community, the ones who had lost a loved one years ago, although not holding out much hope for themselves, offering comfort and support to the others, having been on this road for longer. No one was expecting miracles – the longer someone was lost, the less likelihood there was of a happy ending, and the best many of them could hope for was closure. But the group was there for all, and all were there for the group.

Beth calmed the crowd down by ringing the bell on the counter over and over until it was the only thing left making a noise.

"OK, folks, great turn out as usual." She went quickly through last week's minutes and actions, which sparked off a couple of ideas for the next meeting, before handing over to Bob.

"OK, I have good news for a couple of you! I know you already know, but I'll share it with the group anyway. Lindsey Sharp has been spotted sleeping rough in London. We don't know exactly where she is now, but we have confirmed it was her, and we have CCTV backing this up, so at least we know she is alive and well."

There was a cheer and a few people went over to Lindsey's parents, who were holding back the tears.

"We have possible sightings for our newest members, Tim

and Susan Hampshire. Kim, their daughter, ran off with her boyfriend. We have an anonymous report on our Facebook page saying that they are at the Isle of White Festival, along with a picture. The festival is over now, so hopefully Kim will be heading back up north and should be home soon.

"We have also contacted Sainsbury's supermarket about resurrecting an old idea from the United States: putting missing people's photos on milk cartons, and we have joined missing persons groups in the south that are pushing this. So if you can get your pictures uploaded to Facebook, we'll use them if this comes off.

"And lastly, a big thank you to everyone in the group for making this a happy place in sad circumstances. I know we normally now break off for coffee and chats, but Beth has had an idea which you might be interested in. So can we all gather in a circle – a big circle I know – one seat for each missing person? Everyone else, if you stand behind your loved one's representative, we are going to have a quick chat, if that's OK? You can grab a coffee while we sort the room out."

Bob had a quick word with Beth while the chairs were being set up. "You OK, Beth? All good?"

"Yes, all good, Bob. Regardless of why we are doing this, it's a good idea anyway. We might get all our followers on Facebook to do the same thing in their libraries – it's a pilot and we are piloting it."

"Good idea. You'll smash it – good luck."

Beth stood in the middle of the circle of chairs, Bob looking on. How had he ended up meeting Beth? She had him good and proper, as they say. He had been on this planet for nearly fifty years without really needing anyone; now he could not imagine his life without her. Yes, she could be a pain in the arse, but she was the best pain in the arse he had ever met.

He smiled at her as she put the plan into action.

"I've had an idea and I think it will really gain exposure, locally as well as nationally, for us all." The group members looked on, waiting, hanging on her every word. "So you might have noticed the big display cabinet at the front is empty." There were a few murmurings of assent. "OK, calm down. So, what we plan to do is have a discussion round the group. The cabinet is there to display your favourite pictures of your loved ones and a special object, along with a note you would like to write to them."

Again, the room started mumbling in agreement.

"So we'll start with you, Scraggs. What would be the special object that you would bring in for Lizzy?" They already had the dog lead, but Scraggs was the most confident member of the group, and as such Beth knew he would talk easily and bring everyone else out of their shells.

Scraggs stood up. "Beth, I think this is a great idea. I know this sounds silly… I can't believe I am telling you lot this. OK, here goes. Lizzy used to play with one of those heads – you know, like a mannequin head with loads of blonde hair – doing its hair and makeup." He smiled, reliving the past in front of them. "Well, she got bored of doing the doll up all the time, so I became her doll. She used to sit and make me up – lipstick, eyeliner, the lot." A tear formed in his eye. "I miss her so much, it hurts."

"It's OK, Scraggs, we are all here for you."

He took a couple of deep breaths. "So I am going to bring that bloody head in and the makeup she used to use on me. And if any of you lot mention this to my mates, I'll know where it came from." He pointed round the room to get his warning across.

Scraggs sat down, and the whole room erupted in cheers and laughter in equal measure. Beth looked across to Bob, who smiled a knowing smile. She'd been right again – it was an amazing idea.

The group members on the chairs each took their turns, standing up and telling the others what object they wanted to bring in. There were many tears shed as they all supported each other. John Green's parents said he loved to read and they would bring in the book he was reading when he went missing, *The Lion, The Witch and The Wardrobe.* Again, the room applauded. Each person who stood was gaining strength from the one before.

When Thomas's parents offered up his Rubik's cube, Bob looked over to Beth and winked at her. That only left Harriet Hall's St Christopher and Carl Townsend's PlayStation.

Carl's father was the last in the circle, as he was sitting next to Scraggs who had started the talking. A tall man with a beard, immaculately turned out in a dark suit, he stood.

"Can I first thank Beth and Bob for running this group." He initiated the clapping, and the rest of the room joined in. "They do this out of the goodness of their hearts and we thank them."

The group members quietened down and listened respectfully

to Guy Townsend.

"Our story is a little different from most of yours. Carl only had a week or so to live. The thing is, all we wanted to do was say goodbye to our little boy, but someone took that from us. Like all of you, we have never, since that day, received any news or closure."

His wife Bev stood up next to him.

"I know we normally sit in the background, minding our own business. That doesn't mean we don't gain solace and support from all of you. I would like to thank everyone in this group for your kind words. Look, we know Carl would no longer be with us…"

Guy started to cry. Rubbing his fists into his eyes to try to stem the tears, he took a deep breath.

"I'm sorry. The thing is… as long as there is 0.1 per cent chance… he is still with us, we will carry on and… fight for him. What is life without hope?" Tears streaming down his face, Guy was struggling to breathe, let alone talk. All the emotions of the last six years were flowing out of him. His wife gripped his hand and he gathered himself together.

"And it's groups like this and people like you that make each day that passes with no news a little more bearable for Bev and me."

Scraggs stood up by Guy's side and held his hand. The couple next to Scraggs took his hand, then the next people followed suit. One by one, all the families joined hands and formed a circle of hope. Emotions had been bottling up in all of them for years. It was not grief – there was no one to grieve for – it was hope. Until they knew otherwise. But tonight had been a release for everyone. Tears were flowing as they joined together to remember and pray for their loved ones.

Beth and Bob took a watching brief as the circle had its moment of togetherness. Nothing was said; nothing needed to be said.

They slowly broke off, exchanging hugs before taking their seats. Only Guy remained standing.

"Thank you, everyone, I don't know what Bev and I would do without you. Carl had a PS2, I think you call it – a hand-held PlayStation device. It was the only thing that left his room when he was taken. It was recovered a week or so later by the police, and that will be what we will bring in to represent Carl. Thank you once again, everyone, and Bob, Beth, thank you for doing this for us."

After coffee and a chat, and some more tears, the library emptied, leaving Beth and Bob to pick what they could out of such an emotional night. After showing the last members out, Beth took a coffee from Bob and looked at him.

"That went rather well, Mr Dixon."

"You are amazing, Beth. It's been an amazing night, and you have all the items off our list apart from Harriet's St Christopher. I don't know where we are going to find that."

She shrugged her shoulders in agreement.

Chapter 31 – Picking Up the Pace

Bob took the alarm clock that had arrived with the sleeping pig as a sign that he needed to up his speed. Backing off and keeping tabs on things from afar was one thing, but getting knee deep in the detail was another. Bob's notes had all been transferred to his computer and synced with his iPhone now, but he still had some old-fashioned policing left in him.

He took his old notepad for a walk alongside Skelton Beck, heading towards the Italian gardens, trying to tie up some of the loose ends that had been left dangling throughout his 'back the hell off' years. As he ambled along, the noise of the trickling beck kept him company. He had walked this route hundreds of times, calling it his Kindle walk because it was where he would catch up on his latest piece of fiction. Through the Italian gardens and up to the grassy area near the viaduct, it was an ideal escape from all the factual information he had been reading about ley lines and mermaids, although sometimes it seemed he had his fiction and non-fiction the wrong way around. The fiction he read was far more believable.

Today, as he approached the beautiful Italian gardens and sat on a bench, it was his old notepad keeping him company, the Kindle remaining in his pocket. He read it cover to cover, both from the front and from the back There was still so much out of his control, but there were a couple of things he could influence. Forearmed is forewarned, after all.

The first puzzle concerned Chalky's old barn. Who the hell would pay half a million up front and ten thousand a month, with no questions asked, then go ahead and build a metal barn within a wooden one to keep nothing inside it? He would get Higgins to look at Chalky's finances, not to find out who was paying him – Bob was guessing that the person responsible had the brain power and the financial clout to cover his tracks – more to prove that he *had* covered them. How could anyone build a metal barn inside another barn without leaving some tracks? Again, Bob was guessing that no local builders had been used. And whoever the mystery man had used would not be saying anything about it in a hurry, so he was not expecting much of a result.

Bob moved along and walked up to Saltburn's famous viaduct, which carried the freight trains over Huntcliff to Boulby Potash Mine to pick up and ship out rock-salt from one of the deepest mines in Europe. As he approached, a shipment was heading over the Victorian structure at that very moment.

How did they build that, all those years ago? he thought. Staggered by the viaduct's size and beauty, he took a seat on the grassy bank beneath.

A lightbulb flashed up above his head as the last couple of containers finished their journey across the viaduct. "Ahh, the Aston! The DB5! That might be hard to cover up – it must be registered to someone."

He took out his phone and googled *how many Aston Martin DB5s in the UK?* He was not expecting miracles, but he more or less got one. There was a website, claiming that in quarter two of 2018, there were 346 Aston Martin DB5s in the UK. This information was followed by a chart showing the ones that were licensed and the ones which had a statutory off-road notification. There were eighty-six with SORN, so that left 260 on the road.

Worth chasing up, especially the low mileage ones.

He rang Higgins.

"Hi, Bob, what's up?"

"Hurricane, I need you to chase up a couple of things for me. On the QT, though, son."

"Isn't it always with you?"

"I'll send you the details. I need you to look into Chalky White's bank details and poke around to get me a name of whoever's paying him, or the builders who did his barn up. Oh, and I want the names of all the owners of Aston Martin DB5s and some other stuff – mileage, addresses, colours, although I'm guessing they will all be silver grey. You don't get one of the most iconic cars ever and spray it yellow, do you? You know the form. Is that OK?"

"Of course, Bob. I guess your Lizzy Scraggs case has been woken up again then?"

"You're not wrong, Hurricane. I'll see you in the pub later."

"Will do. See you at eight in The Ship."

Bob put his phone in his pocket, but within seconds it vibrated to tell him he had a text. He took it out again and looked at the screen.

Say, "Cheese".

He looked across the beck. In the woods, a man was pointing a camera at him. The man was wearing dark clothing and a flat cap, a scarf up to his mouth. Bob stood and the man walked down the bank to stand opposite him. Face to face with six years of torment, the fast flowing beck the only obstacle between them, Bob saw the man take out his phone. Then Bob's phone vibrated again.

I have a surprise for you. I found it with my metal detector, exactly where Stephen told me it would be.

Bob looked over at the man again. He could leap across the stream and scramble up the other side, but no. The man would be away up the hill by the time he got across.

The man opposite took something out of his pocket and sent another text. Bob read it out loud.

"*Quack quack!*"

The man placed a yellow plastic duck in the water and waved it on its way, then nodded at Bob and pointed at the duck, which was gaining speed in the beck. Bob looked at the toy duck disappearing into the distance, and then at the man walking calmly back up the hill. What was more important to him right now?

He watched the man disappear into the woods. The yellow duck was nearly out of sight too. He took up the chase, following the river, bursting into a run to catch the duck, hoping it would get snagged on a shallow clearing. No such luck. The duck had decided to have a ball and was in the centre of the beck, hurtling along.

Sprinting, Bob caught up with the duck and slowed to a light jog, following the duck all the way to the road bridge near the beach. It would then have to enter the shallows where the beck hit the sea. Bob headed under the bridge onto the beach, where he had to negotiate a six foot drop.

Three miles chasing a bloody duck, he thought.

Two kids in wellies were looking for crabs under rocks. The duck grabbed their attention, and the bigger of the boys scooped it out of the water as Bob arrived.

"Thanks, son," Bob said, out of breath. "Can you pass it here?"

The young lad spotted an opportunity. "What's it worth, mister?"

Bob thought it was worth a clip around the ear, but having checked his pockets, he found he was all out of clips, so he settled on a fiver. He had a yellow duck in his possession, but what did it mean? It was just a yellow duck.

Bob looked again at the text. *I have a surprise for you. I found it with my metal detector, exactly where Stephen told me it would be.*

He looked at the duck face to face, then rattled it. There was something inside, so he took out a penknife and cut it open along the plastic moulded seam. Inside was a St Christopher, engraved on the back with the initials HH.

"Harriet Hall," he said. "That's the list done."

He headed up to the library to tell Beth the good news.

When Bob entered the library, Beth was reading to some kids from a local school in the children's corner, telling them all about a witch's broom which was running out of space for all the animals it was accommodate. He watched from behind a bookshelf as she had the kids mesmerised. She really did enjoy her work – no one could have that much passion and infectious charisma otherwise. Bob often hid around the corner, listening to her every word.

She came to the end of *Room on the Broom*. "OK, kids, now you have thirty minutes of free time, so go and pick a book and see what magical place it takes you to. Ready? Three, two, one – go!"

Kids ran off in all directions, looking for their next book to immerse themselves into. Beth spotted Bob.

"Have you been listening again, Mr Dixon?"

"I might have been."

Beth picked up *Room on the Broom*. "Mmm, age five to eleven, that's about right." She gave him a sarcastic look. "So, to what do I owe this visit? I thought you were off reading down the Italian gardens."

"I was. Well, reading my notebook. Hurricane is looking into a few things for me, and I have a present for you, Beth."

"Good, you know how I love presents. Especially flowers."

"This is a better present than flowers," he said. Making a mental note to get Beth some flowers sometime soon, Bob placed the plastic duck on the counter and stared at it.

"Well thanks, Bob, you shouldn't have bothered. No, really, you shouldn't have."

"I met him, Beth. He was covered up, but it was him. He

stood on the opposite side of the river up near the viaduct; he must have known I go there."

"And he gave you a plastic duck to mark the occasion?"

"No, he told me via a text that he had a surprise for me."

He showed her the text.

"Well a yellow plastic duck is a surprise, I guess."

"No, it's not the duck, it's what was inside. He made me chase the bloody thing all the way to the beach, and then it cost me a fiver to get it back off some kids."

He took the St Cristopher out of his pocket and dangled it in front of her eyes.

"Is that what I think it is?"

"Well it has HH on the back, so I guess so."

She gave him a hug, then took the necklace and examined it. "Can you believe that all of those kids had these objects with them when they were taken? It's so sad."

"Well hopefully we are going to bring them back to where they belong."

"Follow me." He followed her to the cabinet that was currently covered over with a purple velvet cloth. "You're not the only one with a surprise, Bob Dixon." She took off the cover to reveal the glass-fronted cabinet, full of objects, photographs and letters that the missing persons group members had written. All of the items the group had promised were there, including the magic items on the list.

"So that's everything, Beth. What now?"

"I guess we wait. Maybe we'll get another pig – I have become quite fond of them." She gave him a playful nudge.

"Well done. We have a few months before the big December tide, so I guess you're right – we wait."

Bob met Higgins at The Ship as they had arranged. After exchanging pleasantries with the older man, Higgins got to work,

"OK, Bob, Chalky's barn. There was a payment of half a million and he gets ten grand a month, just as he said. It all checks out."

"Any idea where from, son?"

Higgins laughed. "Whoever you are dealing with seems to be like the invisible man. That money has been laundered more times than your oldest pants. It's been through five offshore accounts, and the trail goes cold in Hong Kong. Whoever they are, they've got some clout."

"I thought as much. What about the estate agent that arranged the deal? Anything on them?"

"Top London firm, they do dealings with the rich and famous. It would take a court order to get anything out of them, and even then, they would have the best lawyers in the world on their side."

"Mmmm, anything on the builders?"

"Fake boards, fake name. They didn't even stay in hotels, but stayed up at the barn. Must have brought their own food in – I don't even have so much as a pizza or parmo delivered up there."

"And everyone loves a parmo."

"I'm guessing they were ex-military engineers hired in, judging by the metal inside the barn and the security system, and the fact no one is spilling any beans. All trails are cold as ice; nothing points to anyone."

Bob looked at Higgins, who reminded him of a young version of himself: logical. They exchanged glances, Bob looking at Higgins like a proud father would look at his son.

"What? What's wrong?"

"Just… you're talking like a proper detective, Hurricane, and I'm very proud of you. Remember that weedy little kid I once went out on the beat with? You've turned into a first class rozzer, son."

"Cut it out, Bob," Higgins said. Embarrassed, he changed the subject. "Want to hear about the DB5?"

"Yes. Nothing there either, I guess?"

"The numbers you sent added up. There were 260 on the road last count. The one we both saw was silver grey, which narrows it down a bit, because eighty-four are other colours. So assuming it's registered, that leaves 176 to look at."

"Well, that's too many…"

Higgins held up his hand to stop Bob. "The mileage on some of them is quite high, so I eliminated the ones that had done over 60,000 miles, leaving 102." Bob went to interrupt. Again, Higgins's hand stopped him. "So 102 DB5s that are drivable in the UK. Six are in museums, so we are down to ninety-six. Then…" Higgins smiled, proud of his work "…these change hands quite a bit. Then it hit me, Bob. Let's not look for the current owner, because we know the previous owner. Bingo!"

"That's my line! I always say bingo."

"Well say it, then."

"Bingo! You're a clever boy, Hurricane. So I guess we have a registration number and an owner?" Bob clapped his hands in anticipation.

"We should have by now, DVLA are running a report for me." Right on cue, Higgins's phone vibrated. He took it out and read the email, his face clouding with confusion.

"They really do have it in for you, that London lot."

"I'm not following, son."

"You own it, Bob. You have been the proud owner of an Aston Martin DB5 for over twenty years."

Chapter 32 – Who the Hell is Bob Dixon?

It was 14 December and the big tide was expected in two days. Bob was getting twitchy – contact should have been made by now – and Beth had been keeping him calm. She was good at that, always the voice of reason.

"He will make contact when he's good and ready."

Bob remembered nearly seven years ago taking Scraggs and Slaven to Marske churchyard a day or so before the high tide. He took Slaven's dog lead out of the drawer and headed to the library to see Beth.

"What's the big surprise, Mr Dixon, you going to whisk me off my feet?"

"Well, sort of, Beth. I want you to see something."

"You know how much I don't like surprises, Bob."

"We are going for a walk along the beach."

He held out his hand for her to join him. Beth was wondering whether he might be about to do the going down on one knee thing – she was hoping he would pop the question, and her mother had been giving her grief about 'living in sin' since Bob had moved in.

They walked and talked, and then walked and talked some more, heading towards Blue Mountain.

"Do you know why it's called Blue Mountain, Beth? It looks brown to me."

"Of course I know, Bob, I read it in a local book. In the spring, hundreds of wild bluebells grow around the side. It's an amazing sight to see. I used to come here with my dad and roll painted eggs down there at Easter."

Beth looked wistful. Her dad had passed away before Bob had moved to Saltburn.

They took the path opposite Blue Mountain, which looked bluer all of a sudden after Beth's explanation, and approached the gap in the graveyard wall. Bob stopped and took out the dog lead.

"Right, Beth, we have travelled around the world, mapping these bloody ley lines. You have believed everything I have put before you, so I need you to see something for yourself. It will only work for whoever holds it. The tide should be high enough, although you may lose the signal now and then."

Beth took the lead in her hand. "Are you coming with me, Bob?"

"No, I'll make sure nobody is coming. I have seen this film twice. I've told you what happens, now it's your chance to see this mad world of ours weave its magic." He kissed her on the cheek, and then on the lips. "This is what you have been waiting for."

"What if it doesn't work?"

"It will. It works with belief, and you have believed in me since the day we met. And remember it's a projection – they can't see you, so get up close and personal."

She nodded and glanced at the dog lead, which looked innocent enough. But when she entered through the gap in the wall, the lead started to flicker blue.

The sky went dark and it started raining, hard. She looked back to Bob; he was gone, she was tuned into a different place in time.

Bob was watching as Beth made her way into the churchyard. She took cover behind the church wall, despite him having told her the projections wouldn't be able to see her, clearly gathering her confidence. Bob imagined the scene in his head as first Slaven, then Stephen and Lizzy appeared through the gap where she'd left him. Bob saw Beth move to the centre of the churchyard and take a look at where Lizzy would be standing, before moving on to Stephen. She then made her way to the gravestone, where Bob imagined the mystery man scoring the date and writing *DIG*. It dawned on him that he had not got a good look at the stranger. However, Beth was doing as he'd suggested and getting up close and personal, by the looks of it.

Beth looked at the man, who was wearing a flat cap and a scarf covering his face up to his eyes. He waved at Stephen as he finished scoring the word *DIG* on the back of the grave and planting the box Beth knew contained the pig and whistle, covering the box with turf. She tried getting a better look at him as he made sure the turf blended in.

"Bingo!" he said.

Beth caught the blueness of his kind eyes. Dropping the lead, she fell to her knees as the projection stopped.

Bob ran over and took hold of her.

"Get off me!" she yelled. "Get off!"

"Beth, it's me, Bob. What happened? What did you see?"

Beth looked at him. "How could you, Bob? It all makes sense now – your fingerprints on the pig, owning an Aston Martin. How could you?"

"Beth, I don't know what you're talking about."

"It was you! You said, 'Bingo'; you *always* say bloody bingo. I heard your London accent, and then I saw your eyes. I would recognise your eyes anywhere. You *knew* all the magic objects. You sent yourself those letters; Frank was never dead. You made it all up."

"Beth, I never, really." Bob was trying to look for answers, but the more Beth accused him, the more it seemed to make sense. Was he going mad?

"Then there is the barn. Did anyone but you see those tractors?"

Well, Hurricane did, and so did Chalky, but they're both unreliable witnesses as they remember a different course of events.

"And then you finding the St Christopher inside a bloody plastic duck. I really hope you got a kick out of all this – you're a madman!" Bob was all out of answers. "Give me one good reason why I shouldn't go to the police?"

Bob knelt next to her; she was in tears.

"You're a conman, Bob, why didn't I see it? And I bloody loved you!"

She stood; Bob got up and tried to hold her, but she pushed him off and he landed back on the ground. "We are over, and I mean it. Keep away from me, you deranged bastard." Bob stood up again and put his hand on her shoulder. "Get the fuck off me, you creep!"

She ran off through the churchyard, crying. Bob sat, glancing at the gravestone, and then watching her leave.

"What the hell happened there?" he said as he slowly got to his feet.

Bob called Higgins, who put him up in the spare room. He just said he'd had a fight with Beth and needed to give her some space. Saying that he'd been helping to kidnap kids for years without having any knowledge of it didn't seem like a good idea when he was desperate for a bed.

The following day, which was a Saturday, Bob headed into town. Seeing the welcoming sign of the coffee shop, he knew facing Audrey would come with consequences, but at least he would learn how Beth was, one way or the other.

"Oh, here he comes with his tail between his legs."

"Audrey, give me a break. How's Beth?"

"You're lucky she has a mother who likes you. She has not told me what went on, but she said it was nothing to do with cheating. In my opinion, you both need to sort yourselves out."

Audrey handed Bob a coffee that he had not even asked for. He accepted it with open arms.

"She said that if you came in here, I was to tell you to meet her in Signals."

Signals was the other coffee shop in town. Bob guessed Beth did not want to be anywhere near her mother's prying ears when they talked.

"What time?"

"Eleven."

"It's twenty-five to eleven now. What would have happened if I hadn't popped in?"

"I was about to text you. She said she has something important to say. Good luck, Bob, I know she loves you. I hope you sort it out."

"Thanks, Audrey."

Bob, thinking the worst, drank his coffee speedily and headed over to Signals. He walked in to see Beth already sitting at the table in the window. She gestured for him to take a seat, and he thought better of leaning over to kiss her.

"Bob, I may have overreacted, but you have some questions to answer."

"OK, fire away."

"OK, we have seen what ley lines can do, we know people have gone missing, we have read books and visited people and places where things don't begin to make sense. So instead of me accusing you of being there, maybe you can tell me how, nearly thirteen years ago, you ended up at the scene of Lizzy Scraggs's murder."

Bob thought better of correcting her. It wasn't murder when there was no body; it was still a missing person case.

"Beth, what you saw was a projection of the past. I have seen two versions of the same thing, once on my own and once with Hurricane, and I told you each one was different. The mystery man only appeared the second time. I never got close enough to see him, but you did, and you claim it was me."

"It *was* you."

"So let's say it was me…" Then it dawned on him. Bob went as white as a sheet. "The eyes! I knew I had seen those eyes."

"What eyes?"

"The CCTV in the Townsend case. Carl's abductor looked up at the CCTV – he *wanted* to be seen. I recognised his eyes, and it's just hit me why."

"What, Bob?"

"Well, let's just say I see them every morning when I have a shave, but they're different."

"Different? And to be honest, Bob, involving yourself in another murder is not really helping your case."

Bob left the 'murder' word alone again, although this time it took a little more effort.

"Older, Beth. They were my eyes, but older."

She looked confused.

"My eyes in the graveyard – you say you had a good look. Younger or older than now?"

Bob looked directly at her, trying not to blink. She looked into his nearly fifty-year-old eyes.

"You were older, Bob, a lot older."

He took out his notebook. "You know ley lines have magic in them?" She nodded; she'd read the books. "What if they can also transcend time? I read a book by a mad Australian Dexter, aghhhh, what was his name, Dexter, something, he mentioned time travel in his book. Broon, that's him Dexter Broon."

"You said that book was crazy and not worth reading, you said that you didn't even finish it."

"I know what I said, maybe I was wrong" He fumbled for a page in the front of his notebook, and then another at the back, both times pointing out the funicular ride as the moment things had changed. "So when I used Stephen's ticket, I released the magic and a man appeared at the top."

"What are you getting at, Bob?"

He took a deep breath; he was not sure what he was getting at, but he knew he was getting at something. The missing piece of the engine had been reconnected, and someone had just turned the key and started her up.

"So, the first thing that changed was the funicular ride. A man appeared at the top, and that man was me. That's why I have two histories – I didn't learn French, he did. I didn't read all of those books, he did. I didn't save Frank Cartwright, he did."

Beth took a few moments to comprehend what he was saying.

He took Stephen's ticket out of his wallet, showed her the stamp on the return portion and pointed to the date. "I think I went back then. There have been two of me since – it all makes sense. Well, sort of."

"That's why your prints were on the pig, and that's why you own a DB5."

"That's why I'm suddenly a genius on computers and can type seventy-five words a minute – it's been there all along. He's been helping me to remember – he's leading me to help Stephen to stop everything."

"That means if he knows things, so do you. You just have to unlock them from your other memory – his memory. Well, you know what I mean."

A man stood up in the corner and walked past them, dropping a newspaper on the floor next to their table.

"Sir, you have dropped your paper."

The man ignored Bob and left the shop. Bob picked up the paper, which was folded in half. He opened it up to find an envelope inside with ***Beth and Bob*** written in bold type on the front. The note inside was handwritten, not typed – the man had obviously been listening to them.

Beth took the note. "It's in your handwriting, Bob."

Bob and Beth,

Well done on getting all the objects, they will come in very handy.

You now know who I am, and well done for working that out, too. And don't fall out – you're a lovely couple. I hope you understand, Bob, I had to tread carefully. Too much too soon could have fried your brain, so I had to tease things out of you. This is new to me too, you know.

Bob, didn't you think my barn looked smaller than it used to? Mmm, maybe it did, maybe it didn't. You and our good friend Hurricane need to pay another visit tomorrow afternoon, before the big tide the morning after, to check it out. I'll turn the cameras off and leave the gate open. After your last attempt at jumping it, we can't have you injured. We need you.

Beth, I need you to gather the magic objects together. I'll be in touch.

A good friend

"What does he mean, *it could have fried your brain*?" Beth asked, reading the letter again.

"I guess having two pasts can screw you over a bit. He had to get me to work things out."

"I suppose so. And what about the barn being smaller?"

"Well, it looked bigger with all the tractors and the like in it. Maybe the metal box they put inside makes it look smaller, but it was enormous when I first went in there. Or first didn't go in there… well, you know what I mean."

"You have to ring Hurricane and go up there tomorrow. I'll come with you."

"You're doing nothing of the sort. Look, we play by his… er, my rules. Either way, you're not coming."

Chapter 33 – The Waiting Game

They walked hand in hand along the top and down the bank to the pier, chatting about what had happened in the graveyard yesterday. It was still a shock to Beth – yes, Bob had told her all about the projections, but seeing is believing, and having seen, she believed. She hadn't been expecting her boyfriend to be in the past she saw, but who was she to rule out the impossible? It made more sense than thinking that the man she had grown to love would have anything to do with kids going missing.

They were wondering what might be in store for them tomorrow as they took a wander across to The Ship, passing the Silent Man.

"Ray, how's it going?"

Ray was knitting an overly large net that spanned his boat. Gill nets, made with light nylon, give off a turquoise sheen, orange floats at the top keeping one end of the net upright, and a string of lead rope allowing the other end of the net to stay on the bottom of the sea. The unsuspecting fish would then bury their gills into one of the array of diamonds that made up the net. It took great skill to knit one, but Ray was a master. However, this one looked different. It looked like he was using piano wire, and the diamonds were bigger than usual.

"Bloody hell, Ray, you off shark fishing?"

Ray took off his gloves, which were stopping the wire tearing into his fingers.

"You could say that, Bob." He laughed. "No, just trying something new out."

Ray grabbed some tin-snips out of the engine box and snipped off a couple of ends he had tied off. Bob and Beth got the impression he was in one of his silent moods, so they left him to it, heading into The Ship for Bob's favourite, scampi and chips, with a mandatory side order of mushy peas.

"So, what do you think is going to happen, Bob?"

"Well, he…"

Bob looked up, confused. It seemed strange to be calling himself 'he', but he could hardly say 'I'. He carried on.

"He has had a long time to plan for this, so I guess he will meet Hurricane and me at the barn, and give you a sign to let you know what you need to do with the objects. Are you scared, Beth?"

"Far from it! We have been waiting a long time for this. It's like reading a book – the end is always the best bit. I'm excited."

"Well, watch your back, Beth, and phone me if you need anything while I'm up at that barn."

Beth nodded. "The tide will be at its highest at four-thirty in the morning, so we have to expect everything and anything before then."

"When was the last time you had a ride on the funicular?"

"As a kid. It's for the tourists really."

"How about we go and have a ride? Listen to Keith's scary tour."

"Is it that scary?"

"What, you've never heard it? It's legendary."

After their late lunch, they walked up the bank to find Keith at the top of the funicular. Bob still had Stephen's funicular ticket in his pocket, but he was not expecting anything to happen today. Anyway, the return portion was punched, and now he knew why: he had sent himself back to the 1980s and had been co-existing with his alter ego ever since.

There was no queue at the top for the ride and Keith had no one to perform to, so Bob asked for more of a technical tour. Keith obliged and showed them around the control hut the brake-man operated from. He explained how to load the upper car's tank with water from the natural spring, saying this took thirty seconds or so. As he opened the lever, they could hear the tank filling quite rapidly.

Once the water gauge was over the green line, it was a simple operation of releasing the brake. The car would slowly head down the grassy bank, hauling the other car up before the brake was again applied as the upper car docked into its station. It took about a minute or so to prepare for the next journey, and then it all started again.

As there were still no passengers, Keith allowed first Bob and then Beth to have a go at driving, or braking, or whatever it was called. It turned out to be a lot easier than it looked.

Bob awoke the next day and opened the curtains, looking out into the back garden. It looked like any other December morning, the winter sun creeping into the garden, trying to look inconspicuous.

But today was not just any old morning. Today was the morning Bob had been dreading and anticipating in equal measure.

Beth rolled over in bed, disturbed by the light that was filtering into the bedroom.

"What time is it, Bob? Have you been for a run?"

"Not today. I have a feeling I may need all my energy today."

She beckoned him across to her. "Whatever today brings, it brings," she said as she hugged him.

"The thing is, I like to know what's happening. He's not been in touch with you, and God knows what he has in store for Hurricane and me later. It could all be a trap."

"If he wanted to get at you, he would have done it by now. Anyway, you don't hurt your own, your family."

He knew what she meant. An older version of himself was family in a way. He tried thinking what he would do if things were the other way round, but his thoughts were giving nothing away. If his older self had a plan, Bob was not feeling the vibes.

"I'll get us some breakfast. We need to be ready for anything today – you saw what happened at the graveyard. Logic has been thrown out of the window."

He made his way to the kitchen and kicked the coffee machine into action.

After breakfast, which he ate while going back through all the notes from his old notepad, Bob called Higgins and agreed to meet him at The Ship at 2pm. It sat uneasily with Bob that 3.30pm was the first high tide of the day, and they were going to be right on top of a ley line in Chalky's barn. He suspected it was going to be a long day. Or night. Either way, it was going to be a long one.

He also did not like leaving Beth on her own, knowing that his older self was going to contact her sometime today with instructions. Then the flip side of his mind thought about Lizzy Scraggs and the Townsend kid. Would they really be bringing all the missing children back home, as he had been led to believe?

He looked out of the kitchen window. The day smiled back at him, holding its arms out and saying, "*Nothing to see here.*"

Bob gave Beth a hug and made her promise to ring him if she received a call, got a message or another porcelain pig with a riddle, and she agreed. Beth was calm; she felt the strangeness of it all, but she was good at reacting to situations. Bob was different; he liked to be in control. He'd felt like a puppet on a string since he'd first stumbled upon the connection between the tides and the disappearing kids. And although he'd tried, he'd not been able to cut the strings to his puppet master.

After a long and frustrating morning, he gave Beth a kiss and walked to The Ship to meet Higgins.

Higgins was already there, talking to Ray.

"Hurricane, Ray." They both nodded. "Have you been out this morning, Ray?" Bob knew the answer, but it was the best small talk he could come up with.

"Yes, I've been out, Bob."

"With that new net of yours? You expecting a whale?"

Ray shuffled uneasily on his stool. "No, that's for another day."

Bob picked up on Ray's body language, but he had bigger fish to fry, even if Ray caught a monster. After a coffee, he and Higgins headed up the hill to the barn. As they approached, Higgins moved into the hedgerow to take cover from the camera.

"No need, Hurricane, we are invited guests." Bob got a look from Higgins, who didn't fancy a CCTV image of him breaking and entering being put in front of his boss in Redcar. "It will be OK, I promise."

"How? We don't even know who owns it."

Bob thought better of saying that he did, and had done for years, even though it made sense of how his fingerprint had worked to open the door last time they had been here.

"Let's just say I've had a tip off."

Higgins left it and joined Bob in the centre of the road. "Your call, Bob."

The camera was not sweeping left and right as it had done before. There was no light on top of it showing any signs of life. As they approached the gate, it clicked open.

Higgins looked over at Bob and tilted his head.

"See, we're guests."

As they walked through the gate, Bob thought about the note: *didn't you think my barn looked smaller than it used to?* He knew there had been something different, and he wouldn't be fooled again.

They reached the barn and started making their way round to the front.

"STOP!" Bob returned to the back of the barn.

That's it, the crafty bastard.

"Do you know what a pin step is, Hurricane?"

Higgins was not expecting the question. "Pin step, Bob?"

"Well, you're a bigger shoe size than me, so it will be quicker if you do it." Bob demonstrated pin step counting. "One, two, three, four," he said, placing one foot in front of the other on each count. "You know! Now we need to measure the barn. See how many of your size elevens long it is."

"You sure?"

"Yes, I'm sure, Hurricane. For me, please."

Higgins set off. "One, two, three. Four. Five, six…"

After thirty or so pin steps, Higgins was losing his balance and put his arms out like a tightrope walker. Bob laughed. Higgins continued until Bob interrupted.

"You only have to walk in a straight line. They would lock you up in America for that. Have you not heard of 'walking the line'?"

"Stop it, Bob, I'll lose count. Is there any point to this, or are you just trying to make me look stupid?"

"Would I do that to you, Hurricane?"

"Yes, you would. I've known you long enough."

"I promise it's important. You're on 107, and we're not even a quarter of the way along it." Bob got a look. Higgins needed all of his brain power right now to walk in a straight line and count at the same time. Bob took the hint.

"OK, I'll keep quiet. From 107. Go."

Bob got another look from Higgins, but the younger man did as he was told.

"…672, 673 and a half. I hope you enjoyed that, Bob. Don't ever ask me to do pin steps again."

Bob was planning on asking him to do exactly that in about five minutes, but he thought better of bursting Higgins's already deflated balloon.

"Right, remember that number: 673 and a half." Bob wrote it

in his notebook, which made his request more or less superfluous. He then opened the hatch to reveal the fingerprint detection system.

"Fingerprint recognition required."

Bob obliged.

"Scanning… please wait. Robert Dixon, welcome back, sir."

"So far, so good, Hurricane," he said as the doors parted smoothly.

Chapter 34 – From the Mind of a Madman

It was dark. It had been dark last time, but this was the daytime. The only natural light came from the gaps in the roof slats, which allowed beams of sunlight to illuminate the dust particles in the air. Bob clicked on the lights, which made their familiar clunking sounds as each bank received a kick of power. The last bank of lights at the far end of the barn clicked on and then off again as if a fuse had blown. As the barn slowly revealed whatever it was hiding, they could just about make out the table at the end in the gloom.

Higgins started to walk towards it. "My mam's flask, Bob! She'll be happy."

"Hurricane, back here, son. This barn has a secret. I can't believe I didn't spot it last time."

"What do you mean, sir? It's just the same."

Bob, didn't you think my barn looked smaller than it used to?

"Pin steps, Hurricane, let's go."

"Bob, you've just made me look stupid outside. I'm not doing that again."

Bob put his serious face on and squared up in front of Higgins. "Would I ask you if it wasn't important? How long do you think this barn is?"

"Er, 673 steps would be my guess. Oh, and a half."

"I bet you it isn't. Pin steps, for me."

Higgins sighed and made his way to the corner of the barn with all the enthusiasm of a drowned rat.

"One, two, three…"

Bob did not interrupt this time. As Higgins approached half way, he was at 230. Bob had his game face on – he was going to need it.

"…465, 466, 467 and a quarter. But how? Have I miscounted?"

"No, son, this barn has a false wall. That's why we found nothing last time. There are over two hundred pin steps of secrets behind this wall. Clever bastard!"

"So what now?"

Bob's attention moved to the table and the flask. They walked across together.

"That's not my mam's flask."

"Can you remember what your flask looked like? It looks like your mum's flask to me."

"It has a cup on top. I took the cup outside, remember?"

"Well done, Hurricane. See, all those detective lessons I gave you have paid off. But it could still be your mum's flask with a new lid."

Higgins took the cup off the top.

"It's not. My mam's had rust under the lid. Should I open it, Bob?"

Bob, not having a better idea, agreed. As Higgins took off the lid, a blue light appeared from the flask.

"It's a torch, Hurricane, a UV torch." Bob held out his palm for the flask. "That's why these lights blew. There must be some writing somewhere." Bob shone the ultraviolet light onto the back wall. Nothing showed up. He then made his way along the back wall to where Higgins had finished his pin step marathon.

And there it was.

A handprint showed up on the wall, level with their eye line. It had *George Higgins* written above it.

"Well, that's your way in, son."

As they moved away, the handprint disappeared. Bob made his way to the other corner, and a handprint with *Bob Dixon* written above it appeared.

"Well, I'll go first, son. Light it up."

Higgins shone the light onto the wall to show the handprint. Bob took a deep breath before placing his hand directly on top of the print

"*Bob Dixon engaged.*" It was the same computer-generated lady's voice as the one on the entrance. Bob took his hand away.

"*Bob Dixon disengaged.*"

"What does that mean, Bob?"

"I'm guessing it takes two to tango. Look, son, you don't have to do this."

"Bob, this has been bothering me all these years as much as you. You may still have Lizzy Scraggs's case on your desk, but I have Carl Townsend's on mine." Higgins lit the wall up again for Bob to locate the handprint. "Engage, Bob, then I'll join you on the other side."

Bob placed his hand back on the handprint. "*Bob Dixon engaged.*"

Higgins left Bob with his hand on the wall and took the flask to locate his handprint.

"You ready, Bob?"

"Yes, son."

Higgins lit up his print and placed his left hand onto it.

"George Higgins engaged. Opening in three, two, one."

There was a *whoosh* and two doors slid open right next to where they were standing.

"What now, sir?"

Bob stood looking at the open door next to him, which had seven years of answers behind it.

"Your call, Hurricane."

"I'll see you in there, sir. I'm guessing they will close if we disengage."

"I guess so."

"OK, Bob, on my mark, three, two one."

They disengaged together, and as their respective doors started to close, they both rushed through. The doors made another *whoosh*ing sound as they closed behind them.

Higgins walked into a six foot square dimly lit metal box.

"Bob? Are you there, Bob?" he shouted. No answer. "Bob?" he tried again, louder this time. Still nothing.

In an identical space on the other side of the barn, Bob was also shouting, asking Higgins if he was OK. Nothing came back.

"Bloody brilliant," Bob muttered. If he'd thought he was out of control of the situation before, the puppet strings were stronger than ever now. "So what do you want with me?" he said, assuming that whoever was playing games with him would be watching him right now. "If you lay a finger on Higgins, I'll kill you, you sad bastard."

A plasma screen lit up in front of him. He could see Higgins feeling his way around his metal cell, but there was no sound. Then Higgins's floor slid away, and Bob saw him disappear from view. A new camera angle appeared, showing a long corridor. Bob watched Higgins slide down a chute and land on the floor, then the sound kicked in.

"What the hell is going on, Bob? Bob?"

"Hurricane, can you hear me?"

No reply confirmed that he couldn't.

Higgins was talking to himself. "OK, calm, George, calm." He was trying to rationalise his thoughts. "What the hell is this place?" He slowly walked down the corridor to an L-shaped turn leading into another corridor. There were a number of doors on both sides of the wide passage. Higgins went up to the nearest door and read the name on it.

"Carl Townsend?" There was a spyhole to look through. Higgins moved the brass cover to the side and peered in. "My God." He could see a bedroom and make out a body under the covers on the bed, but he couldn't see the face. The angle of the spyhole wouldn't allow it. However, he could see the chest moving up and down and a medical drip by the side of the bed.

"My God, Carl's alive!" Noticing the red camera light behind him, he said, "You fucking sick bastard! How could you do this?"

Higgins made his way to the next door. "Lizzy Scraggs." He didn't know if he should be happy or sad. The missing kids were alive, but their childhoods had been taken. During his training, he had done a course on psychological profiling, learning how psychopaths would take trophies from their victims. This madman had taken kids as trophies and kept them alive for his pleasure.

Higgins looked inside Lizzy's room to see that it was identical to Carl's, complete with the drip he now assumed was keeping them in whatever state they were in. He checked out the other rooms, reading the names on the doors as he did.

The last door was open, so Higgins looked inside. The drip was ready and waiting, as was an empty bed. Higgins's head poked back out into the corridor to look at the name on the door.

"Oh my God," he said, slumping to the floor. "George Higgins. You bastard."

The view on the plasma screen changed camera angles as Higgins appeared around the corner. As he read the names on each door, Bob checked them out, too. They were all on his list.

So why would he say he wanted to stop?

Then Bob saw the name on the last door. "You sad bastard! You wait until I get out of here," he shouted to the screen."

"Bob? Bob, is that you?"

Bob saw Higgins stand. "Can you hear me, Hurricane?"

"Yes, Bob, you won't believe what's down here."

"I can see, Hurricane, I've been watching you on a screen. Are you OK, son?"

"I'm fine, Bob. The last one has my name on it."

"I know, son."

"Listen, Bob, they're all alive. All of them on the missing persons list we took all those years ago. You need to get out and let someone know." For someone who had just seen a room that he could be entombed in for the rest of his life, Higgins was very upbeat. He'd always been a brave lad. "They're alive, Bob, and we need to get them out."

Bob remembered when he'd found out Frank was still alive. That was the game changer, the convincer. Of course he would play a convincer card on himself!

"I'll sort it, son, I'll sort it." Bob could normally plan things and make the cards fall in his favour, but this time he'd had a bum deal. He was stuck in a metal box with no way out. His reassurance was enough for Higgins, though.

"I know you will, Bob, you always do."

Bob shook his head. Higgins had always had his back, always looked up to him, and look at the situation he had got the young man into. He took a deep breath and logic kicked in.

"Hurricane, sit tight. We'll get this sick bastard."

Nothing came back; the sound went dead.

Right, Bob thought, *he wanted us to speak. There has to be a reason for that. When I see him, there will be trouble.*

Then the wall holding the screen slid aside and he walked through the gap.

Chapter 35 – Bob, Meet Bob

Bob entered a large open space flanked by a bank of computer screens. His alter ego, complete with scarf and a flat cap, was attending to the computer. Bob ran in his direction. Hurtling head first into a clear glass partition, he fell to the floor. The force he hit it with nearly knocked him out. Lying dazed on the floor, eyes blurred, he shook his head, trying to regain consciousness.

He slowly got to his feet, eyes gaining clarity, and felt the glass wall.

What now? he thought.

"I know you can hear me, you sad bastard."

The man left his computer and walked over to the glass partition.

"Now that's no way to speak to someone who is trying to help, is it, Robert?"

"We both know what you are – you're a freak of nature. A version of me with all the evil elements. Does the funicular ride only allow evil through the ley line portal?"

"Ah, so you read my book."

"Your book?"

"*Ley Lines: The ancient travelling companion.* It was on your list."

"By Dexter Broon, not you." Bob was looking directly at his tormentor of nearly seven years. He was even blinking quickly, fearful of missing something that might be important.

"Dexter I. Broon, actually."

The man took out a fluorescent pink pen and wrote backwards on the glass so Bob could read it: D-E-X-T-E-R I B-R-O-O-N. Crossing out one letter at a time, he wrote underneath R-O-B-E-R-T. Bob was already ahead of the game before he wrote D-I-X-O-N, but there was one letter uncrossed in the upper name.

"And what's our middle name?"

Bob sighed, annoyed that he hadn't spotted it. "Edward."

"You didn't just read that book, Robert, you wrote it."

Bob remembered it had been the strangest book on his list. He'd been expecting a book on ley lines, but it was way more unbelievable. As such, he'd failed to take it all in.

"OK, enough of your games. You have my friend down there and have kidnapped, or at least assisted in the kidnap of kids around here for years. You're one evil son of a bitch."

The man took off his cap and scarf and went nose to nose with Bob against the glass.

"Do I look like a kidnapper, Robert?"

It was the first time, apart from the glimpse on the CCTV footage, that Bob had managed to get a good look at his nemesis. He looked into his own face, but older, his hair salt and pepper and a thinness around the features. Bob looked down. The man in front of him was wearing a tight muscle tee-shirt – he was very fit for his age.

The man picked up on the direction of his stare. "Did you not wonder how you got fit and lost weight overnight, Robert? Your mystical diet was kicking in. I worked for forty years for this body and you were a benefactor. I'm sure we could sell fitness DVDs on the back of that – send yourself back in time, work out and live healthily for forty years, and you will benefit."

"Oh, so you want thanks? You're a madman and need stopping. Those poor kids! You were with Stephen on the Lizzy Scraggs abduction and you still let it happen."

Something caught his eye on the big screen behind his other self. The older Bob turned around.

"I wondered how long it would take. He's a bright boy, that one."

Higgins had jammed his shoe under the door and was searching his cell for anything sharp he could use as a weapon.

"Excuse me, Robert, I have some fishing to do."

"Bastard."

The man turned and headed for the bank of TV screens, computers and keyboards, pressing a couple of buttons. A metal door slid across, blocking Higgins's escape route from his cell.

"George Higgins, welcome. Make yourself at home." The man walked back to Bob, whose anger levels were off the chart. "I need one thing from you, Robert: trust. I am not asking for much."

Trust? After what he had witnessed over the past hour?

"And why should I trust a madman?"

"Robert, I need to tell you some things, and you need to free your mind and trust me."

"Bollocks."

"If you had read my..." he left a gap "...and *your* book properly, you would have seen a couple of paragraphs on adjoining lives, where if a time-slip were to happen, the person who went back would have to be careful not to change anything. More importantly, they should never touch anything. Skin to skin contact would... well, let's just say it would not end well for me. It happened once in the Amazon. I visited them..."

"Why should I give a shit?"

"Just give me a chance to explain! That's all I ask, then I will lift the screen."

What do I have to lose? Bob thought. *If what he has just said is true, that would flip control to me. Besides, more time behind the glass will do me no favours.*

"Deal."

The man put his cap back on, raised his scarf and put on some black leather gloves. He then went to the control desk and pressed a couple of buttons. The glass screen disappeared into the floor. Bob was free.

"So what is stopping me jumping at you right now, touching your skin and wiping you out? Then this whole thing would be over."

Bob did not expect the reaction he got. The man took off a glove, threw it onto the table.

"Nothing. Be my guest." Bob took a step forward. "Before you do, I hope you don't think I have lived my life again since the beginning of the 80s, befriended Stephen and worked together with him to try to get out of this mess for nothing. But if you do think that, go ahead."

Bob took another step forward, thinking about Higgins, Lizzy, Carl and the rest of the missing kids. He was one step away from his black-clad puppet master.

"I'll tell you what, Robert, let me show you something. Then if you want to shake my hand, I will let you and it will be done. And you will be on your own."

Bob's anger slowly moved from boiling point to a simmer.

"May I?" The man took his glove as if to ask permission to put it back on.

"For now, yes. What have you got to show me?"

"Things are not always as they appear, Robert. You have heard the term convincer? You and I are both masters at it."

"Yes, of course."

"Do you think Lizzy Scraggs, Carl Townsend and the rest of them are down there with Higgins?" The man laughed.

"Yes, and why is that funny?"

"Come with me, Robert, and put these on." He gave Bob some leather gloves, and then pressed a button on the control panel. Making his way to a metal wall, he pressed his finger against an illuminated panel.

"*Robert Dixon, welcome back, sir.*"

The door slid open with a now familiar *whoosh*. The room they entered contained an old friend. The Aston Martin was gleaming under the lights beaming down on it.

"So this is where you keep it. Registered to me, I see."

"Well, of course, you and I are the same person. When this is done, she's yours, if you want her."

They moved past the Aston to another door. Bob followed his alter ego closely; he could trust nothing and no one, especially the older version of himself. They walked down a steep staircase and were presented with another door. This time, the door slid open silently.

The corridor looked like the one Higgins had been in earlier, but with only one door. They walked past it and Bob stopped.

"Stephen Farrell? But that's who is taking everyone – your partner. He's here?" Bob thought of Silent Man, telling him he would speak to Stephen out at sea before each big tide. Was Ray in on it, too? Was it all a big con?

"Take a look, Robert."

Bob opened the door. The room was empty. The drip was lined up ready, but nobody was in the bed.

Bob got a better look at the room. There was a wardrobe full of gowns of different sizes.

"Is this for when they grow up?" he asked.

"It looks that way, Robert."

"Why would you do it? I know you are a version of me, but I'm very disappointed in you."

They left Stephen's room and went around the corner. The next room was Higgins's. The man kicked away Higgins's shoe and closed the door. The metal that had trapped Higgins slid away as the door shut.

The man put his finger to his lips. "Shhhh."

Bob looked in through the spyhole. "If you touch him, I'll kill you, you know that," he whispered.

"You're not the only one who is fond of Higgins, you know."

They walked past all the other rooms, Bob peering in each one to see the bed, a body breathing and a drip. When they stopped at Lizzy Scraggs's door, Bob tried to work out how old she would be now. Twenty-six-ish?

"This is what I want to show you." The man beside Bob pressed his finger on the door, and it opened.

Bob walked into Lizzy's room. Seven years after first hearing about her disappearance, which had happened six years before that, he was finally going to see her.

He walked to the bed. "Is this meant to be a fucking joke?"

"It's what you call a convincer, Robert."

The 'body' had no head. Bob pulled the covers back to reveal a rubber torso hooked up to an air pump.

"But why? Why would you do that?"

"Well, you believed it, and more importantly, so did Higgins. In the Amazon, I met a tribe. I was told they managed to get missing kids back who had no recollection of anything having happened. If we succeed tonight, in the morning, it will be the same here."

"So this is your convincer?"

"Well it convinced the best detectives Saltburn and Redcar have to offer."

"But the police will see the air pumps, and the lack of heads might give the game away."

His alter ego laughed.

"That was just for Higgins. He needed to believe that the kids were really here so when it's all over, he can be the hero. The real people will be here by the time he comes to rescue them, if it all goes to plan."

"But someone has to take the flack."

"Well that will be me. I'll take the can for all of it."

"But I'm you, fingerprints and everything."

"That's why you're here. They will expect your prints to be everywhere except down here, hence the gloves."

The penny dropped.

"I'm not you, I'm an eccentric Australian author called Dexter I. Broom. I wrote a crazy book on ley lines." The man laughed briefly, then turned serious. “In the back of the book is a plan of the labyrinth under this barn. I have created an ID, birth certificates, passports – everything. We have a fall guy, Robert.” He left a gap for sinking-in time, and then added, “Let’s go back upstairs. I need to run you through the plan.”

“How have you afforded all of this? Buying the place, the builders – everything is covered up. We’ve tried looking.”

“Money, Robert, it’s amazing what you can accomplish with money.”

“But where did you get it all?”

“When you know every FA Cup winner and goal scorer, every Grand National winner, the results of every boxing match for over twenty years, it’s amazing what you can do. I even bet on an election once. Remember when you went to Goodwood with work down in London? You, Frank, all of them?”

“Yes.”

“I was in the box next to you, and do you know what? I backed every winner in an accumulator – £250,000. I had to be careful not to meet you. The only dodgy thing I have done to change the past is to save Frank. I had to, Robert.”

Bob nodded. He would have done the same. Well, technically he did do the same. They were one and the same person, after all.

They moved back upstairs, Bob gaining confidence in his older version’s motives all the time. And keeping Higgins out of the picture made sense. The fewer people who knew the truth, the better.

Chapter 36 – Pleased to Meet you, Stephen

Beth had not really been concentrating on her library duties; she was too concerned that she had not heard from Bob. She had rung him five times and Higgins twice, but all her calls went to voicemail. Either they were avoiding her or they were in trouble, and she feared the latter.

She looked at her watch. It was 4pm and getting dark. She tried to convince herself that everything was going to be OK. Her imagination had always been overactive.

Just then, a man entered the library. "I'll be with you in a sec, hun." Beth ran around the counter. "I was just sorting the books into alphabetical order. The people round here – you know what they're like. Can I help you?"

She looked up at the man, who stared back at her. He had a deep diamond-shaped scar on his cheek. She went pale and backed away from the counter.

"It's you, isn't it?"

"Sorry, have we met?" He held out his hand, but she moved further away. Then she took a deep breath before stepping forward again to shake his hand.

"Beth… I'm Beth. I… I run this place."

"You said, 'It's you, isn't it?' Well yes, it is me, but I can't recall where we could possibly have met. I don't visit here that often."

Only every six or seven years, Beth was thinking, her defence mechanism kicking in.

"I know who you are, Stephen, and what you have done, but I saw you say you were sorry in the graveyard. And do you know what? I believed you."

"Thank you, Beth, and I am sorry. I'm done with it all. It's now or never for me – I can't go back to that place and take my children with me."

"Your children?"

"That's what I call them. Once the person who took me died, I became the master. All the kids I take are my generation. They follow me, and if I were to fail, they would step in, starting with the youngest. Which would be Carl. He's seventeen now."

"What, he's still alive? I thought he only had a week to live when he was taken."

"That's why we targeted Carl. It's amazing what a bit of magic can do. He's doing fine." A smile broke out across Stephen's face.

"So why are you here, Stephen? I have been waiting all day for instructions, but I wasn't expecting you to be delivering them."

"Look, we only have one chance at this, Beth, so you need to listen to me, and listen carefully. I need you to be ready at the funicular for the high tide at four-thirty am. This is what you need to do…"

In the barn, Bob was listening intently to the plan which his older self had drawn up. It sounded like madness – how could it possibly work? But who was he to challenge the ways of the world? He was staring at an older version of himself, and if that wasn't breaking the rules, what was?

Occasionally, he would look up at the TV and see Higgins sitting on his bed, his head in his hands. But there was only one part of the plan he questioned, and it involved Beth.

"There is no way that's happening."

"We have no choice, Robert. It's only you and Beth who know anything. Oh, and Ray. He's made the net."

"I thought you said that when Stephen hits land, he has amazing powers. I know that net looked strong, but I saw him jump off a multi-storey car park. I doubt it will hold him."

"It doesn't need to hold him." Bob looked confused. "It just needs to look like it's holding him. If he is in trouble, the youngest of his generation – that's Carl – will step up to the plate. That's the rules. We have been working on drugs to allow Stephen to remain calm."

"Will that stop him? I've seen his eyes when he gets angry."

"It will take a lot of willpower on his part, but he wants this to stop. Robert, Stephen and I have been friends for over twenty years. He and his children are captives of the Masters of Atlantis. He's forced to take one child back every high tide to energise their underwater city."

"But using Beth as bait? She's not a kid. I thought you said they would only take the very young."

"She doesn't have to be a kid, she has to look like one. Stephen has a school uniform for her – he's taking her through the plan right now."

"She will never agree."

"She already has, Robert."

The door opened and Stephen and Beth walked in. She ran over to Bob.

"Are you OK, Beth?"

"Yes, Stephen and I have been talking through what we have to do. Look at this place! It's so James Bond."

Stephen gave her a pair of gloves to put on.

"You haven't seen the car yet." Bob then continued more seriously, "You don't have to do this."

Before she could answer, the older Bob took off his cap and scarf and the glove on his right hand.

"Pleased to meet you, Beth."

She shook his hand and took a good look at him, and then at Bob.

"Bloody hell, Bob, you're gonna be a handsome bugger when you're older. How lucky am I?"

"I already am a handsome bugger."

"Mmm, I know, but can you hurry up and go grey? You look so distinguished."

"Can we get back to the plan?" he said, trying to stop her eying his other self up. "Beth, are you sure you want to do this? You could… well, you could end up like one of them." He looked over to Stephen. "No offence."

"None taken." Stephen smiled back at them both.

"I know the risks, Bob, but we can get these kids back. Is Hurricane OK?" She looked up at the screen. "It makes sense. If we get them back, we need a hero."

Bob looked at Stephen and his older self. "So, Stephen has taken soothing drugs to quash his urge to take someone, but I guess the rest haven't. What if one of them gets Beth over the ley line? They are going to have powers. What if… well, you know."

Before they could answer, Beth answered for them. "I know the risks. I know what to do and I will have a practice to master it before we trap Stephen. We must do this, Bob, for those kids."

"OK, Beth. But I swear if she gets caught, I'll blow this thing wide open. I don't care who does or doesn't believe me."

"Robert, this has been going on for thousands of years. And not just here, but all over the world. If we can stop this now, it stops for ever in this village. Only the kids of the master – Stephen at the moment – can hit land. The older ones are lost to the sea for ever." The older Bob looked pensive for a moment. "I need to show you something. Stephen, make our guest a cup of tea."

Stephen, showing no monster characteristics whatsoever, went into the corner and put the kettle on to boil.

"Oh, and pass me that bucket, please." Stephen brought the bucket across and gave it to Bob with a grin on his face. "We should still be OK. The tide is on the turn, but we have a two-hour window. It should be high enough."

"High enough for what? And why do I need this bucket?"

"It's all questions, questions, questions with you, Robert. You'll need it, trust me. OK, follow me." They left the hi-tech room and returned to the empty barn. The older Bob walked into the centre, and younger Bob followed. "Stand here." His older self moved six foot away, facing him.

Nothing was happening.

"What now?"

"Can you feel it, Robert?" He was not feeling anything. "Remember when you first came to this barn? You felt it then."

"The ley line?"

"Yes, you are right on top of it. You need to close your eyes, empty your mind and feel its energy."

Bob closed his eyes.

"Concentrate. Let the power in, Robert."

He felt his body being absorbed by the ley line's energy from the feet up. Opening his eyes, he could see himself opposite, glowing blue. He looked down at his arm – he was glowing, too. Then it faded.

"You lost concentration. Focus. It's easier with your eyes closed. Try again."

This time, he picked up the energy more quickly. Eyes shut tightly, he assumed he was glowing. He was correct.

"OK, I feel connected. What now?"

"Well, think of it like the Underground in London. There is a Tube map in your head, and we have many stops: Marske beach, Monks' Walk in Marske's Valley Gardens, the graveyard, Blue Mountain, then we have the funicular and this barn."

Bob, eyes still closed, was willing to believe in anything right now. He could feel the power of the ley line crawling all over his body.

"So where are we going?"

"We are going to the final stop, the cave."

"The cave?"

"Channel your energy. Think cave… cave… cave..."

Bob stood glowing blue, bucket in hand, saying, *Cave, cave, cave*, over and over in his mind.

"OK, you're hooked in. Three, two, one."

There was a flash of blue light that bounced off the metal walls of the barn, then they were gone.

Bob felt queasy. He opened his eyes, looked at his opposite number, and threw up in the bucket. Trying to look up, he immediately threw up again.

"I guess I now know what the bucket was for."

The older man laughed. "It got me the first time, too, but you get used to it."

Bob put the bucket down; he was feeling better and his dizziness had abated. Looking around, he saw that they were indeed in a cave. It was dark, but he could hear the echoes of dripping water. His older self lit a lantern, hung it on the wall, and then lit another.

"Where are we?"

"We are underneath Huntcliff. This cave has been here for thousands of years. Follow me. You have to see this to realise how important it is that we stop what's been going on."

Old Bob walked down the side of the cave and into a corridor which was already illuminated by large lanterns on either side, pointing to the wall. Bob saw hieroglyphics showing men, mermaids and sea creatures.

"Atlantean hieroglyphics. Stephen told me that the same symbols are in the caves in Atlantis. They use them as slaves, you know, the kids they take. The elders, the original dwellers, are thousands of years old – too old to do their own dirty work now. That's why they started to drug their captives, so Stephen says, to do their bidding. And to compel the youngest of each generation to carry on the tradition of taking a child from a coastal ley line each high tide." He stopped and looked at Bob. "We have to stop this, Robert. They whip their captives if they disobey any order. And they keep the kids alive until they're over two hundred."

"Two hundred?"

"Two hundred years as a slave – can you even begin to imagine it? We can stop this, Robert, at least here in Saltburn. Are you ready?"

"Yes, I am. What is it you need to show me?"

Younger Bob followed Old Bob into a large cavern, which was lit by twenty or so old-fashioned evenly spaced flame torches. Bronze caskets, which started small and gradually increased in size as they walked around the room, were sitting between each torch. In the centre of the stone floor was a large pool of water.

"Look at this first, Robert. Follow me." Old Bob's mood was sombre, and his younger counterpart could feel the tension in the air. Bob followed him to the edge of the pool and looked in the water. At first he could only see his reflection, then his eyes adjusted and he looked deeper.

"My God, is that what I think it is?" The pool was full of skulls. "There're hundreds of them."

"I know, and there will be hundreds more unless it stops tonight. Follow me." Bob followed his older self to one of the bronze caskets. "Robert Dixon, meet Lizzy Scraggs." Old Bob opened the casket, and there she was, breathing and alive, wearing a gown similar to the ones Bob had seen in the bedrooms. She looked peaceful, calm and beautiful.

"They're all here – all the ones Stephen has taken. He looks after them when he is here, moves the smaller ones into bigger caskets so they can grow in the six or seven years until the next big tide. That's how we know they can survive outside the caskets."

"What about the ones before Stephen?"

"Once they can no longer function on land, their bodies have no reason to be here, so… well, you know."

Bob looked over to the pool where the skulls were.

"So tonight, Stephen and I are going to take them to their rooms. If all goes well, Higgins will… you know the plan."

"Do you think it will work?"

"I don't know, but we have to try."

"How will you get them up to the bedrooms in the barn?"

"Here, I'll show you. I'm glad you have been working out."

They went through a gap in the rocks to find a staircase, of sorts.

"What? This goes all the way to your barn?"

"Yep. I had a mining company come in, told them I was looking for Whitby Jet. I did the last bit myself so they didn't see the cave."

"Wow, you have been busy!"

They clambered their way up to the top of the makeshift staircase, which took an hour, then entered the control room where Stephen and Beth were waiting.

"OK, you two, you need to get some rest. We'll meet as planned at four am."

Chapter 37 – Putting a Plan into Action

Bob and Beth went to bed, hoping Higgins's girlfriend would not call, asking where he was. Bob hated leaving Higgins alone in the barn, but he knew it was essential. Higgins was the convincer – he would testify as to what he'd seen in the barn: the missing people kept alive, hidden in the bedrooms. And who better than a detective to do this? Higgins had even left evidence on the CCTV camera of himself visiting the rooms. Bob's older self had thought of everything.

Bob still did not know how the plan was going to pan out, though. There was something missing. Was the older man going to have to give himself up and face questioning, the press and prison? That bit of the plan had been conveniently glossed over.

Bob did not sleep. He tried to, but he was like a kid on Christmas Eve. After nearly seven years of waiting, he was not in a sleeping mood, so he spent all night looking at his watch and turning things over in his mind.

Eventually, the hands on his watch approached 3.30am and he was up in a flash, making Beth a coffee. Beth joined him in the kitchen and took her coffee.

"Well, this is it, Beth. Are you sure you're going to be OK? It doesn't seem right, using you as bait."

"I'll be fine. I know what I have to do." She gave him a nervous smile – knowing what she had to do and actually doing it were not the same thing, and they both knew it.

They headed, as planned, to meet Stephen and Old Bob at the top of the funicular at 4am. The tide would be at its highest at 4.30am. As they approached, they could see two figures standing waiting for them.

"You ready?" asked Old Bob. She nodded. "And you, Robert?"

"Ready as I will ever be. Where's Ray?"

"He's down at the trap in the car park."

Bob peered over. A street light in the car park allowed him to see a solitary figure. He took a deep breath and held Beth's hand. She was wearing a black mac, which she took off to reveal a school uniform: short skirt, tights, a white shirt, tie and a blazer.

"Can I have a practice, or at least a look at the trapdoor?"

Stephen took her into the car at the top of the funicular.

"Both cars are the same." He took out a fifty pence piece. "It's spring loaded, Beth. Simply use the coin and turn a quarter turn on the floor here." As he turned the coin in the metal groove he was pointing to, the floor sprang away into the empty water tank beneath.

"You can jump in and push the lid back into place. The tank will be empty as you'll be in the bottom car." Stephen demonstrated, jumping into the water tank, which was itself currently empty, waiting to be filled for its journey to the bottom of the slope. He secured the floor back into place, then seconds later, he was waving at her through the car window. He came back in to join her. "There is a T-bar on the right of the tank which opens it up. You can then roll out before it sets off up the slope. Here, have a go."

He gave her the fifty pence piece.

"I already have one, thanks."

"It's a spare. Put it in your blazer pocket."

"Thanks, Stephen. Right, here goes." She practised the simple manoeuvre twice. It worked like a dream. "Easy."

Bob was still unsure about the 'using a carrot to attract the donkey' approach, especially when his girlfriend was the carrot. "Are you sure you're OK, Beth?" he asked.

"Yes!"

"Right, we all know our jobs," said Old Bob. "Let's see if we can get these kids back home, and… well… just be careful. They will be angry and desperate when they hit land. It took Stephen years to control it, and that was with the drugs we gave him to calm him, so keep your eyes peeled and stick to the plan. Have you got the objects, Beth?"

She took her school satchel from Bob. "Here, all of them."

As she opened the satchel, they could see that the objects were already feeding off the tide, and the ley line was gaining in power only twenty feet down the bank. Beth closed the satchel again.

"And remember the order, Robert, youngest first, Stephen last, and we must be done by daybreak. The drug the Elders in Atlantis gave to Stephen means he has to be done by sunlight; he is never to get the sun on his back. The latest Stephen has taken anyone before was two am, and by then the drug seemed to be making him more powerful and angry, as if desperation was taking hold. This is the latest the tide time has been, and consequently the nearest to sunrise."

Stephen's blue eyes gave a tiny flicker of red. Bob was the only one who spotted this.

"Are you OK, Stephen?"

Stephen took a second to calm himself before replying, but he still looked nervous, avoiding eye contact with anyone, especially Bob. He was nearly there – his dream to end the taking of Saltburn's children was within his grasp. All he had to do was hold it together, but he was struggling with the urges in his body to take someone. And he found himself looking at Beth.

"I'm fine, Bob. Let's get this done."

"Bob – Stephen's ticket," Beth reminded him. Bob took the ticket out of his wallet and added it to the objects in the satchel. Stephen looked at the magic that he left behind as it dropped in. The objects were now all dancing with blue lights, except Stephen's ticket, which looked like it had not been invited to the party. They all picked up on this, including Stephen, but nobody said a word.

"Come on, Beth. Good luck, everyone. I'll see you all on the other side."

Stephen smiled a false smile. He knew that the ticket should be glowing blue like the rest of the objects. Then he thought about the children he had taken and the lives he had ruined, and his urges abated. He was back on plan.

"OK, I'll head back and make sure they arrive safely in their rooms," said Old Bob. "Their heads will be all over the place." He left for his car, the silver Aston Martin DB5. "Good luck, everyone."

Bob took hold of Beth. "You are the bravest girl I have ever met. Good luck – I love you." She hugged him back. "And, Stephen, you make sure you hold it together, understand?"

"I'm fine, Bob, really."

"Ignore him, Stephen, he's nervous for me. Isn't that right, Bob?"

"Sorry, Stephen. I hope to see you back here real soon – for good this time, not just every six years."

"Thanks, Bob. Beth, let's go."

Bob put the first object on the shelf of the funicular. It was

Carl Townsend's PSP PlayStation, which was fizzing and spitting out blue sparks. He then filled the tank with water before releasing the brake with his foot and sending the car down to the bottom, loaded with the magic object for the youngest of Stephen's generation, and bringing the next car to the top.

Looking at Slaven's dog lead, he again noticed the ticket was out of place. It was just a red ticket. Shaking his head, Bob took out the glowing blue lead and loaded into the empty car which had just arrived from the bottom.

Beth and Stephen, who seemed to be in control of his emotions once again, were walking towards the end of the pier. The moon was lighting up the night, casting its reflection on a calm sea. This high tide did not have the anger of the last one.

As they reached the end of the pier, Stephen gripped Beth's hand tightly and whispered, "Are you OK?"

"Yes… yes, I'm good. I think." She was not good; she was nervous as hell.

"OK, I need to show you off. They will be about a mile out there, waiting for me to take someone and increase the family. Not today, though, hey?"

Stephen could feel the ley line calling him and was staring at Beth noticeably longer than he should have been. He turned his head to look out to sea as he felt the power running through his veins.

"Give me a sec, Beth."

He took a glass bottle containing a cannabis oil, tea tree and lavender concoction out of his coat pocket and rubbed it onto his temples. As he calmed, his eyes reset. Beth joined him looking out to sea, where fluorescent blue and white objects were getting closer under the water.

"Put your hands over your ears." She did as she was told. Stephen let out a loud shriek, and Beth went down on her knees, covering her ears even more tightly. "I've told them that I have you and will be bringing you with me."

A screeching chorus came back at them.

"What did they say?"

"They said they will be waiting just in case and wished me

luck. OK, that's enough. They know you're the target. You ready?"

She took a deep breath and took the fifty pence piece out of her pocket, gripping it tightly as they walked back across the pier.

"I've waited nearly forty years for this. You know what you have to do, Beth. Head over to the funicular. Ray will have opened the door for you. Good luck."

Running over to the funicular, Beth looked up at Bob in the control room and gave him a thumbs up.

So far, so good, she thought. Gripping her coin even more tightly in the palm of her hand, she turned, ready for round one.

Ray left the funicular door open so Beth was in full view. Bob filled the upper car, the water hit the levels on the gauge, and his foot hovered over the brake, ready to release it. The net was laid out on the beach near the surfing hut, and Ray was now inside the hut, waiting for Stephen to walk into position. The only thing no one could control was the anger of the landing merpeople, drugged up to their eyeballs with rage and compulsion to abduct yet another innocent child.

Stephen looked at Beth in the funicular car, his eyes flickering blue and red. Trying to quell the urges within him, he shook his head to regain control of his thoughts. It would be so easy to give in and take Beth right now…

Stephen, not now. Concentrate!

He walked onto the wire net, and Ray pulled the ropes. As the net gathered around Stephen, Ray pulled with all his might, lifting him off the beach and tying the rope off. Stephen was caught.

Stephen let out an ear-splitting screech, and one of the pod of blue sea creatures broke away from the group, making its way down the side of the pier. It was now or never. The creature landed and slowly took the form of a young man, clothed all in black like Stephen. Beth gripped her fifty pence piece, but as she moved it to her fingertips, she dropped it on the floor.

Chapter 38 – Holding Out for a Hero

The young man ran, jumping the six foot wall with ease and landing on the promenade. He then stopped running and glanced across at Stephen, trapped in the net. It was now his time to shine; the urges he was feeling were uncontrollable.

His eyes a fiery red, he looked at the schoolgirl in the funicular car. He had been waiting for this moment. The ley line, like a blue river across the landscape, was intersecting the funicular tracks. He needed to take her.

He started to run once again.

Beth was on her knees, fumbling around, trying to find the fifty pence piece, breaking a nail in the process. As she scrambled on the floor, the young man entered the car, and Bob kicked off the brake.

The young man smiled – this would be his first recruitment, and he would be rewarded back in Atlantis.

"You have to leave some magic behind."

He raised his hands. The funicular was gaining speed up the grassy bank, heading for the ley line. Beth looked at her arms – she was glowing blue. As the fifty pence slid down the car, she remembered her spare. Taking it out of her blazer, she knelt up. She was losing her earthly body and the fifty pence was fizzing and crackling, turning blue and absorbing her soul.

The young man opposite her started laughing. "There is no escape. Let your magic go and join us."

She looked down and located the release catch on the floor. With all the self-control she had left in her body, she made the quarter turn as Stephen had instructed.

"Not today, Carl."

The hatch opened and she slid inside the empty water tank.

"No, no!" Carl shouted as Beth closed the hatch. She turned the T-bar and rolled out of the water tank, continuing her roll down the grassy bank to the bottom.

"Bloody hell, that was close."

Carl, now alone in the funicular car, turned and saw his PlayStation on the shelf.

"It can't be…"

The PlayStation was glowing blue, and he remembered leaving his magic in it when he was taken. As the funicular car crossed the ley line, his eyes cooled and turned back to normal. He picked up the PlayStation. A blue flash was followed by rainbow colours bleeding out of the Victorian stained-glass windows.

Beth looked up from her prone position at the bottom of the slope just in time to see the flash. Bob also saw it from the brake hut at the top of the lift. Then the lights disappeared and the car made its way to the top. Bob opened the door. Carl was gone, the car was empty apart from his PSP on the floor.

In the barn, Old Bob was in Carl's bedroom. The figure in the bed suddenly sat up and gulped in as much air as his lungs would allow.

"You're OK, Carl, you're safe."

Carl looked at his arms and his body.

"What the hell? I'm grown up! What's gone on?"

Old Bob gave him a smile and left him. Locking Carl in his room, he peered back in through the spyhole. Carl was struggling to stand. The last thing he would remember would be waiting to die as a sick child in a hospital bed, almost seven years ago. Old Bob smiled again and made his way to Lizzy Scraggs's door.

Bob loaded the empty car at the top of the funicular with John Green's book. *Come on, Beth.* He could see her struggling to regain her composure. Ray was helping Beth back over the white picket fence, opening the door for her to get into position. Bob saw the mermaid that was Lizzy Scraggs leave the pod at great speed and land, standing up all clothed in black. The anger in her red eyes was fierce. She paid no attention to Stephen; she was on a mission and ran straight to Beth in the funicular car.

Bob kicked off the brake. Beth slid out of the funicular in seconds.

Lizzy saw the lead and took hold of it. She remembered the graveyard and smiled just before she disappeared forcing the lead to drop to the floor as her soul rejoined her body in the barn. Old Bob watched from the spyhole as Lizzy sat up, looking confused, and on the beach, Stephen let out a yell as Lizzy's power was transferred to him, topping up the power injection he'd already received from Carl. He called for John Green while he still had the willpower to hold himself captive.

John Green with his book and Harriet Hall with her St Christopher both followed to plan before the last of the pod, Thomas Hawthorn, was lured to the shore. His beloved Rubik's cube in place, he also transferred safely to his room.

But Stephen's rage was now uncontrollable.

Beth was hugging Ray at the door of the funicular. The sun was not yet visible, but the sky to the east was getting lighter. Stephen's eyes were blood red, the veins pulsing on his temples. He could see a shimmer of light on his skin and desperation overcame his willpower; he *had* to take someone, and take them now.

Breaking free from his wire net, he landed in a crouch on the beach. He looked over at Beth with Ray. Stephen's ticket had been loaded into the funicular car ready for him, but it was not glowing blue. It was as if it had no power to give.

Stephen looked at his hands, which were drifting in and out of focus. *I need to take one before sunrise.* He looked across to the sea, where the first hints of a new day were gradually lightening the horizon. His eyes scorching with venom, he felt more powerful than he ever had before.

He headed off with purpose towards Beth. Ray noticed the look in his eyes.

"Stephen, they're all back. It's your turn."

Stephen picked Ray up and threw him against the sea wall. The Silent Man was out cold. The raging man then grabbed Beth and threw her into the funicular car, holding her down with his foot on her neck.

"Stay still, Beth, I don't want to hurt you, but you're coming with me. I have to take one."

Beth tried to scream, but Stephen pressed his foot further onto her neck. She could not breathe, let alone scream.

Stephen gave Bob the thumbs up, and Bob, his view of the attack on Ray and Beth's predicament obscured, kicked off the brake.

"Beth, you need to leave some magic behind. You know the rules."

Stephen allowed her to roll onto her knees. She looked at her fifty pence piece, her body already losing the fight. Stephen was far more powerful than Carl had been earlier. Slowly the coin started to absorb her energy; she was in a trancelike state. Stephen had a new member of his family, and her boyfriend had unknowingly delivered her to him.

There was a flicker of blue in Stephen's eyes, and for a second Beth regained some form of control. Then the funicular car approached the ley line and Stephen looked upon his prey, raising his hand, ready to take her to his other world. But as he looked down upon the helpless soul on her knees, his eyes flickered blue once more.

Then he looked at the ticket and remembered when he had been taken.

He took the fifty pence piece out of Beth's hand. "You're not for my world, Beth." Unlocking the trapdoor, he threw her in. He then took hold of his ticket as the car crossed the ley line.

Nothing happened.

Bob met him at the top.

"Stephen, I think we used the magic in your ticket to send me back to help you. I'm so sorry."

Stephen had regained some of his composure.

"I am ready to go. I'm the one who made this all happen – I'm evil."

The sun was peeking its head over the eastern horizon. Its light hit Stephen as he left the lift, and he collapsed into a heap on the ground.

"I'm sorry for everything, Bob. At least they are safe."

Stephen slipped from consciousness as Beth made her way to the top, along with a somewhat dazed Ray. They looked at the crumpled body lying beside the vacant funicular car. Stephen's hands looked like they were crawling in the sunlight as the flesh started eating away at itself.

"Let's get him inside," said Bob. "The light seems to be burning his flesh."

"Why didn't the ticket work?" asked Beth. "It was his magic object. Everyone else's objects did the job."

An Aston Martin screeched to a halt and Old Bob leapt out, a smile beaming on his face. Then he saw Stephen and his mood changed.

"Why didn't it work?"

Sheltered from the sunrise by the funicular car, Stephen opened his eyes and looked at his friend.

"Bob, did they all get back?"

Old Bob entered the car and knelt next to him, cradling his head in his arms.

"Yes, Stephen, it worked. They're all back and well."

Bob took the ticket from the shelf. "It didn't glow blue when I put it in there, like the rest did."

Old Bob looked confused and took the ticket from his younger self. Stephen's skin looked like it was melting; the daylight and he were not the best of friends, it seemed. Beth put her school tie in some water and mopped Stephen's brow.

Old Bob looked at the ticket where the return portion had been stamped.

"Robert, I have an idea. What is the time?" It was approaching 8am. "There might still be enough power in the tide. Right, there is no magic left in the ticket. We used it to send me back – that's why the return portion is stamped."

"So, if there is no magic, what can we do?"

Stephen, starting to breathe unsteadily, opened his eyes. "Just let me go. I'm tired and I caused this mess. I'm a monster."

His eyes closed. Beth took his pulse and looked up at the two Bobs, a tear forming in her eye.

"He's gone."

"Maybe the magic is in me, Robert. I took the magic from the ticket when I went back in time – maybe it's been in me all along. It's got to be worth a try." Old Bob took out his phone. "We have not got long. Hurricane will be out soon."

As he pressed a code into his phone, there was an explosion on the hilltop where the barn was located, then another and another. The loudest of them was to their right at the base of Huntcliff.

"What was that?"

"I set explosives in the pathway to the cave and blew it up. The electrics are off, so I am hoping Hurricane will be starting to do his hero thing right about now. There will be cops crawling all over here soon. You know what we need to do, Robert, Beth – you need to get out of here."

Bob charged up the funicular for its last journey of the night. His older self was kneeling next to Stephen, checking his pulse. Again, nothing. Bob closed the door and kicked off the brake, and the car started to slide silently down the hill. He hugged Beth in the control hut as his older self smiled through the window and waved goodbye. There was a flash of blue, then they were gone.

Bob fell to his knees, holding his head. All the knowledge his older self had gained over the years was flooding into his brain. He let out a yell of pain.

"Aghhhhh!"

Beth knelt next to him and helped him to his feet. As the mental download abated, he had vision upon vison spinning around his head. His eyes were tightly shut, fighting the pain.

He let out a large breath as the pain and the visions dissipated.

"I'm OK."

"Are you sure? You had me worried."

Bob regained all of his senses. "I'm good, Beth, honest."

She hugged him into her chest.

"Did it work, Bob?"

"I really don't know." He cleared his mind of thought – they had some tracks to cover. The plan was now crystal clear in his head – it should have been, as he had formed it. And the plan was not to leave an Aston Martin that he owned for all to see on the top of Saltburn bank.

"Beth you need to get the items back to the display cabinet, then go back and get changed, and await my call." She nodded and took the satchel with the items inside. "Ray, lose the wire net and lock up the funicular."

"Will do Bob."

"I'd better get the car back and go see how our hero is getting on."

As he drove down Saltburn bank and up the other side using the sleeves of his coat to ensure he left no prints on the steering wheel, Bob felt different. Since his other self had disappeared, all the gaps in his life had gone, too. He was thinking more clearly, as if the knowledge he had gained and the knowledge his older self had gained had combined. The plan had not been his plan to start with, but he knew how to wrap it all up. And the first thing he had to do was get the car back to the barn, undetected.

He approached the back of the barn, typed the PIN into the keypad situated on a pole outside without questioning how he knew it, and drove the car into position. Donning a pair of gloves and making his way to the control room, he calmly switched the power breaker back on, and the room lit up.

He could see Higgins on the CCTV, helping Lizzy Scraggs out of her bed. All the missing children, all now adults, stood behind him. Bob smiled – they had done it. He pressed the release button for Higgins to escape and jumped over the glass partition as it was raising from the ground, shoving the gloves into his pocket. Now he was once again a prisoner, waiting to be saved by Higgins. He lay on the floor and pretended to be asleep.

Ten seconds later, Higgins appeared and ran over to the glass partition. Bob awoke from his fake sleep.

"Bob, are you OK?"

"Yes, sunshine. I think the release button is the green one on the control desk. That's how he locked me in here."

Higgins pressed the button as ordered, the partition disappeared into the floor, and Bob gave him a hug.

"Bob, the sad bastard had them here all along."

One by one, Higgins introduced Bob to the people behind him, all of whom had gone missing as children each time the tide was high. The last two to be introduced were Lizzy Scraggs and Carl Townsend, both looking confused and disorientated.

"What do you remember, Lizzy? Carl?"

Lizzy went first. "The last thing I remember was being late back with our dog. A man offered me a lift home. And now I'm… not a kid anymore? But how?"

Ignoring Lizzy's questions for now, Bob turned to the young man beside her. "Carl?"

"The same. I was in the hospice, and the next thing, I'm here."

Bob's older self had been right. None of the missing persons could remember any strange goings on at sea.

"Well, you're all safe now, thanks to Detective Higgins here. Your brother has never stopped looking for you, Lizzy."

Lizzy smiled for the first time, still trying to take it all in. It would take time for them all to come to terms with the ordeal they had been put through.

Higgins turned his head at the sound of sirens getting closer.

"He's kept them down there for years, Bob. Looks like he's done a runner – bastard!"

"All of them, Hurricane? You said all of them, but where is Stephen Farrell?"

Higgins looked down, and then back at Bob. His eyes looked slightly damp.

"We were too late to save Stephen. He's gone. I've called an ambulance."

"Where is he?"

"He's in his room, through that door."

Bob left Higgins to tend to the group and walked down to the bedrooms. Higgins was going to be hailed as the hero, but there was only one hero in Bob's eyes.

He entered Stephen's bedroom and checked for a pulse, but still there was nothing. Lying on the bed before him was the bravest man he had ever met – a man who had been planning for nearly forty years to stop the tragic cycle of children being taken from Saltburn every high tide. Bob sat on his bed and cradled Stephen's head in his arms, kissing him on the forehead as two paramedics burst in.

"Let us handle this, sir."

Bob moved aside as they worked on Stephen's limp body, frantically trying to revive him. He could hardly believe they had pulled this off against the odds – they had made Stephen's wish come true and returned the missing people home to Saltburn. It should have been a happy time, but in so doing, they had lost the very man who had made the whole daring rescue possible. Bob could not even force a smile.

He joined the others as Stephen's body was wheeled out on a stretcher, covered in a blanket. One of the paramedics looked Bob's way and shook his head.

The police went through the place with a fine-tooth comb, gently quizzing all the people who had lost their childhoods, but no one could remember a thing. The story broke and the media went into a frenzy, spreading the news about the hidden lair and the people whom the sicko to end all sickos had kept alive as trophies. An international alert went out for one Dexter I. Broon – the most wanted man in the world. All the CCTV footage in the barn pointed back to him as the culprit. He was a lone wolf, and clearly guilty as sin.

Bob was in Redcar police station, going over his statement. Taking a break, he went to the bathroom and inhaled deeply. Cupping his hands, he splashed water into his face. As he looked in the mirror, for the briefest of seconds, he thought he saw red flickering in his eyes, then they were as blue as a clear summer's sky again.

Shaking his head to clear his mind, he took out his notepad and calmly wrote, *Book a holiday 2024/2025 high tide.*

Better to be safe than sorry.

The End

Acknowledgements

Claire Lince - For being my wife and putting up with me
Alison Jack (Editor) - For turning water into wine
Julia Gibbs (Proofreader) - Ensuring the wine was not corked

Readers who I forced to read it early on and contributed;

Martin Gibb - For reading and feedback
Phil Lince (Brother) - For reading and feedback
Jennifer Lince (Mam) - For reading and feedback
Ian Hutchinson - For reading and feedback
Graham Megennis - For reading and feedback
Gillian Petrie - For reading and feedback
Michelle Ryles - For reading and feedback
Maria Tate - For buying me a book on 'How to write a novel

Early reviewers;

5 * Michelle Ryles - AKA on Twitter - @thebookmagnet
5 * Gillian Petrie - AKA my No 1 fan

About The Author

Trev Lince originates from Marske-by-the-Sea on the north-east coast of England, but now lives in Darlington with his wife, Claire. Their daughter, Annie, is a very good guitarist and is setting up a band, playing every pub in the north-east that she can. She's so rock and roll, living the dream while her father is approaching his mid-life crisis.

A keen golfer and frustrated Middlesbrough FC fan, Trev gets to as many matches as work and leisure time allow. He writes in what little spare time he has, when not working as an IT Consultant for a major oil company in Surrey.

Funicular is Trev's second book following on from *Room 119 – The Whitby Trader* which was released December 2017

He would like to thank you for reading his second novel and if you can find the time, he asks that if you could please leave a review.

Follow on Twitter - @Room119TFLince

Printed in Poland
by Amazon Fulfillment
Poland Sp. z o.o., Wrocław